Darius James
Monster Hunter
Campfire Stories #1

By

D Glenn Casey

www.DGlennCasey.com

The novel *Darius James – Monster Hunter* is a work of fiction. Names, characters, places and incidents either are the product of the author's imagination or are used fictitiously. Any resemblance to actual persons, living or dead, events, or locales is entirely coincidental.

Copyright © 2022 by D Glenn Casey

All rights reserved. No part of this publication may be reproduced, stored in a retrieval system or transmitted in any form or by any means, electronic, mechanical, recording or otherwise, without the prior written permission of the author.

Cover design: D Glenn Casey
Cover art: Tino Serraiocco
Model: Florio Cocconi

Other works by D Glenn Casey
(All titles available in ebook and paperback)

The Chronicles of Wyndweir
The Tales of Garlan - Prequel
Wicked Rising ~ Book One
The Wrath ~ Book Two

A Cold Shivers Nightmare
Beware The Boogerman
Shattered Prisons
Crossing The Veil
Demon Hunter Academy

Campfire Stories
Darius James: Monster Hunter

Other full-length novels
Into The Wishing Well

My Amazon Author page

My writer's blog

Darius James ~ Monster Hunter
Table of Contents

1 – A Hunter Rides Into Town..1
2 – Darius, We Have a Job For You..................................15
3 – Treat No Woman With Unkindness...........................26
4 – The Trouble With Wendigos......................................35
5 – The Braves Are Restless..47
6 – You Are Not The Help I Need....................................61
7 – Alone In The Dark...70
8 – Reliving Old Memories...79
9 – Sniffing For Blood...86
10 – And You Brought Her?...97
11 – Mountain Battle..105
12 – More Vampires Than Thought..............................119
13 – Preacher, We Are Going To Have Words.............138
14 – Pigheadedness Is Hard To Argue With................149
15 – You Didn't Deserve This..158
16 – A Change Of Heart...167
17 – Two To Become One..174
18 – Ramping Up His Game...182
19 – The Aftermath..191
20 – Stirrings Best Ignored...204
21 – Entering The Vampire's Den................................209
22 – Help Comes While You Sleep...............................225
23 – On Becoming A Squire..242
24 – More Pine Boxes..248
25 – The Bait Is Taken...262

26 – The Underground	275
27 – What's He Done Now?	290
28 – Like Shooting Vampires In A Barrel	296
29 – Took Your Eyes Off The Ball	310
30 – Not Wanted Anymore	320
31 – A Plan Is Hatched	326
32 – Please, Don't Make Me Do This	334
33 – Final Battle	345
34 – Returning To Normal	352
Coming in late 2022 - The City of Time	363
Other books by D Glenn Casey	373

Darius James
Monster Hunter
Campfire Stories #1

1 – A Hunter Rides Into Town

Time is a funny thing. Some say that it flies, while others say it crawls. Well, it certainly can't do both. Can it?

Time also marches on, like an army across the face of history, leaving in its wake the detritus of humanity scattered across the landscape.

It has been many centuries since any person witnessed more than a few decades of time slipping by. If you read the Bible and believe in that sort of thing, people used to live hundreds of years; some even reaching more than a thousand years old.

But now, a person was lucky to see their sixtieth birthday, most succumbing to the harsh life of this world in less than forty years. The real old-timers might see their fiftieth, but not much more than that.

This was the world of steam-driven locomotives and ocean-crossing ships. The age of gas lamps and wind-up pocket watches. In the old west, it was the day of traveling for days on horseback to reach a destination that wasn't served by the railroads.

It was the world that passed before the eyes of the man in the dirty brown duster, leather boots and two Colt six-shooters on his hips. His silvery gray eyes looked out across the barren landscape of Northern New Mexico and saw little to his liking.

His horse, black as the bottom of a coal

mine, plodded along and snorted a few times to chase the flies away from its nose. But, the flies of New Mexico are an insistent bunch and would cause the horse to waggle its head now and then to shoo them away.

"I know, Midnight," said the man. "We've been on the trail for far too long."

One of us a lot longer than the other.

"Are you saying I'm old?"

Your eyes have seen many centuries that mine have never seen or hope to see.

"There are days when I wonder if that's a curse or a blessing," the man mumbled.

You can always say you're done with this life.

The man laughed and patted the horse on the neck.

"If I did that, I would get sent straight to Hell and you wouldn't have anyone to keep you company."

That's true. And I wouldn't be able to watch you get into and out of trouble like you do.

"See there, I am here for your amusement."

Midnight snorted and waggled his head again. The sun was falling behind the mountains to the west and these two travelers knew they were walking toward their next adventure.

Holding his Colt six-shooters waist high, the man looked back and forth across the scene. It took a few seconds for his eyes to adjust to the darkness before he set foot inside.

The gloom in the abandoned farmhouse was almost complete, but not quite. The full moon outside shone through a few holes in the roof, giving him just enough light to see his targets.

At the moment, he did not know where those targets were. He could feel them with his senses; could almost smell them, but see them? Nope, couldn't do that.

His eyes swept across the rafters of the old house, having learned at a young age that his enemies liked to hang out there and drop on top of him. It only took about a half a dozen times of that happening for him to learn. That and having his mentor laugh at him every time it occurred.

What the hell does that old coot know? He's dead and I'm not.

Stepping as quietly as possible, he crossed the open room of the farmhouse and could hear the old floorboards creaking under his boots. His spurs jingled each time his heels hit the ground. The cavalry sword hanging from his waist knocked gently against his leg.

His heart would race, but he'd been doing this for so long, it was hard for him to get it pumping any faster than normal. There was only one thing that could get his heart rate up and this wasn't it.

Moving to the center of the open room, he turned in a circle, his eyes looking for any movement that shouldn't be there, but he had no doubt they were close.

Come on out and play, you mangy sonsabitches. I ain't got all night.

Then he laughed to himself. He had all the time in the world and then some. He just didn't appreciate being kept waiting. Not that he had anywhere else to be. He had seen the lights of a small town in the distance and he realized he was hungry and was going to have a nice, hot dinner this evening.

If he could get this task taken care of before it got too late.

"Inconsiderate bastards! Come out and meet your doom," he mumbled to himself.

Oh yes, that should bring them right out.

"You hush out there."

Incoming!

Before he had time to register what Midnight had said, something crashed through the roof of the farmhouse, landing in front of him. Make that *two* somethings.

The gunslinger backed away from the two late arrivals and found himself in a corner. Not the most ideal spot to be in, but it kept his attackers from flanking him.

With two targets on different sides of the room, he wondered how he always got himself into situations like this. The answer was quite obvious.

You're an idiot! No doubt about it!

"If you don't shut up, I'm making you gallop to town when I'm finished."

If you get hurt, I'm not picking you up.

"You can't pick me up, anyway," mumbled

the man.

The situation he found himself in wasn't new. This was something that he had been doing since he was a young man. Never mind the fact that it had been over four hundred years since he could call himself a young man. That thought alone caused him to laugh to himself. Obviously, age brought no more wisdom than experience.

Backed into the corner, he could keep both of his attackers in sight without having to turn his head. Just a shift of his eyes kept both of them at bay.

The two assailants, one male and one female, shifted back and forth on their feet, their dark cloaks swinging in the slight breeze coming in through the broken door. Both were bald and their bare heads glinted in the moonlight. Their fingertips came to sharp points as they curled into claws.

"You two really don't want any of this," said the man as he raised his pistols and trained them on each one.

Both of them hissed at him like feral cats, baring their fangs. They each took a step toward the stranger, trying to come at him from different directions.

Deciding it was time to put an end to this, the man pulled both triggers. The Colts erupted with the fire and thunder of Hell itself. He didn't need to aim. He knew exactly where his pistols were pointing, having done this for so many years.

Both bullets found their targets. Each one

exploded through the heads of his attackers. He infused his bullets with silver and crafted them in six segments each. This caused them to fragment when they hit their targets, with each piece staying embedded. When they hit their targets, they did what they were designed to do, which was to spall in different directions inside the heads of the demons he had spent most of his life hunting.

Before their bodies hit the ground, he twirled the pistols in his hands and slid them into their holsters on his hips. He could feel two heavy thumps through the floor of the desolate farmhouse, as the bodies fell onto the decayed planks of wood. As the echo of the shots died away, he couldn't hear anything. Even the crickets outside had gone silent. The only sound was his horse softly nickering at the full moon.

As he walked across the room, he could hear the crickets starting their symphony again. Firing his guns always seemed to put the world on hold for a few seconds.

He stopped and looked down at the two headless bodies and just shook his head.

Damn vampires will never learn.

As he walked through the broken door and onto the porch, Midnight just eyed him and waggled his head.

"If I ever want your opinion, I'll ask for it, you old nag."

I'm younger than you, you old geezer. And if you continue to act in this manner, I will outlive you.

"You wish."

He stepped down off the porch and moved to his saddlebags. Reaching in, he pulled out a cloth bag and walked back into the house.

Untying the knot at the top of the bag, he dumped part of its contents on each body. Pulling a cigar from his pocket, he struck a match and lit the end. After a couple of puffs, he dropped the burning match onto one of the bodies and the gunpowder flared to life.

Turning around, he walked casually through the ramshackle door and onto the porch, stopping to enjoy the taste of the cigar. He looked at Midnight, who just stared at him.

You're quite pleased with yourself, aren't you?

"Why yes, Midnight, I am."

You realize you're not finished.

"I know that. Don't you think I know that?"

I'm just checking.

Stepping down off the porch, he stuck the cigar in his mouth and pulled both pistols from their holsters. As the flames consumed the house, he walked about twenty yards away, into an open space.

Would you like some help?

"And just exactly what would you do to help?"

Oh, I don't know. Maybe tell you where he is.

"I know where he is," said the man in exasperation. "I'm just waiting for him to show his ugly face."

Okay, just thought I'd ask.

"You just stand there and look pretty."

Midnight just snorted. He did that whenever he thought the man was being a knucklehead, which seemed to happen a lot lately.

Standing in the clearing, turning slowly and looking all around, he held his Colts at waist height; the hammers cocked and his fingers on the triggers.

Knows where he is, does he? Yeah, sure he does.

The solid black stallion just watched as his rider searched the area for the coming attack. Deciding he was a little too close to the action, Midnight moved a few steps away and found a clump of green grass to munch on.

Might as well grab a snack and enjoy the show.

The area was now lit up by the flames and the roof caved in on the house, sending sparks a hundred feet into the air. The man detected no attacker. He kept turning slowly, looking for any movement.

It probably would've been better if he had focused some of his attention overhead.

Out of the darkness came the sound of a fluttering cloak and before he could raise his pistols, a vampire slammed his heels into the man's chest, knocking him to the ground, his pistols skittering away in the dirt.

Rolling quickly, he jumped to his feet and realized the Colts were out of reach.

Would you like some help now?

"Stay out of this or I will put you in the stew tonight!"

Whatever.

The man and the vampire began circling each other, with the demon bearing its long, pointed fangs. Its bald head shone in the moon's light, with the flames adding their own little accent.

"You guys get uglier every day."

The vampire just screeched at him.

"You know, one of these days you guys are going to have to learn to talk."

"Oh, we can talk," growled the vampire. "We just don't think you're worth the effort."

"Are you trying to hurt my feelings?"

"The only way I'm going to hurt you is by ripping your heart out of your chest and drinking your blood from it."

"That sounds rather painful. Wouldn't you rather just shake hands and call it a night?"

The vampire glanced at the burning building and paused for a second. Looking back at the man, he hissed.

"You just killed my son and daughter. I told them to wait for me, but they never listened."

"Kids, am I right? They always think they know everything. But hey, why don't I just arrange for you to join them. One big, joyful family reunion."

The vampire screeched at him and lunged.

"Okay then," muttered the vampire killer as he reached under his vest. When his hand came out, he held a twelve inch spike, made of steel and coated with silver.

The vampire batted the spike out of his hand and grabbed him by the throat, lifting him off the ground. As his leather boots swung back and forth, trying to find something to stand on, the man stared the vampire directly in the face.

"You're a tall one, ain'cha?" gasped the man through his closed off throat.

The vampire brought his face in close, their noses almost touching. Its fangs extended out of its mouth and were dripping with vampire spit.

"We've put up with you hunting us for far too long," said the vampire. "It ends tonight with your death. Then me and the others will rain horror down on this valley."

"Phew! Damn, your breath stinks, I thought Midnight's breath was bad, but you… ew… you win the prize."

Need some help now?

"Yeah, just a little."

A questioning look crossed the vampire's face as he tried to figure out who the man was talking to. Then he felt something slam into his back, knocking him forward, causing him to lose his grip. He swung around to see the horse walking away. If he could see his back he would see a really nice imprint of a horseshoe.

As he prepared to leap after the animal, someone behind him yelled, "Hey!"

Swinging around, he was met with the sword through the right eye. He went down with a screech loud enough to wake the dead and flopped around on the ground. The sword remained embedded in his head.

"Kinda stings, don't it?" asked the man. "It has a really nice coating of silver along the edges. I understand you vampires don't like that sort of thing."

The man calmly walked over and picked up his two pistols, blew off the dust and put one back in its holster. Looking around, he found the spike the vampire had so carelessly batted away. He stuck it back in the leather belt that crossed his chest under his vest.

Walking back to the writhing vampire, he pointed the other pistol at its head. Placing a boot on the throat of the vampire, he yanked the sword out of its head.

"I'd ask you to deliver a warning to the rest of your kind, but that would be hard to do without a head."

Without another word, he squeezed the trigger and blew the top of the vampire's head clean off. One more shot at the neck and what remained of the head rolled away from the body.

Holstering the pistol, he walked over to Midnight, who had returned to casually munching on the grass and patted him on the neck.

"Good job, buddy."

After wiping down the sword and returning it to its scabbard, he pulled another bag of gunpowder out of the saddlebag and returned to the vampire. As he poured the contents over the dead body, he searched around for his cigar.

Seeing a small wisp of smoke a few feet away, he walked over, leaned down and picked up the cigar and just shook his head. It hung limp in his fingers, broken in half.

Walking back to the vampire's body, he looked down and said, "You know, you ruined a perfectly good cigar."

He dropped the broken cigar into the gunpowder and walked away. There was just enough ember left to ignite the powder and set fire to the vampire's body.

"Anymore words of wisdom?" asked the man as he put the half-full bag of gunpowder back in the saddlebag.

I have plenty of words of wisdom, but I wouldn't waste them on you.

"Ooooo, getting a little snarky in your old age, are you?"

Just as he was about to swing himself up into the saddle, they heard a new sound above that of the flames consuming the house.

The sound of approaching horses.

Stepping back around Midnight, he stood in the clearing, near the burning body. He pulled another cigar from his vest and scratched a match on his belt buckle. As he lit the cigar, five men rode into the circle of firelight.

One man had a shotgun resting on his thigh and pointing into the sky. That man also wore a badge that said SHERIFF.

"Evenin', sheriff. What brings you out on this lovely night?"

"Well stranger, we see fire off in the distance and hear some gunshots and, well, we feel we might need to take a look. Suppose you tell me what you're doing out here, with what looks like a burning body behind you?"

The man half-turned and looked at the burning body and scratched his cheek.

"Oh that? Just taking out the trash, sheriff."

"Well, around these parts, we don't take kindly to one man killing another. Kinda sets my teeth on edge."

The man just smiled at him and walked over to what was left of the vampire's head. He could hear the hammer being cocked on the shotgun, so he made no sudden moves. He knew getting shot with the shotgun wouldn't kill him, but it would still hurt like the dickens.

Reaching down, he grabbed the remains of the head and picked it up by one of the pointed ears. Walking back over and standing in front of the men and horses, he held it up.

"Does this look like a man to you, sheriff?"

The sheriff looked like he was about ready to retch as he looked at the gory sight. Most of the top of the head was gone, but there was still enough left to see the fangs and the pointed tongue hanging from the mouth.

All of a sudden, the head snarled, causing a couple of the men to scream in terror. The man in black pulled one of the silver spikes from his chest belt and stabbed it through one of the eyes. The head squealed in pain.

"Sorry about that," said the man as he pulled the spike from the vampire's head.

"Sometimes they don't die like they should."

Whispers were exchanged among the rest of the men as he turned back to the burning body and dropped the head into the fire.

"It's Darius James," whispered one man.

The sheriff heard that and looked at the man and then back at James, who was wiping down the silver spike and placing it back in his belt.

"Darius James? So the stories aren't just made-up legend."

"No, sheriff, I'm afraid not," said James as he touched the brim of his hat. "If you have a mind to, there are two more bodies of vampires in the house, but the fire is going to take good care of them."

James looked at the rest of the men and then walked over to Midnight and climbed into the saddle.

"Now, if we're finished here, I'm heading into town to get a bite to eat and a little sleep. If you would like to continue this conversation, you'll find me at the boardinghouse."

Without waiting for an answer, he turned Midnight toward the town in the distance and they sauntered off.

As he disappeared into the darkness, he heard one man say, "If he's here, trouble can't be too far away."

"I don't know, Clem. Trouble has been here for a couple of months and it looks like he just took care of it."

All the horses whinnied in fright when one wall of the burning house collapsed.

2 – Darius, We Have a Job For You

Darius walked through the door of the boardinghouse with his pack over one shoulder and his saddlebags over the other. He carried his Winchester repeater rifle under one arm. His spurs jingled as he crossed the dining room, which he had to pass through to get to the desk.

He could feel the eyes of at least a dozen diners on his back. It happened every time he made an appearance in a new town.

Stepping up to the desk, he reached out and rapped the bell one time. A few seconds later, a woman came out of the back and gave him the once over.

"Yes sir, what can I do for you?"

"Well, pretty lady, I am looking for a room for a couple of nights."

The woman, easily over forty years old, blushed and said, "Young man, we have several rooms and I would be happy to set you up with one."

"And how about bath facilities around here?"

"We have those," she said. "We have two bath rooms, one on each end of the hall upstairs."

"You actually have bathing facilities here in the hotel?"

'Yes, sir. First boardinghouse in New Mexico to have the tubs indoors, complete with running hot water. How long are you planning on staying with us?"

"I shouldn't think more than a couple of nights. I'll be back on the trail day after tomorrow."

"Alright, that will be one dollar for the room, fifty cents for each night and twenty-five cents for the bath. Should I have a hot bath prepared for you?"

He pulled a dollar coin and a quarter dollar from his pocket and set it on the counter.

"Yes, ma'am, but after I've had some of that fine dinner you appear to be serving."

As she turned the ledger toward him for his details, she said, "Best dinner in all of Hell's Gate."

He cocked an eyebrow at her as he filled in his name.

"Hell's Gate, huh? You should really consider changing the name of this pretty little town. You're just inviting trouble with that moniker."

She took the ledger back and read it.

"Don't I know it, Mr. Ja ... Darius James?"

The dining room went completely silent when she said the name. James didn't have to look around to see everyone was looking at his back. He could hear the whispers and knew every set of eyes was on him.

"Yes, ma'am. Just came into town to take care of some business a short time ago and now I'm looking to relax for a couple of days before moving on."

"Has the business been taken care of?" she asked, with a stutter in her voice.

"It has," he said with a smile. "Should be

rather quiet now."

"Oh, thank the Lord," she said as she crossed herself. Then she looked up at him and said, "And thank you, Mr. James. The past few weeks have been full of terror."

He smiled and said, "That's why I came to town. Now, do you have a houseboy?"

"Not a houseboy, but a housegirl," she said as she stepped to the door leading to the kitchen.

"Anna Marie, could you come out here, please?"

A young woman, looking to be about twenty-five years of age, stepped out and said, "Yes, mother?"

She pointed to Darius and Anna Marie stepped up to the counter. As soon as their eyes met, Darius could feel his heart rate climb. Only one thing could do that to him and that was a beautiful woman.

"Can I help you, sir?" she asked in one of the most musical voices he'd heard in a long time.

"Uhh… yes, you can," he said as he pulled another dollar from his pocket and slid it across the counter to her.

"I tied my horse up outside. Can you see he gets down to the stables and taken care of?"

"Yes, sir. It would be my pleasure," she said as she picked up the dollar. "But it won't cost nearly this much."

"You can keep whatever change there is. Call it payment for putting up with my horse's attitude. If he gets too uppity, just smack him upside the head."

"Oh, sir! I could never hit a horse."

James laughed and said, "You might change your mind after you've dealt with Midnight."

She giggled and said, "I'll take care of him now." She scurried toward the door and out to find the horse in question.

"Now, Mr. James, if you'd like to take a seat at a table, I will bring you some dinner."

"Thank you kindly, ma'am."

He chose a table in the corner of the dining room, near a window that gave him a good view of the dusty cattle trail that served as Hell's Gate's main street. He stacked his belongings in the corner and sat down, just in time to see Anna Marie lead Midnight down the road, toward the stables.

He watched the beautiful woman walk along the dusty road, leading the black horse by the reins. Midnight looked like he would have followed her anywhere.

"Sleep well, Midnight," he said under his breath.

You, too, Darius.

With a belly full of dinner, James soaked in the warm water of the bath and relaxed for the first time in over two weeks. Two weeks on the trail, being sent to Hell's Gate because of reports of vampires terrorizing the locals.

He took a moment to gaze around the

room as he laid back in the hot water. For Hell's Gate being a tiny, dusty town in northern New Mexico, it appeared the owner of the boardinghouse had spared no expense in creating accommodations that would rival those in Europe or the East Coast.

The tub he was soaking in was a thick, hammered copper that could not have been inexpensive. There was even running water that came in hot to fill the tub. Anna Marie explained there was a small, elevated tank in back of the building that had a fire going under it constantly. She warned him not to put any part of his body under the hot water tap when he opened it.

Closing his eyes, he laid his head back against the edge of the copper tub and slowed his breathing. His thoughts drifted, like they usually did when he wasn't in any immediate danger.

Four hundred years? Had it really been that long?

As the fog of time cleared from his memories, he was no longer soaking in a bathtub in Hell's Gate. He found himself in the middle of a battle, not armed with his trusty pistols and rifle, but with a longsword. No longer did he wear the garb of an American western cowboy, but the armor and colors of an Old World soldier.

And as usual, when he revisited this battle

in his mind, things weren't going very well for him. It's usually not a very good day when you find yourself surrounded by six men, all armed to the teeth and looking to deprive you of your life.

Swinging his longsword with everything he had, he decapitated one man, but all he got for his troubles was a sword stabbing him in the back. He could feel the blade slice through his body and exit his chest, only to slam into the inside of his metal chest plate.

Finding himself laying on the ground, another man stabbed him in the gut while the others laughed.

Then, to add insult to injury, he was stripped of everything of value, which meant everything. Fighting this battle in one of the poorer villages of France meant even his undergarments had value. His underwear would probably be used to make a scarecrow or the like.

As he felt the life inside his body slowly dripping into the dirt beneath him, he found himself more irritated than anything. He was angry that they hadn't finished him, deciding to let him die slowly and naked on the battlefield.

Allowing his head to fall to the side, he could see the men walking away with his things. They stepped through the remnants of the battlefield, congratulating themselves for their heroism.

Waiting to die, which was taking a hell of a lot longer than he felt it should, he thought back on his life and realized he was probably heading to warmer climes.

That's okay. I'll give the devil so much trouble he'll kick me out of Hell.

In the throes of death, he hallucinated. That was the only explanation for what his fading eyes were seeing.

Walking across the blood-soaked battlefield, he saw a priest in pristine white robes with a red cross on his chest. The man of religion would stop every few steps and look down at the body of a dead soldier, make the sign of the cross and then continue on. He seemed to be searching for someone in particular.

When he stopped and looked down at the still-breathing soldier, he smiled and his blue eyes cut right through him.

"Darius James. How fortuitous it is that I have found you and still among the living."

"I must apologize, padre, for I find myself at a loss," gasped James. "I do not know you and I appear to be dressed inappropriately to meet you."

"I'm sorry," said the priest. "My name is Father Ferdinand Drake and your attire means nothing to me."

"What can I do for you, padre. As you can see, I'm busy at the moment, preparing for a journey to the other side of the veil," wheezed James.

"I need you to postpone that journey for the time being. I ... we, have need of your services."

"I'm not sure if I'm going to be of much use to you or anyone else within the next few minutes."

"Allow me to get right to the point."

"Yes, I really wish you would so I can die in peace."

Father Drake just shook his head and sighed.

"Darius, I can offer you a second chance at life and the opportunity to escape the clutches of Satan and the fiery depths of Hell."

James laughed and coughed up some blood.

"Are you some kind of wizard?"

"No, I am a man of God and God has some work that needs to be done. Work that it appears He thinks you would be perfect for."

James felt his body stiffen with a bout of pain, driving the breath from his body.

"I'm dying, padre," he gasped. "I don't think I can help you or your boss."

"Do you want to live?"

"Can't you just let me die in ..."

"Do you want to live!" stormed the padre.

"Wow. I didn't think a man of the cloth would raise his voice like that," croaked James with a raspy breath. "Yes, given the immediate circumstances, I'd prefer to live."

Father Drake pulled a rosary from his waist and began saying something in a tongue James didn't recognize.

Ah yes, the Last Rites ... HOLY SH ...!

His body was wracked with pain as he felt his injuries knit themselves closed. He could feel dirt and grime pushed out of his body and what felt like fire coursing through his veins.

After what seemed like an eternity of burning flames, the pain subsided and James found himself able to breathe easily. Running his hand over his bare chest, he found no gaping wound and when he looked down; he didn't even see a scar.

"Shall we go?"

Looking up, he saw Father Drake holding out a hand to help him up. Taking it, the padre pulled him to his feet and then turned and started walking out of the battlefield.

"A moment ago, you said we had a job for you. Who are *we*?"

"Ever heard of the Knights Templar?"

"Of course. All soldiers have."

"Well, we're not them."

"What?"

"We are a small group of men and women called Heaven Sent. We fight the enemies of God that cause most men and women to have nightmares."

Without another word, the padre continued walking toward the small village.

As James hurried to catch up, he said, "Uh, padre, I'm not exactly attired to be walking through any villages right now."

Drake stopped and looked up at him.

"Adam and Eve walked through the Garden of Eden dressed in nothing but the skin on their bones."

"Yes, and if I remember correctly, they got their butts kicked out of the garden for doing something stupid."

The padre smirked at him and sighed.

Waving his hand across the battlefield, he said, "If you can find something suitable to wear, be my guest."

James looked around, seeing the naked bodies of his company of soldiers and realized they had fared no better than him. Walking over to the nearest body, he looked down and felt a pang of guilt wash over him. It was a young boy, no more than twelve years of age, staring up at him with lifeless eyes. He was lying on top of the flagstaff and flag he had been bearing into battle.

"Oh, Sebastian," he whispered. "You should have stayed home."

Reaching down, he closed the boy's eyes and then pulled the flag out from under him. Wrapping the dirty cloth around his waist, he tied it off and turned back to the padre.

"You all should have stayed home," said Father Drake. "Trying to impose your will on others never seems to work out like you planned."

Without waiting for a reply, the priest turned and began walking away and James hurried to catch up.

"So, what is this job God has for me?"

"You left home, Darius James, looking for adventure. Well, you're about to have more adventure than you ever dreamed of."

James opened his eyes and realized the

water in the bath had gone cold and it was time to get out.

Adventure, you old coot? You didn't say a damned thing about vampires, werewolves and demons!

3 – Treat No Woman With Unkindness

Stepping out of the bathroom, Darius heard a fuss at one end of the hall. Looking to his right, he saw Anna Marie was being accosted by a man at least a hundred pounds larger than her.
Instead of heading for his room, he decided to see if she required any help.
"Can I be of assistance?" asked Darius as he neared the couple.
Anna Maria glanced over her shoulder to see Darius standing there.
"This is no worry of yours, mister," said the man.
One look from Anna Marie told Darius that he was about to make it his concern. He stepped around her, easing her behind him and confronted the guy.
"I have done some pretty black-hearted things in my time. Things my mama would be mighty disappointed with me for. But one thing I have never done is mistreat a woman or a child."
The man looked Darius up and down. He stood at least six inches taller and outweighed James by at least fifty pounds.
Having just stepped out of the bathroom, James was barefoot and his long, black hair was hanging wet and limp from his head. Hardly an intimidating sight.
"I will not put up with that kind of

conduct from another man, especially one the likes of you."

The man stepped forward and got right in James' face.

"Just who the hell do you think you are?"

"I ordinarily like to keep my name to myself," said James. "It makes it a little simpler for me to move through life."

"Well, I'll tell you what, Mr. No Name. I'm giving you exactly two seconds to get out of my sight and then I'm going to rain holy hell down on you."

"Please," said Anna Marie as she placed a hand on James' shoulder, "just tell him who you are so this doesn't go any further."

The warmth of her gentle touch sent a shock through his body, just as if he had gripped hold of a telegraph line.

He glanced back at her and could see she desperately wanted this to end without violence. Then he saw her flinch and knew what was coming.

Snapping his head back around, he was able to duck the crashing right hand being thrown by the big guy. As he felt the man's massive arm swoosh over his head, he heard Anna Marie yelp in surprise.

Dropping his bundle of dirty clothes to the floor, James came up with a forearm under the chin of the man and pushed him back against the wall. The entire boardinghouse shook from the collision of the man's body with the heavy wood timbers of the hallway.

Holding the man against the wall, Darius

looked over his shoulder to see that Anna Marie hadn't been so lucky to avoid the man's fist. It hadn't been a squeak of surprise, but of pain. She had caught the punch on the side of her face, knocking her against the opposite wall.

As she rubbed her face, she could see the fire growing in Darius' eyes and knew he was going to kill the man if she didn't stop him.

She rushed across the hall and put both hands on his arm.

"Please, just tell him who you are and this will end right now," she pleaded.

"He hit you," said James with as much control as he could muster.

"Oh please, horses have kicked me harder."

Darius perked up, still holding the guy against the wall by his neck.

"Midnight didn't kick you, did he?"

"Are you kidding? Midnight loves me," she said with a small smile.

"Well, I'm glad he loves someone."

Turning back to the problem at hand, Darius looked up at the man, focusing his dark brown eyes into the inebriated eyes of the attacker.

"In deference to Miss Anna Marie, I am going to introduce myself, so you better listen carefully. My name is Darius James."

At the sound of his name, the man's eyes went wide and it seemed like he was trying to push himself through the wall to get away from the legend.

"Now, because this sweet lady would

probably be the one to clean up the mess, I'm going to forego killing you right here, right now."

Again, he felt Anna Marie's hand on his shoulder.

"So, a couple of things are going to happen to keep me from doing that. First, I want you to reach way down deep in that dark soul of yours and dig up an apology to this little lady. And it better sound sincere to me."

The man looked back and forth from James to Anna Marie. He was shaking from the fear of having this man in his face.

"I'm sorry, Miss Anna. I'm sorry, I don't know what came over me."

Darius chewed on his tongue for a second and then glanced over his shoulder.

"I don't know, Anna Marie. I'm not sure that sounded sincere. What do you think?"

"I think ..."

"Please, I swear to God in Heaven I am sorry for having hit her."

"You're not supposed to be apologizing to me," said Darius.

The man looked Anna Marie in the eyes and begged her forgiveness. She patted Darius on the shoulder.

"That's acceptable."

"That's good with you?"

"Yes."

Darius turned back to the man and said, "What you really should do is thank her for saving your life."

The man nodded at her and squeaked,

"Thank you."

"Now to the second thing," said Darius. "How long are you planning on staying in Hell's Gate?"

"I will be back on the trail day after next."

"When are you planning on leaving?" asked Darius.

"Day aft ..."

He stopped when Darius raised an eyebrow and slowly shook his head.

"I was thinking of getting on the trail right now," he said. "No sense waiting for two days."

"Well," said Darius as he let the man come away from the wall, "don't let us keep you. I'll tell you what, I'm going to my room to put on some boots and make myself a little more presentable. Then I'll come back and walk with you to the stables. You know, because there are some dangerous things that creep around at night and I'd hate for you to encounter any of them."

He patted the man on the chest and turned him toward his room. Bending down, he picked up his dirty clothes and Anna Marie held her hands out for them.

"I was going to go out and see if there is a laundry service that can take care of these," he said.

"I can do that, Mr. James. It's part of the service."

She reached to take the bundle from his hands, but he pulled back.

"Don't you have a bag for nasty things like these?"

"We do and I'd be happy to bring you one."

"That would be great, because I have more dirty laundry in my room."

"I shall return momentarily," she said as she turned and whisked down the hallway.

He returned to his room and was putting his boots on when she returned. She saw the pile of dirty clothes in the corner and began stuffing them in the bag.

"Phew," she said with a groan.

"Yes, miss, I've been on the trail for two weeks and haven't had time to stop and take care of the niceties. These clothes I'm wearing are the last clean ones I have."

"Well, by tomorrow noon, that will be remedied," she said as she tied the offending clothes into the bag.

He stood up from the bed and pulled his pistol belt down from the hook on the wall and strapped it on. She watched and he could see she was a little afraid of his guns.

"Do you really think those will be necessary for a short walk to the stables?"

"Anna Marie, I learned very early on never to go anywhere without my weapons. When you do a job like I do, you are a target everywhere."

"That sounds like a terrifying life."

He picked up his hat and walked over to her. Looking at the side of her face, he reached up and stroked the back of one hand over her cheek. Her eyes closed and she sighed at his touch.

"That is going to be a right, nasty bruise."

"Which is another reason we need to get Mr. Sully out of here and out of town. If mama sees this, she'll kill him and won't be nothing you or I can do to stop it."

Darius smiled and said, "Well, let's get him out of town. For his own protection."

Stepping into the hallway, they almost bumped into Sully as he was heading for the stairs. He took a wide berth around Anna Marie and came to a stop.

He looked at her and said, "I really am sorry. I get that way when I've had too much to drink."

She nodded and Darius motioned to the stairs.

"After you, Mr. Sully."

As Sully started down the stairs, Darius took the bag of dirty laundry from Anna Marie, much to her consternation.

"I can carry a bag of dirty laundry, Mr. James."

"And so can I," he said. "I'll carry it until we part ways with you heading for the laundry and Mr. Sully and I heading for the stables."

As they walked through the dining room and out onto the porch, she held out her hand.

"Hand over the bag, Mr. James. I am going this way and you're going that way."

"Yes, ma'am," he said as he handed it to her and fished another dollar out of his pocket and gave it to her.

"Again, this is way too much, sir," she said.

"They can keep the change. Call it paying

extra for a job well done."

Turning and walking away, she left Darius and Sully standing there, watching her dress sway back and forth as she walked. James felt something stir deep down in his soul; something he hadn't felt in a long time.

Looking at Sully, he saw he was also staring after her.

"It's that kind of look and thinking that got you into trouble in the first place. Let's go."

As they walked along, heading for the stables, Sully said, "That is one mighty fine woman."

"Yes, she is," said Darius, "and you need to remember one thing about her. Because she is an exceedingly fine woman, she saved your life tonight."

Sully shut up and didn't say another word from then on. He was silent through the time it took him to get his horse saddled, climb up and head out of town.

As Darius watched him disappear into the darkness, he looked up to the sky and took a deep breath.

Mama. I'll never let what happened to you happen to another woman. I promise.

As he brought his gaze back down and stared into the darkness, his reverie was interrupted.

Talking to your mama, again?

He walked across the stables and looked in one stall.

"Shouldn't you be sleeping?"
Shouldn't you?

"I'm getting to it," said Darius. "Just you relax. We're going to be here for a couple of days."

No word from the padre, yet?

"I'm sure we'll hear something soon. Goodnight, Midnight."

He left the stables and headed back to the boardinghouse and a long awaited night of sleep.

Hopefully without dreams.

4 – The Trouble With Wendigos

The sun bore down on Hell's Gate as if it were trying to live up to its moniker. Small dust devils swept down the street, raising the red dirt into little funnel clouds that stretched thirty feet into the air.

Sitting in a chair, propped back against the wall of the boardinghouse, Darius rested two crossed boots on the railing in front of him. He watched as the citizens of the small town hurried from one place to the next, trying to get out of the scorching sun.

He was itching for a cigar, but Abbie, Anna Marie's mother, had stepped out earlier and asked him to not smoke just outside the door of the building. The smoke was being blown in the door and causing her some discomfort.

His only reply to her was, "Yes, ma'am."

He had been sitting out there for about two hours, relaxing for the first time in over a month, just waiting for word on his next assignment.

Anna Marie had made it a point to step out every fifteen minutes or so and bring him a fresh glass of cold water for which he was extremely grateful.

It did not escape his notice that she was spending a lot more time on him than any other customer.

Another thing he saw was the bruise on the side of her face. Every time he saw it, he felt an urge to jump on Midnight, track down Sully and put a bullet through his head. The only reason he didn't was because he was sure it would disappoint Anna Marie.

When Abbie saw it, she was ready to spit fire and go after the man herself.

The heat of the day caused him to close his eyes for a moment and was almost ready to drift off.

"Mr. James?"

Cracking one eye open, he tried not to be irritated as he had just about fallen into a slumber. Standing at the edge of the wooden porch was a young boy, maybe twelve-years-old.

"Yes, son, what can I do for you?"

"I was told to give you this," said the boy as he held out a folded, yellow piece of paper.

James leaned forward and took the paper and flipped it open and immediately saw it was a telegram.

> *Nothing of note to send you after. Rumblings in the west. Will know more soon. Relax while you can.*
>
> *Fr. Benedict*

He sighed as he read the words. One thing Darius James was not good at was relaxing.

"Can you remember my reply, or do I need to write it down?" he asked the boy.

"I kin 'member it, sir. I got a good memory."

"Good," James said as he fished a quarter dollar from his pocket. "Tell the old coot, I don't like relaxin'. If you don't find something soon, I may settle down here and take a wife. Darius."

He flipped the coin to the boy, who stood there dumbfounded.

"What's the problem?"

"Well, Mr. James, I know that Fr. means Father Benedict. I don't know if you should talk like that to a priest."

James laughed and said, "Believe me, boy. If I didn't talk like that to him, he'd take it that something was amiss and come looking for me. That's the last thing I want. Now repeat the message back to me."

When the boy repeated it perfectly, James sent him on his way.

"Take a wife, will you?"

He glanced over his shoulder to see Anna Marie standing in the doorway with his next glass of water.

"A man could do a lot worse," he said as he took the glass from her.

She walked around in front of him and leaned back against the rail his boots were resting on.

"And just who might the lucky woman be?"

"I was thinking about your mama. She's a mighty fine woman."

He raised the glass to his lips, trying to keep a straight face. It became impossible when he saw her mouth had dropped open and her eyes were as wide as the dinner plates inside.

He started laughing and her eyes came together in a scowl.

"Mr. James, that is not funny. No sir, not one bit."

"I thought it was funny, especially by the look on your face."

She sighed and crossed her arms under her breasts. He could tell she was not amused.

"Anna Marie, you are an exceedingly fine woman and I would venture to say, would make a fine wife to just about any man. Any man, but me."

She cocked her head and looked at him.

"And why would you think yourself undeserving of a wife?"

"Well, first and most importantly, that telegram could easily send me on my way and it's possible I might never come back this way. As a matter of fact, I'm sure the next telegram will do just that."

She looked at him with a wisp of sadness in her eyes.

"That sounds like a very lonely way to live."

He took a deep breath and let it out slowly.

"Anna Marie, truer words have never been spoken."

"Then why do it?" she asked. "Why not settle down and take a wife?"

He closed his eyes and fought with his inner emotions before answering her.

"Because that isn't part of the deal I made," he said in a softer tone.

He drained the rest of the water from the glass, hoping to wash the lump down his throat. Stepping forward, she took the glass from him and for some reason, took hold of his hand. The warmth that passed between them was something he wasn't prepared for. He felt a small bit of electricity travel up his arm and straight to his heart.

"Sometime, before you leave," she said, "I'd like to sit and talk with you and hear about some of the things you've seen."

Looking up into two of the kindest, bluest eyes he'd ever seen, he said, "Most of what I've seen are things I will never tell you about, m'lady. Those are things not meant for gentle ears such as yours."

She looked down at him and smiled.

"Darius, I was born and raised in Hell's Gate and I can assure you I've heard and seen many things that would change your mind about that."

She let go of his hand and disappeared through the door.

That is more of a shame than you know, Anna Marie.

It surprised Darius just how long it took for the sheriff to seek him out. After the events of the previous night, he thought the sheriff would have come to him almost immediately. In fact, the sheriff didn't come around until Darius was enjoying an early evening meal.

Sitting at the table that had quickly become *his* table, he looked up to see the sheriff walk into the boardinghouse. He looked around and when his eyes settled on him; he made a beeline for him. Without even asking, he sat down in the chair directly opposite.

"Afternoon, sheriff. To what do I owe the pleasure of your company?"

"I was just talking to Hank over at the telegraph office and was told you may stick around here for a little while."

"That would appear to be the case, but I can assure you, it's not my choice."

The sheriff bit his lip and Darius could see he was trying to come up with some words.

"Spit it out, sheriff. It don't do no good to hold it in."

"First, I need to know if the stories about you are true?"

Darius laughed and said, "I guess that would depend on which stories you've heard and from who."

"I'm talking about the stories of you being a monster hunter."

"I should think what you saw last night would answer that question."

"What I saw last night I can't explain," said the sheriff. "I ain't never seen no demon like that before."

"Vampire, sheriff. Demons are a whole different kind of monster."

The sheriff shook his head as he gazed out the window at the street of his little town.

"I never would have thought such things

were real until a few weeks ago," he mumbled.

He turned back and Darius was staring him in the eyes.

"Suppose you tell me what's troubling you?"

"I don't know if this is something I should even bring to you, but it might be just the thing you're familiar with. Those vampires you killed last night ... uh, thank you, by the way ... don't seem to be the only monsters we have around here."

Darius sat back in his chair and placed his hands on the edge of the table.

"Alright, tell me more."

"Before the vampires started causing trouble here, we were hearing some troubling news from a mining camp just north of here. It's a small operation, using some of the local indians for labor."

"By using, I hope you mean paying them to work the mine."

"Oh, of course. Mr. Stalls, the owner of the mine, is a fair-minded man and wouldn't consider not paying them."

"Okay, so what is this troubling news?"

"About a month ago, some of the mine workers began disappearing. Now, Mr. Stalls figured they had just grown tired of working the mine and left, heading back to their homes a little further north. But then, they found a body. Then another. Mr. James, these bodies were destroyed, torn to pieces worse than any wolf or mountain lion could do."

"But it could just be an animal attack," said

James as he took another bite of his steak.

"I thought so, too," said the sheriff. "but the indians aren't believing that. They are scared out of their minds, to the point of not even wanting to go into the mine anymore."

"Were the bodies found in the mine?"

"No, and that's the strange thing. They were found just outside the mining camp, in the woods around the camp. The indians say they don't want to be trapped in the mine if it ever comes back."

"Okay, you say they don't believe it's an animal that's done this. Have they said what they think it is?"

"When Mr. Stalls asked them, they just said one word. Wendigo."

Darius dropped his fork and knife on his plate at the sound of the word. The clattering of the utensils hitting the plate stopped all activity in the dining room. Anna Marie looked up from behind the counter.

"A wendigo is a monster that is believed to haunt the northern and northeastern woods of this country and Canada," said Darius in a low voice. "I would have a hard time believing there is one here in New Mexico."

"I can only tell you what I've heard, Mr. James."

Darius sat back and could see the sheriff was dead-straight honest with him. All kinds of thoughts were crashing through his brain, including one that he had never battled a wendigo or even knew how to battle one.

"How far is this mining camp?"

"It's about a two-hour ride north of here. It's about a quarter way up the mountains."

Looking outside, Darius could see it was getting late in the afternoon and the sun would set within the next hour.

"Well, it makes no sense to start right now with darkness coming on," he said. "First thing in the morning, after breakfast, I'll take a ride out there. I don't know the way though."

"I'll send a couple of my deputies with you."

"That would be much appreciated."

"Well, I'll leave you to your supper, Mr. James. I'll have the deputies here at nine sharp."

Standing up, the sheriff looked like he wanted to say something else, but ended up walking out of the boardinghouse and back to his office across the street.

James watched him go, still trying to figure out if a wendigo really could be here in New Mexico, and if so, what was he going to do about it?

It startled him when Anna Marie slipped into the chair the sheriff had just warmed. Her eyes were wide as she looked at him.

"What are you going to do?"

He laughed and said, "Anna Marie, you need to stop eavesdropping on my conversations."

"Mr. James, there …"

"Darius."

"What?"

"My name is Darius, not Mr. James."

"Oh ... okay. Mr., I mean, Darius, there is so little that goes on here in Hell's Gate that could even remotely be considered interesting. I mean, what the sheriff just said about, what was it he said, wendigo?"

"Yes, a wendigo. A frightful monster that would scare even the bravest of indians."

"So, what is it?"

"You remember I said there were things not meant for your ears? This would be one of those things."

She folded her hands in front of her and leaned on the table.

"I am not leaving here until you tell me."

"I could call your mama over here and she'll lead you away by the ear."

"You wouldn't," she said in surprise.

James looked at her and then smiled.

"Okay. A wendigo is a beast that roams the forests of the north and northeast. Supposedly, it looks like a skinny bear, with a wolf's snout and a set of antlers coming out of its head. It walks on two feet and has claws about a foot long. Some say it doesn't even have a head, but a skull."

"It sounds a little scary."

"It is rumored a wendigo is created when a man turns to cannibalism. It feeds on the soft parts of the human body after it kills you. I guess sometimes, it starts eating before a person is actually dead."

James took the last bite of his steak and washed it down with some cold water. Looking across the table, he saw her eyes were wide open, as was her mouth. She was trying to keep her breathing under control and was fighting a losing battle.

"A little worse than getting kicked by a horse, wouldn't you say?"

"And you're going after this monster?" she asked with a quiver in her voice.

"No. Like I told the sheriff, it is very unlikely a wendigo is roaming the forests of northern New Mexico. It's probably nothing more than a rabid mountain lion or something like that. I'll see if I can find it and take care of it. At least it will give me something to do."

He could tell by the look in her eyes he didn't convince her of how minor this problem was.

"Relax, Anna Marie. I know this will be taken care of easily. Besides, the sheriff has said he's sending two of his deputies with me. So, I'm not going alone."

"Oh! None of the sheriff's deputies are worth a plug nickel," she said. "Well, except for one, but even the sheriff is nothing more than a paper pusher."

"I'm sure he would disagree with you."

"When those vampires started causing trouble a few weeks ago, his solution was to tell everyone to stay in at night and lock their doors. Something he did quite nicely until you showed up."

"Hunting vampires is not something most men are cut out for."

"Yes, but he's supposed to be the law around here and he just cowered in his office like the rest of the town."

"Anna Marie, do you really think those vampires cared one bit about the law? Hunkering down inside your homes was the best thing a person could do until help got here."

"Help? Meaning you."

"It took me about fifteen days to get here once I received word of the problem. How many people died because of the vampires?"

"Nine. Well, we think ten, but we never found the first one. Joshua Dalton. His wife said she heard him scream when he went out to take care of the animals one night and she never saw him again."

"No blood or anything to show he had been killed?"

"No, nothing. It was like he just disappeared into the darkness."

"Anna Marie!"

They looked over to see Abbie had decided her daughter had rested long enough. She jumped up and looked at Darius. She wanted to say something, but couldn't find the words.

As Darius watched her walk away, he had some troubling thoughts running through his mind.

No blood, no body.

That could mean any number of things, but the most logical was also the most horrifying to think about. Darius drank the last of his water, trying to keep his hands from shaking, praying to God in Heaven he was wrong.

Joshua Dalton was turned.

5 – The Braves Are Restless

The next morning, after Darius had eaten his breakfast, he walked out of the boardinghouse and saw three men waiting for him. One was the Sheriff and the other two were obviously his deputies. He recognized both of them from two nights before.

Midnight had already been brought from the stable, saddled and ready to go. Darius walked over and put his rifle into the scabbard on the saddle and then looked at the three men.

"Good morning Mr. James," said the sheriff. "Let me introduce Clem Barker and Seth Gooding, two of my deputies."

"Gentlemen," said Darius with a nod.

Behind him he heard some steps coming from the boardinghouse and he turned to see Anna Marie coming down the steps. She had three cloth sacks in her hands and she handed one to Darius and one to each of the deputies.

"You be careful, Seth," said Anna Marie.

Seth was the youngest of the three men that was going on this mission and when Anna Marie talk to him, he blushed as he took the sack from her.

"Yes ... Anna Marie."

"What about the rest of us?" asked Clem.

Anna Marie laughed and said, "You too, Clem."

She turned and looked at Darius and could see a darkness in his eyes that told her he was all business now.

"Please bring him, I mean, them back safely."

"Yes, ma'am," he said as he touched the brim of his hat.

He looked at the sheriff and said, "I'm guessing we won't make it back tonight, so look for us sometime tomorrow afternoon."

"Will do, Mr. James."

Darius climbed up into the saddle and looked down at Anna Marie and could see the concern in her eyes. It had been a long time since a woman worried after him as he was going on a hunt.

Of course, he could tell she was more worried about Seth than either of the other two. Looking at Seth and looking at her, he realized they were about the same age and probably better suited together than he and Anna Marie would be.

What about me?

"You hush," said Darius. "You always come back unscathed."

Not for your lack of trying to get me killed.

As they headed out of town, Midnight kept looking back and could see Anna Marie was standing there watching them go.

"Stop looking back," said Darius.

She is worried about us.

"And you looking back isn't helping matters."

As they put the town behind them, Darius could see the mountains in the distance they were headed for. Though they looked a long

way off, he trusted the sheriff's estimate of it being a two-hour ride to the mining camp.
They followed a dusty trail that looked like it ran straight to the mountains and Darius didn't have to do anything to keep Midnight on the trail.

"So, Mr. James, do you really think we're going to find a monster or is it going to be some animal?" asked Clem.

"I don't know, Clem. I'm hoping it's an animal, because if it's what the indians are saying, we're going to have a fight on our hands."

"I ain't never heard of this thing. What did they call it, a wangdingo?"

"A wendigo."

He spent the next few minutes explaining to them what a wendigo was and how he had never fought one before. He also told them that when it came right down to it and there was a fight, to let him do most of the fighting. In his own mind, he wasn't expecting either of them to be much help if it really turned out to be a monster.

He turned and looked at Seth and asked, "So, tell me about you and Anna Marie."

Seth immediately went red in the face and couldn't say anything. Clem started laughing and Darius looked at him.

"That boy's got it real bad for Miss Anna Marie, but he can't get two words out whenever she's around."

Darius looked over at Seth and asked, "Is that true? You can't speak to a pretty woman?"

"I don't know, Mr. James. Every time I'm around her I get all choked up inside and can't get the words out."

"Well, I'll tell you," said Darius, "I sometimes know how you feel. Sometimes I feel I'd rather go up against a vampire than have to talk to a pretty woman, such as Miss Anna Marie."

"Really? I would think you'd be brave enough to do just about anything, Mr. James."

Darius laughed and said, "Monsters are one thing, but women are a lot scarier."

Clem snickered and said, "I ain't got no trouble talking to women."

Seth looked at him and said, "Clem, when was the last time you ever talked to a woman about anything other than what you wanted for dinner?"

Clem scratched his chin and said, "Well, boy, I don't rightly know. I never had much use for a woman in my life. Not since my Rosie Belle passed on."

After he said that, Clem went silent as if he had dragged up some old memories that he had been trying to push way down.

Darius looked at him and then at Seth.

Seth said, "Miss Rosie Belle was one of the sweetest little ladies you ever saw, Mr. James. Why she ever took up with an old coot, like Clem, is beyond anyone's imagination."

"Love is a strange thing, Seth. It will take two people that you would never dream would get together and slap them into a relationship that befuddles the mind. Maybe Miss Anna

Marie is your Rosie Belle."

"Do you think so?"

"I saw the way she looked at you. She looks at me and sees a man who lives a life of adventure, fighting monsters and trying to keep the world safe. But that is not what she is looking for in a man to spend the rest of her life with. She is looking for a man who is safe and will treat her like the queen she is."

"I don't know, Mr. James. I don't think I could measure up to be the man that she deserves."

"Well, Seth, let me tell you something about women. They have no problem telling you what you're doing wrong and what you need to do to fix it. The trick is listening to them and realizing they are almost always right and you are almost always wrong. You learn that one little secret and you will have the key to happiness with a woman."

Seth nodded and went silent, as did Darius and Clem. They rode on quietly for the next hour until they reach the foothills leading into the mountains.

"We'll be at the mining camp in about thirty minutes," said Clem.

"Gentlemen, when we get to the camp, let's keep my identity to ourselves initially," said Darius. "I like to get an idea of the situation before that gets out."

"Sure thing, Mr. James," said Clem. "How should we introduce you?"

"Just say I'm James. That way you're not telling lies and no corrections need to be made later."

As the trail narrowed going up the hills, Clem took the lead and Seth followed at the back. The two deputies kept their heads moving from side to side, watching the trees, searching for anything that might come at them by surprise.

Darius rode easily, having been in this sort of situation before. He didn't feel any danger close by, but he didn't want to tell them that, so they would stay alert and ready for anything.

True to his word, Clem led the three of them into the mining camp about half an hour later. It was a minor operation, set in a small draw between two slopes. There was a small creek running down the middle of the draw, with the camp set up on both sides.

Darius could see the opening to the mine above the camp, on the east side of the creek. There were rope and cable systems coming out of the mine and down to the slough area. The operation was obviously too small to warrant building tracks and using ore carts.

There were half a dozen tents set up below the mine for the workers. Each looked big enough to house six to eight workers. There was also a small wooden building which was the office for the people that ran the mine.

Based on what they could see, there should have been fifty to sixty men in the camp, working the mine. It was possible most of the men were in the mine, but there still should have been a couple dozen above ground.

Darius counted less than ten as they rode in. For a place that should have been making enough noise to raise the dead, this place was almost as quiet as a ghost town.

"I've never seen it like this," said Seth.

"Not what I was expecting to see," said Darius.

As they stopped outside the office and dismounted, a man came out and looked them over. Then he stuck his head back in the door and said something to someone inside. A few seconds later, another man came out.

"Clem, Seth, what brings you men up here?"

"Mr. Stalls," said Clem, "we've come to see how things are going. We wanted to find out if you still had that trouble you were having a couple of weeks ago."

"Well, as you can see it's not going very good. Most of my men have left, heading home. Said they couldn't stay if this creature was still in the area and killing them."

"How many men have been lost?" asked Darius.

"And you are?" asked Stalls.

"This is James," said Seth. "He's trying to help."

"Well, James, we lost almost a dozen men in the last two weeks."

"A dozen? Now, the sheriff told me when this started, you had workers disappear and figured they may have just gone home."

"That is true, but I don't think the sheriff was being truthful with you. Those men disappeared, but no one here ever thought they left for home. They wouldn't do that and leave their belongings here."

"So, if this started a month ago as I was told and you've had a dozen workers killed in the last two weeks, how many would you say that adds up to? I mean, assuming those who disappeared are also dead."

Stalls looked at the other man standing beside him and asked, "What, twenty? Twenty-one?"

The man nodded and said, "Twenty-one."

The number floored Darius.

"Twenty-one?"

He couldn't believe he was just now hearing about this when it should have been a top priority for Heaven Sent. When he got back to town, he was going to be sending a strongly worded telegram to Father Benedict, asking why they didn't know about this.

"Are any of the bodies still here?" he asked.

"Yes, sir," said Stalls. "We have two that haven't been taken back to the village yet. The rest of the indians are leaving within the hour and will take them."

"How long have these men been dead?"

"One was killed two nights ago and the other four nights ago."

"I'd like to see them," said Darius.

"You're welcome to try, but it may not be that easy," said the other man.

"And why is that, Mr ... ?"

"I'm Jericho and the reason is that the indians have already wrapped them for their journey to the village. They will probably not take too kindly to disturbing their fallen brothers."

"Even if it helps to catch this creature?"

"I can order them to let you see the bodies," said Stalls. "They will usually do whatever I ask of them."

"No, sir," said Darius. "You need to stay on good terms with your workers. If you order them to do something they may not like, it will hurt that. Let me talk to them."

"Suit yourself. This way," said Stalls as he turned and led them over a small bridge to the other side of the creek.

Walking through the camp, they came to a small group of men sitting around a fire. A couple of them jumped up as Mr. Stalls approached and greeted him.

As the group came to a stop, Darius stepped out from behind Jericho and stood near the fire. As he looked at the men, one of them shouted something in their native tongue and made some gestures with his hands.

The other Indians looked at him and back at Darius. They all took a couple of steps back as the oldest one among them stepped forward. He waved his hands in front of Darius, as if he was trying to feel something in the air. He was talking, almost chanting, saying something no one else could understand.

"He says you are a spirit walker," said one

of the other indians.

Darius nodded and said something to the old man in his own tongue. Clem and Stalls both sucked in quick breaths as he began talking to the old man.

After a few seconds, the old man turned and motioned to the others and they disappeared into a tent.

"What's going on?" asked Seth.

"They are bringing out the bodies for me to see."

The old man said something, motioning to the men behind him.

"He's also saying that you four need to leave. This will be for my eyes only."

Darius looked at the four of them and saw it wouldn't take much convincing to get them to leave. Seth looked especially ready to head back across the creek. He was not ready to witness two bodies that had been torn to pieces.

The four of them turned and headed back over the bridge and Stalls invited the other two in for some coffee while they waited.

"Did you know he could speak Pueblo?" asked Seth quietly.

Clem said, "Boy, I have a feeling he can speak any language he wants."

Darius turned back to the old man and saw four men carrying two wrapped bodies out of the tent and placing them on blankets on the ground. As they were getting ready to unwrap the bodies, Darius stopped them.

Unbuckling his pistol belt, he walked to a

tree and hung it on a broken branch. He pulled his vest off and hung it up, too. Checking that he was suitably disarmed, he walked back to the group.

Dropping to his knees near the heads of the wrapped bodies, he nodded to the men and watched as they carefully unwrapped them.

As the full horror of what happened to the men became visible, the old man chanted in a low, singing voice. The other men dropped to their knees and bowed their heads. Darius followed suit, waiting until the medicine man finished.

When the shaman finished, Darius opened his eyes and looked at the remains in front of him. Something had torn both men to pieces, from their upper chests to their waists. Most of their organs were missing, leaving nothing but empty cavities.

Darius reached out and moved his hand slowly over the space above the open cavities. At first, the others watched him and saw nothing, but the shaman just nodded.

A few seconds later, a small glow formed around Darius' hand. His hand absorbed the glow until his hand was shining.

Darius placed his hand on the forehead of one man and closed his eyes. At first, his mind's eye was foggy, but the mist cleared away and the vision darkened.

He was seeing through the eyes of the dead man and it was nighttime. He was walking away from the camp, heading for the pit to relieve himself. The pit was about fifty yards below the camp and it took a minute or two to get there.

As the man did his business, he heard a snap of a twig and swung around to see what had made the sound. A loud screech burst into his ears and something slashed him before he saw it. The vision went black immediately.

Darius opened his eyes and looked down at the tortured face of the man. He brushed the hair off the man's forehead before reaching and laying his glowing hand on the forehead of the other dead man.

This was a young man, maybe not even twenty years old. As he closed his eyes, he let his mind sink into the vision again. This time, the circumstances were different. The young man was sitting near the base of a tree about a hundred yards above the camp. He had a large knife in his hand and he was whittling away on a piece of wood.

Though he was working the wood, he kept his eyes moving all around, as if he was waiting for something. And something was what he got.

Again, a loud screech broke the silence of the night and the young man jumped up. Brandishing the knife, he turned to face where the sound had come from. A large paw with long, razor-sharp claws came out of the darkness at his head and he ducked. He could feel the claws disturb the air as they passed over his head.

As he came up, he was face-to-face with the demon. It looked exactly like what a wendigo should look like.

He stabbed at it with his knife, driving the blade into the body of the beast. It horrified him that his attack had no effect on the demon. It was almost as if he was battling the surrounding air.

Before the young brave had a chance, the wendigo brought the claws of one paw up and into his chest, driving the air from his lungs. The demon lifted him off the ground and stared into his dying eyes.

The warrior tried to scream, if for no other reason than to alert the rest of the camp, but he couldn't draw a breath. He watched as the wendigo licked its lips and he prayed to the Great Spirit to take him fast, so he wouldn't be alive when the beast feasted on his body.

After a few seconds, the brave's sight dimmed and Darius felt the connection break between them. He sat back on his heels and let his head drop, trying to draw slow, even breaths.

The Pueblos sitting near him said nothing. After what they had seen, they knew they were in the presence of a man of spirit and didn't want to intrude on his thoughts.

For five minutes, they sat quietly and waited for him to speak. Finally, he opened his eyes and saw six pairs of eyes staring back at him.

"Wendigo," he whispered.

Fear crossed the faces of the men and he went to stand up. When he tried to get up, his knees were wobbly and he almost fell. Before he knew it, two of the men were at each side and holding his arms to keep him from falling.

They led him to the fire pit and had him sit down on a log and another brought him some water. Not realizing how dry he was, he drained the mug of water and asked for more. He drained two more mugs before his thirst was quenched.

Looking back at the two bodies, he motioned for the others to re-wrap the bodies. As the men prepared their brothers for burial, the shaman sat down across from Darius and looked him in the eyes.

"That was unnecessary," said the old man. "I had already seen what those warriors faced."

"I needed to see it for myself, grandfather. But, if it makes you happy, I wish I hadn't seen it."

"It does not make me happy. What can we do to drive this evil spirit away?"

Darius took a deep breath and stood up. He walked over and took his pistol belt down from the tree and strapped it on and put his vest back on, checking to make sure he had a full set of spikes.

Looking back at the old man, he said, "I'm going to kill it."

He turned and walked down and across the bridge and headed to the mine office. He patted Midnight on the neck as he walked by.

Didn't like what you saw, did you?

"No, Midnight, I did not."

6 – You Are Not The Help I Need

"You two gentlemen can head on back to Hell's Gate. I'm going to be here for a little while."

Clem and Seth looked at Darius, still in shock from what he told them about what he had seen in his vision. Mr. Stalls looked down at the floor and shook his head.

"Wait a minute," said Seth. "Why are you staying?"

"Because I told those men out there I was going to kill this beast and that's what I intend to do."

Jericho looked at his boss and said, "I'll go out and get the horses ready to leave. You and I can go back with Clem and Seth and wait for this to be over."

Stalls looked up at him and nodded. The big guy stood up and walked out the door.

Clem pulled out his pocket watch and said, "If we start back now, we'll be back in Hell's Gate before dark."

"That'll be good," said Darius.

He looked at Seth, who was shaking his head.

"Something eating at you, young man?"

Seth looked up at him and said, "I don't run, Mr. James."

"I'm not asking you to run. I'm asking you to ride protection on Mr. Stalls and Jericho."

"Clem and Jericho can look after Mr. Stalls. I'm staying to help you."

"Like hell you are!" yelled Darius. "One

thing I will not put myself into a position of doing is having to explain to Anna Marie why you were killed."

Seth raised his voice and said, "And I'm not going back to explain to her why I left you out here by yourself!"

"This will not be the first time I've faced a demon like this by myself. It's how I usually work, as you and Clem saw the other night."

"Boy, I think you should listen to him," said Clem. "You'll probably just get in the way."

"Why? Because he's the great Darius James? Seems to me the safest place is going to be right by his side."

"You're Darius James?" stammered Mr. Stalls.

Darius closed his eyes and shook his head.

"Now I definitely don't want you around here," said Darius.

"I'm not going," said Seth through gritted teeth.

"That sounds pretty final," said Darius. "If you get yourself killed, I'm going back to tell Anna Marie what a fool you were."

"Anna Marie would think me even worse than a fool if I ran and left you here."

Darius wanted to figure out a way to get Seth on a horse and headed back to town, but short of wrapping him up like one of the indian's dead bodies and tying him to the saddle, he couldn't see any way of doing it.

"Alright, you're a grown man, but if you don't listen to me, I'll shoot you myself.

Understood?"

Seth nodded, wondering if the legend would really shoot him.

Stalls got up and started putting some papers in a small pack and grabbing his gun. He and Clem stood up and headed out of the office, as Jericho was walking up with two saddled horses.

As the three of them climbed up, Seth said, "Clem, do not tell Anna Marie what we're really facing here. Just tell her it's a mountain lion or something like that. No need to worry her."

"Boy, that little lady would worry about you if I told her you two were going after a rabid squirrel. Like Mr. James said, don't get killed or you are going to have stories told about your stupidity and I'll be the one telling them."

Darius nodded to Jericho and the three of them headed down the trail and back toward Hell's Gate. Looking up at the sky, he could see there were about three hours left before sundown, so he knew they had plenty of daylight to get there safely.

Sounds coming from the other side of the creek interrupted his thoughts and they looked to see the indians were finished loading their own horses and were coming across the bridge.

He walked over to the small group and they stopped in front of him.

The old man said, in his native tongue, "The Great Spirit walks with you. I can see it with my old eyes."

He held out his hand and said, "Be brave."

Darius took his hand and nodded, relaying they would send word when it was safe to come back.

The old man looked at Seth and said, "The fool will need looking after. He does not know the Great Spirit and won't ask for his help."

Darius smiled and nodded. They watched the small band of warriors head down the same trail the first three had gone down. When they reached the bottom of the mountain, they would head north and back to their village.

"What did he say about me?"

Darius looked at Seth and said, "Same thing I've been saying about you for the past twenty minutes."

With no further explanation, Darius turned and headed across the bridge and down the hill about a hundred yards. Seth followed along behind him, keeping his Winchester at the ready. Darius wasn't in the mood to tell him that his Winchester would be of no use against a wendigo, but he let the boy continue if it gave him a sense of protection.

The two of them walked down the hill and found the spot where the second brave had been killed. Darius looked around and recognize the spot from the vision that he had had.

Closing his eyes, he tried to get a picture in his mind, of which way the wendigo went after it had killed the brave. He knew it hadn't gone down the hill, because if it had, the other indians would have seen it.

Looking to the sides, he saw the slopes were very steep and even though he couldn't imagine a wendigo going up the steep hills, he couldn't discount that.

And going down the hill, the wendigo would've ended up out of the mountains and out of the forest. That was something he didn't think the creature would want.

He looked back at Seth and asked, "If you were a wendigo, which way would you go after leaving this spot?"

Seth looked around and came to almost the same conclusions that Darius had. Going back toward the camp would've caused the wendigo to be spotted.

"Well, I doubt it went down the hill, because from what you've told me it likes to live in the forest, in the trees. If it has animal instincts, it will not want to give that up."

"Very good," said Darius. "Maybe you're not the fool that I think you are."

When Seth's face blushed, Darius couldn't tell if it was from embarrassment or from anger.

"Alright, the last thing we want to do is go traipsing all over this mountainside looking for it when we don't know where it is. So, we're going to have to wait for it to come to us."

"And how long is that going to take?"

"Why? Do you have someplace else to be?"

"No, I was just wondering."

Darius turned and started heading back up the hill toward the camp. When they got to the bridge, he crossed over and headed for the office.

I think the boy asks a good question.

Darius stopped and looked at Midnight.

"If I want your opinion, I'll ask for it."

"Do you always talk to your horse?" asked Seth.

"Only when he's getting a little uppity."

"And does he talk back to you?" asked Seth with a raised eyebrow.

"Almost constantly."

Walking into the office, Darius took a seat behind the desk and Seth sat down in the other chair across from him.

"In answer to your question," said Darius, "we're going to stay here as long as it takes. That may be one night, that may be three or four nights."

Seth looked around the small office and said, "Not much for accommodations around here."

"We have our bedrolls and we have enough food to last us. I'm thinking it won't be much over one or two nights, anyway."

"What makes you say that?"

"It's been four nights since it killed that last brave and I believe it's going to be getting hungry. With everyone gone, that leaves the two of us."

Seth wasn't sure he liked the sound of that and was thinking he should've left with Clem, Mr. Stalls and Jericho. Fighting and defeating the wendigo sounded like an adventure to him, but being bait wasn't exactly what he had in mind.

Darius reached into the small pack that he had brought in and pulled out a small journal, a pen and a small inkwell.

As he opened the book and was prepared to write, Seth asked, "What are you writing about?"

Darius looked at him and said, "Anything and everything. It's a good habit for a man to have. You should think about it."

Seth hung his head and Darius sat back in his chair, looking at him.

"What's the problem?"

Seth looked up at him and said, "I don't know how to write."

"You can read, can't you?"

"Sort of. Not very good, though."

"How old are you, young man?"

"I'm twenty-five years old, sir."

"And in those twenty-five years you've never learned to read or write? Didn't your mama teach you?"

"My mama died when I was a baby."

Darius bit his lip and nodded his head.

"I'm sorry to hear that. A boy needs his mama, just as much as his father."

"My pa was a good man, but reading and writing weren't exactly skills he was prepared to teach. I got some of it during the couple of years of schooling that I had, but pa needed me to work at the farm more than going to school."

Darius stared right through him, making him feel uncomfortable.

"Well, it is not too late to learn. I'm sure if you applied yourself, you could learn to read and write quickly."

Holding up the journal, he said, "This is a good habit for any man, or woman, to get into. This will allow you to look back over your life and see where you were and where you've come to."

"And what does your journal tell you about yourself?" asked Seth.

Darius set the journal down and put his hand on top of it. He closed his eyes and thought for a moment before he said anything.

"My writings tell me I was not an honorable man when I was your age."

Seth sat forward in his chair and rested his elbows on the edge of the desk.

"All the stories I've ever heard of you have always been of a good man."

"Well, the stories are incomplete."

Darius told him about his life before becoming the legendary monster hunter. Seth was on the edge of his seat the whole time, taking it all in.

"Wait, you're telling me you're over four hundred years old?"

"Four hundred and thirty-seven years old, to be exact."

"How is that possible?"

"As the Holy Bible says, with God all things are possible."

"So, you work for God."

"Yes and no, I work for the men who work for God. They tell me where there's monster trouble and I go there and take care of it."

"And that's how you ended up in Hell's

Gate."

"Correct."

Seth sat back in his chair, folding his hands in front of his face.

"Until a couple of nights ago, I would never have believed monsters existed. But then I saw with my own eyes when you held up that vampire's head."

"Well, now you know. Now you know the devil isn't the only monster that roams the face of the earth."

Darius studied the young man for a moment and then changed the subject.

"Seth, tell me about Joshua Dalton."

7 – Alone In The Dark

The first night passed without incident. The only excitement came when Darius needed to get up in the middle of the night and relieve himself outside. Seth almost jumped out of his bedroll when he saw him getting up to go out and showed he was going to go with him.

"I don't really need someone to watch over me while I take care of business," said Darius.

"You don't, but I've been holding back for a couple of hours now."

"Why didn't you just get up and take care of it?"

When Seth didn't answer, Darius just smiled and said, "Come on, get your boots on and let's get this done."

When they were outside, Darius had his gun belt slung over his shoulder. He almost laughed when he saw how fast the boy got done and was ready to head back to the office. And Darius, being who he was, just took his own sweet time, enjoying the cool, crisp night air.

As he finished, he just walked a few feet away and then stopped, taking in the beauty of the night sky and the sound of the night critters all around them.

He could feel the nervousness rolling off Seth and just wanted to see how long it took for the young man to bolt for the office. After a couple of minutes had passed and Seth was still there, he gave him a break and headed back to the warmth of their bedrolls.

Seth bolted the door and checked it twice just to be safe. Darius laid down on his back, his head resting on his pack and drifted off to sleep with a smile on his face.

Seth woke up with a start, with a couple of sun rays shining in his eyes through some gaps in the wall. Looking over, he expected to see Darius still sleeping, but was surprised to see an empty space. Even his bedroll was rolled up and stowed away.

Jumping out of his bed, he listened and could hear some small noises coming from outside. Walking over to the door, he saw it was not bolted and he peered through the gap and saw Darius.

The monster hunter was across the creek, sitting near the fire pit the indians had built. Seth could see some smoke coming from the pit and it looked like Darius was cooking something.

Getting dressed as fast as he could, he left the office and headed across the bridge. He could smell the wonderful aroma of frying bacon.

"Well, good morning, sunshine," said Darius. "I was wondering what kind of farmer sleeps when the sun is up?"

"You could have woke me."

"Why would I do that? We're not going anywhere and we're not doing anything. So, you might as well rest while you can."

"What do you think the chances are of the wendigo attacking during the day?"

"Pretty much zero. During the daylight hours it's going to be hiding in whatever cave or hole it's found for protection."

Seth looked at the bacon and eggs in the frying pan and then wondered where Darius had got them. He didn't think he had carried it in his pack.

"You hungry?" asked Darius.

"Sure am, but where did this food come from?"

Darius pointed with the large knife in his hands and Seth turned to see the small blockhouse built next to the creek. It was actually built partly over the creek and was using the cold of the mountain water to keep the provisions cool.

"You raided their food locker?"

Darius sat back and looked at him.

"Do you really think they would begrudge us a little food while we sit here and try to solve this problem for them?"

"Well, no, but we should have asked."

"Seth, when we finish this task and head home, I will not be asking Mr. Stalls for any payment. All I will want from him and the others is a simple thank you. So, providing a little something to eat will be the least they can do. The last thing we need to be doing is trying to fight the wendigo on empty stomachs. Now sit down, grab a plate and dig in."

Seth sat down on the log across from

Darius and picked up a metal plate and fork. After filling his plate, he took his first bite and thought he had died and gone to Heaven. Obviously, four hundred and thirty-seven years had been plenty of time for Darius to learn to cook over a campfire.

"So, what are we going to do today?" asked Seth.

"A whole lot of nothing."

"Really? That's the plan?"

"Look, kid, part of this job entails a lot of waiting. These monsters rarely work on my schedule. They keep to their own time."

"But you don't think it will attack us during the day."

"Not having ever dealt with a wendigo before, I can't rightly say. But, from what I could gather from the old man before they left, it did all the killings at night. I'm guessing this wendigo likes to keep itself in the darkness. Gives it the advantage."

"What kind of advantage can we get for ourselves?"

"Our biggest advantage is we know what we're dealing with. It's a flesh-eating monster that stands about ten feet tall, has claws about a foot long and teeth that can rip the meat right off your bones with very little trouble."

Seth's hand had stopped about halfway to his mouth with a fork full of food. He just stared at Darius with wide eyes. The monster hunter was just casually stirring some more eggs to keep them from burning in the frying pan.

Darius looked up at him and saw the young man's hand was shaking, losing all the food back onto his plate.

"What's the matter?"

"I just ... I ..." stuttered Seth as he tried to control his breathing.

Darius' eyebrows raised as he looked at the scared man. Then he started laughing.

"I'm just kidding, Seth. Take it easy."

"You're joshin' me?"

"Yeah, it's not nearly as bad as I just said," said Darius with a laugh.

"That's not funny!"

"Wow, nobody in Hell's Gate seems to have a sense of humor."

"I'm out here with you, scared out of my mind that we'll actually meet up with this thing and you're funnin' me!"

"I'm sorry, you're right. That was completely uncalled for, but remember this one thing. You wanted to stay and I wanted you to leave."

Darius went about dishing up some food onto his own plate and sat back to enjoy it. As he filled his mouth with some hot, tasty bacon, he looked at Seth, who hadn't gone back to eating yet.

"Wendigos never get to be ten feet tall," he said as he chewed on the bacon.

"They don't?"

"No," he said as he put a fork full of scrambled eggs in his mouth.

"How tall?"

Darius gave a little half-shrug and said

with a mouthful of eggs, "Eight feet, tops."

He almost wanted to laugh as Seth set his plate down on the log. It appeared the boy had lost his appetite.

You know, you're not very nice sometimes.

"Hey, I want him scared. If he's scared, he'll jump at every snapped twig. There's no way a wendigo will be able to sneak up on us."

You could still be nicer to him. He could die on this mountain.

"He will not die on this mountain!" yelled Darius at the horse across the creek. "I'm here and won't let that happen."

Seth was looking back and forth between the two, wondering what one half of the conversation was.

That's what you said about Carlos last year.

"Hey! Carlos got stupid and went after that demon by himself!"

Midnight looked at him and then waggled his head before going back to munching on a sparse patch of grass.

"Who was Carlos?" asked Seth, with a hitch in his voice.

Darius looked at him and pointed at his plate.

"Eat. You're going to need your strength."

Seth picked up his plate and began eating again, albeit with a lot less enthusiasm.

"About a year ago, I got a message of a demon terrorizing a small town in Mexico. So, I headed down there and found a village full of people more terrified than any I've ever seen."

He took another bite of bacon as his mind

slipped back about a year. Somehow, these people figured out who he was and they looked to him as if he were some guardian angel sent from Heaven.

As the events quickly rolled through his mind, he felt a pang of guilt and pain course through his soul.

"What happened?" asked Seth softly.

Darius snapped out of his thoughts.

"What happened was this kid, Carlos, about the same age as you, decided he wanted to help me kill the demon. He got it in his fool head he could become a hunter like me. I told him he would not come with me and he was going to stay in his home and protect his mama."

He stopped talking again, but this time Seth kept his mouth shut. He could see it was a painful memory for the monster hunter to relive.

"Later that night, as I was getting ready to head into the hills and kill this demon, his mama came running to me, telling me Carlos had left, saying he was going to find this demon and kill it, proving he could do it."

He set his plate down on his knee and closed his eyes. The memory was still vivid in his mind, even though it was over a year old.

Then he raised his head and looked Seth directly in the eyes.

"When I found what was left of that kid, there wasn't enough to have a decent funeral. That demon went through him like a wildcat through a lamb."

Seth dropped his head and stared at the ground.

"I'm sorry, Mr. James. You're right. I should have gone back with Clem and the others."

"Well, that time has come and gone. Now, listen to me and listen good. Do not get yourself separated from me when the wendigo comes. Do not take it on yourself. Stay close to me and do everything exactly as I tell you. Understood?"

"Yes, sir."

"You do that and I'll deliver you back to Miss Anna Marie, safe and sound. But, you have to promise me one thing."

"What's that?"

"The very first moment you see her again, you take her hand, you look into her beautiful blue eyes and you tell her exactly how you feel about her."

Seth looked at the ground and swished it around with his toe.

"What's the matter?" asked James. "You're ready and willing to go into battle with me, but you can't talk to a pretty lady?"

"Yes sir, that pretty much sums it up."

"Allow me to let you in on a little secret. Yes, women are some of the scariest creatures on this planet. They can reach right into your chest and grab your heart and never let it go. But, if you treat their heart with gentleness and love, they will do the same with yours. I can tell by the way she looked at you, she's hoping you will step up and be the man she hopes you are. Don't disappoint her."

Seth took another bite of food and then asked, "Have you ever loved a woman?"

Darius took a deep breath and then said, "Yes, I have. But it doesn't work for me. I don't allow myself that luxury anymore."

"Why not?"

"Because I will always outlive any woman that hitches herself to me. I've buried four wives now and it is the most painful thing I've ever had to do. I won't go through that again."

The conversation ended on that note. For the rest of the day, Darius wrote in his journal and Seth kept a watchful eye on the surrounding hills.

8 – Reliving Old Memories

It had just crossed midnight, not the horse, and Darius was wondering if this wendigo had moved on. He looked over at the sleeping form of Seth, curled up against one wall of the small office. The young man had spent the entire day scanning the mountainside for the wendigo and by the time the sun went down, he was exhausted. He was snoring within five minutes of laying his head down.

The soft glow of the candle on the desk illuminated his journal. Hunched over the book, he was reliving the events of a year ago when Carlos tried to prove his bravery. The young man had heard all the legends about Darius and was convinced he could be just as good a monster hunter. No matter how much Darius tried to get through to him he had to be chosen, it never swayed the young man. He couldn't make the kid understand you can't volunteer for this job.

The day he found the young man's body was one of the worst in his long life. Not just the finding of the body, but also when he had to face the boy's mother. Though he killed the demon and ended its reign of terror, it didn't bring the solace he usually experienced when a job was finished.

The next day, when he rode out of that small village, the mother raged at him, that her baby was dead because of him. She screamed she hoped he burned in Hell for the rest of eternity.

As for the others, most of the people living there couldn't even look him in the eyes. They knew Carlos' death wasn't his fault, but they somehow felt the hunter had let them down.

That was the last hunt he had gone on before being sent to Hell's Gate. There had been a few telegrams from Father Benedict, but he just ignored them. He was thinking he might never get back in the saddle again.

He tried hiding his troubles in bottles of whiskey. Drink after drink didn't quench the flames of guilt he felt. If nothing else, they added fuel to the fire, causing him to wake up screaming in the night. His nightmares were crowded with demons and vampires, all on the attack. But they weren't attacking him. He got to witness them tearing Carlos apart every night.

It all ended when Father Benedict showed up in a small town in south Texas, near the border. The padre walked past Midnight, asking if he was inside. The horse told the padre he had been in the saloon for three straight days now.

It took another three days, with the help of the faithful in that small town, to get Darius off the fire water and sober again. The sheriff was a God-fearing man. He and the padre led five men who grabbed the monster hunter and hauled him out of the saloon, across the street and dumped him in a jail cell.

For two straight days, Father Benedict didn't leave the jail, sitting on a stool just outside the bars that contained Darius. While James raged and swore, demanding to be let out, the padre just sat on the stool and quietly read his Bible.

On the morning of the third day, Darius had pushed all the whiskey out of his body and became more subdued. When the sheriff unlocked the cell, Father Benedict stood in the doorway, looking at Darius and started laughing.

"What are you laughing about?" growled Darius.

The padre held up three fingers.

"What?"

"And on the third day He arose and walked out of His tomb."

"You think you're being funny?" asked Darius as he draped his arm over his eyes to shut out the light.

"Oh no, I'm just trying to provide a small amount of levity before we begin."

Darius moved his arm and stared through one blood-shot eye at the padre.

"Begin what? Look, I'm in no mood for this right now."

Father Benedict walked across the cell and leaned over and said, "You know, I really don't care if you think you're ready or not."

Then he reached down and clamped a hand on the top of Darius' head and the hunter's body stiffened as if in pain. Instantly, his vision of the cell vanished and he felt like he was falling through darkness. And this falling felt like it went on for hours.

Then Darius saw an orange glow below him and he screamed as he fell toward it. It only took him a few seconds to realize what he was falling toward.

The roaring fires of Hell.

As he slammed into the molten lava, the flames engulfed him, burning every inch of his body. The searing pain caused him to scream as he expected to see the flesh burn off his bones.

But it didn't happen.

Though he could see the flames and feel them burning his body, they did not consume him. Then he realized they never would. He was consigned to the fiery flames of Hell that would burn him forever, never letting up on the torment.

Through his pain-filled eyes, he saw the devil standing at the edge of the lava river, laughing and jeering at him.

"I've been waiting for you, Darius James! Now you are mine!" bellowed the devil.

Darius screamed in pain again, knowing he was going to be screaming like that for the rest of eternity. No matter how long he was in the fire, he would never numb to the pain.

Then, as quickly as it had begun, it ended. Father Benedict removed his hand from his head and Darius found himself on the floor of his cell. He was face-down, his nose rubbing in a pool of his drool. His body was shaking uncontrollably, weakened from the ordeal he had just been through.

While he laid there, trying to summon the

strength to move, the padre stepped over to the cot and sat down.

Finally, Darius could roll over onto his back. He rubbed the sleeve of his shirt across his mouth and nose, clearing away the spittle and snot.

When his eyes could finally focus, he saw the padre had tears streaming down his face.

"You send me to Hell and you're the one crying?" croaked Darius.

The padre opened his eyes and looked at him.

"I didn't just send you there, Brother James. I went with you. I witnessed everything you experienced in that vision. I felt your pain every time you cried out. I felt your body burn in the fires of Hell."

Then he reached his hand forward and Darius took it. He pulled the hunter up and had him sit down next to him.

"For the last three days, I've been sitting outside your cell, praying for the strength to do what God was asking of me. I already knew of the torture you would experience and I begged Him not to subject you to it."

Darius hung his head and sighed.

"Father, the flames of Hell are exactly where I belong," he whispered.

"What in the world are you talking about?"

"A young man is dead because of me."

The padre stood up and paced back and forth in the cell.

"Is that what you think? That this young man died because of something you did?"

"Or something I didn't do."

"You did nothing wrong other than being great at your job. And being really good at the job you do makes a man a legend."

"He looked up to me, like I was some kind of hero," said Darius, with pain in his eyes.

"You are a hero to the people you help."

"Just not to everyone."

"Did you really think you'd be able to do this job and never lose someone? Well, allow me to let you in on a little secret. Eventually, you were going to lose someone you cared about. It's part of the life we've chosen. I'm surprised it's taken this long to happen to you."

"I don't expect you to understand."

"I don't understand?" asked the padre. "Darius, you are not the only one to lose someone. All of your brother and sister warriors have lost people they cared about. You're not the first one to do so."

"And how did they handle it?"

"Well, a lot of them tried the same method as you. To burn the memories out of their brains with alcohol. I can assure you, it doesn't work."

Father Benedict stepped in front of him and reached his hand out to place it on Darius' head, causing him to jerk back.

"Give me a break, padre. Once was enough."

The padre smiled at him and said, "I had no intention of subjecting you to that again."

Darius relaxed and sat forward again, feeling the priest's hand settle down on his head. Instantly he felt a warmth wash over his body, bringing him relief from the pain in his soul.

After a couple of minutes the padre removed his hand and patted him on the shoulder.

"Shall we go? I have something that may put a smile back on your face."

"What's that?"

"How would you like to kill a few vampires?"

The padre was correct. Darius couldn't keep the corners of his mouth from turning upward. Nothing made him happier than ending the lives of some blood-sucking demons.

A scraping sound outside the small office building brought Darius out of his reverie. Then the sound of Midnight screeching in the darkness drove every bit of exhaustion from his eyes. In an instant, his eyes were open and his ears were alert to every sound in the night.

He heard another scrape, this time sounding like it was coming from the other side of one of the walls. The wall Seth was curled up against.

"Seth!" he hissed at the sleeping man as he grabbed his pistols.

Seth roused a little and turned over, looking at him through sleepy eyes.

"Get away from that wall! Now!"

9 – Sniffing For Blood

Just as Seth realized what James was saying, the wall next to him shattered in a torrent of splintered wood and dust. A set of sharp claws grabbed at him, catching him in the shoulder.

He rolled away from the wall and jumped to his feet just as James fired three shots from each of his pistols. He didn't have time to register the blood running down his arm as he grabbed for his Winchester.

"Don't bother!" yelled Darius as he handed his pistols to the young man. "You have three shots left in each!"

Darius pulled his rifle up from behind the desk just as the wendigo ripped an enormous hole in the wall. Right where Seth had been sleeping. A second sooner and Seth wouldn't have gotten away from the wall in time. James' bullets did no damage to the terror because they exploded against the wall.

The beast screeched loud enough to cause both men to cringe in pain.

"Wait until you have a clear shot before you shoot anymore!" yelled Darius.

He could see the kid having a hard time holding the gun with his left hand. That was the shoulder the wendigo had clawed. The fear was just rolling off the boy and Darius swore at himself for not forcing him to leave.

James had his rifle up and aimed at the opening in the wall, just hoping for one good shot. The bullets in the rifle were bigger and had more stopping power.

He did not know if their bullets would do anything to the wendigo, but it was a start.

A movement at the hole in the wall brought a hasty shot from both men. It impressed Darius that Seth had only fired one shot, knowing he needed to conserve his ammunition.

He didn't know about Seth's shot, but he knew he had hit the beast dead center and had done nothing but cause it to be angrier. It screeched as the bullets tore into its body and then it slammed against the rickety office, causing it to shake and creak. Dust wafted down from above and Darius instantly knew the wendigo's intention.

To bring the building down on top of its prey.

The wendigo cut loose with another ear-piercing screech and then slammed into the outside of the shack again. The sound of cracking timbers followed the collision. Both men knew the building couldn't withstand too many more of those.

Darius jumped around the desk and moved to the hole in the wall. Thrusting the barrel of his rifle into the darkness, his eyes adjusted to the gloom. Seeing some movement in the black of the moonless night, he fired again. The bullet exploded against the side of the beast, driving it back.

Climbing over the broken timbers of the shattered wall, he brought the rifle to bear on the target again and fired. The impact of the bullet was clear as it drove the wendigo back and to its knees.

The beast tried to get to its feet and charge Darius, but he fired again. This time, the bullet missed and hit a tree a few yards away, showering the area with splinters.

The wendigo turned and disappeared into the night, the sound of its hooves pounding away. Darius tried to draw a bead on the fleeing beast, but lost it in the darkness.

As he scanned back and forth, he saw Midnight a few yards away. The black horse blended into the darkness of the night.

"Are you okay?"

Midnight didn't answer, causing Darius to move to his side.

"You're not hurt, are you?"

I have been better.

"What's the matter?"

Midnight moved his head and motioned toward his other side. Darius moved around and looked to see a couple of deep gashes in the horse's side. Red blood was glistening in the bit of light from the overhead stars.

"Aw shit!" cursed Darius as he ran his hand over the wound.

I will survive. It is not as bad as it looks. Where is the boy?

"He's in the shack. The wendigo got him in the shoulder," said the hunter as he examined the horse's wound further.

Go to him. I'll be fine. Take care of me after.

"You sure?"

Yes.

"I'll be right back to take care of this," he said as he turned and walked back to the office.

Stepping back through the wreckage of the wall, he looked for Seth and didn't see him immediately. The candle was still burning on the desk, casting a warm glow in the small space.

Moving around, he saw a boot sticking out from behind the desk.

"Seth?" he said as he knelt down to check on the man. All he got was a groan from the young man.

He rolled him onto his back and could see the shoulder wound was a lot worse than he initially thought. It was very clear Seth was suffering from a loss of blood and from the paleness of his face, he wouldn't last much longer.

"Did you kill it?" groaned Seth.

"No, regrettably it got away."

"That's not good."

"No, it's not, but we need to do something about you first. I need to get you out of here."

He grabbed Seth by his good arm and pulled him into a sitting position.

"I don't think I'm going to be able to get up."

"You don't have a choice. If I leave you lying down, you'll bleed to death. If I leave you in this shack, it could collapse on you. Besides, if I get you up, it will slow the bleeding to your shoulder."

"I'm a goner, Mr. James," slurred Seth.

Next thing he knew, a sharp slap across his face jolted him awake.

"You say that again and I'll shoot you myself," growled Darius. "Now let's get you up."

Darius stood up and put a hand under Seth's good shoulder and hauled him to his feet. As he was pulling the young man up, Seth reached for the two pistols laying on the floor.

"Leave them," said Darius. "I will come back for them."

Walking Seth to the door, he pulled it open and led him out of the building. The cool night air was enough to refresh Seth a little and he could walk with a little more strength.

The two men crossed the bridge and moved to the fire pit and Darius lowered him to a sitting position, his back against a log.

"You stay sitting upright, you hear?"

"Yes," mumbled Seth.

Darius grabbed a few sticks and dropped them into the embers of the fire pit. Getting down close, he started blowing on the coals and within a minute a flame sprang up around the sticks. As it got bigger, he added some bigger sticks.

Then, he reached over and picked up a piece of iron the Indians had been using as a fire pit poker and set its tip into the flames.

"What is that for?" groaned Seth.

"We have to stop the bleeding."

"Oh Jesus," said Seth as he realized what Darius intended to do. "I'll be alright. We don't need that."

"Really? Tell me, boy. What is your mama's name?"

Seth stared at him with a blank look on his face.

"What is the day of your birth?"

Blank.

"You've already lost too much blood. We are going to stop it the only way I know how."

"Just let me die."

Darius lashed out again and slapped him hard across the face.

As he groaned from the impact, Seth looked at him and gasped, "Is that some new treatment of the wounded I'm not privy to?"

Darius got right in his face and growled, "Every time you talk of giving up, I'm going to pop you good. If you think I'm going back to Hell's Gate and telling Anna Marie that you died, you can get that fool notion out of your head right now."

"I guess the world is damn lucky you didn't decide to become a doctor."

As the iron heated, Seth looked across the creek and saw Midnight staring back at him. He could barely make out the red sheen on the side of the horse.

"Did Midnight get injured?"

Darius looked at the horse and then back at Seth.

"Yeah, seems like it."

"Why don't you go take care of him. I can wait."

"No, you can't, but Midnight can. He's as strong as a ... well ... as a horse."

Seth sat up and looked around.

"Wait, where's my horse?"

I've never seen a horse move so fast.

"Took off, did she?"

Darius, I would venture to say she's back in Hell's Gate by now.

Darius looked back at Seth and smiled.

"Seems your horse has more brains than you and I put together. She took off when the wendigo showed up."

Want me to go get her?

Darius looked back at the black stallion.

"Not just yet. I don't need you bleeding out trying to catch her. Once I'm finished with the boy, I'll take care of your wound and then you can go after her."

You know, you really should stop calling him a boy. He's old enough to be called a man.

"Midnight. I'm over four hundred years old. Everyone looks like a child to me."

Darius looked back at Seth and his wounded shoulder. He shook his head and looked back at the horse.

"Point taken."

He reached into the fire pit and pulled out the metal rod and held it up. The last six inches were glowing a nice reddish-orange. And Seth's eyes were so big they were about to pop out of his head.

"Midnight thinks I should stop calling you, *boy*. You piss yourself and I'll never stop calling you that."

"I can't promise I won't. Hell, I'm about to lose control right now!"

Darius reached over and pulled Seth's shredded shirt off his shoulder, exposing the full extent of the wound. It was still bleeding at a good clip and he knew it needed to be stopped immediately.

He reached down and picked up a stick with some thickness to it and held it up to Seth's mouth.

"Open."

The young man did and Darius set the stick between his teeth. As Seth bit down on the stick, his breathing became raspy and his whole body started shaking.

"Look over thata way," said Darius, pointing to a spot up the hill.

As soon as Seth took his eyes off the red hot poker, Darius grazed it across one slash in his shoulder. Seth screamed through clenched teeth, but didn't pull away.

In just a few seconds, the hunter had swept the hot metal rod over the four slashes and the bleeding stopped. He set the poker back in the fire and then reached out and put a hand on top of Seth's head.

"It's over," he said in a much softer tone.

Seth's head dropped forward, the stick falling from his mouth. He was about to fall over, but Darius held him up.

"I still need you to stay upright for a few minutes. Try to get your strength back."

Seth nodded feebly as drool fell from his mouth. James pulled a handkerchief and wiped his face and mouth.

"I didn't piss myself," said Seth in almost a

whisper.

Darius chuckled and said, "Then you did a damn sight better than I did."

"What?" asked Seth, looking through bleary eyes.

Darius reached up and pulled his own shirt off his shoulder. The skin was ravaged by scars from the outside of the shoulder to the middle of his chest.

Seth looked up at him and asked, "What kind of monster did that to you?"

"Werewolf. Mean bastard, too. 'Bout two hundred years ago."

He stood up and looked at Midnight.

"Now, just sit here for a moment and I'll be back to help you lie down. I need to take care of Midnight."

As he started walking away, Seth asked, "Don't you need the poker?"

"Nope."

He walked across the bridge and stepped up to the side of his horse. He dropped his head and began chanting a prayer. Midnight just stood silently, waiting for him to continue.

After a moment, he reached up and ran his hands slowly over the open wounds. His palms began glowing and Midnight nickered softly at his touch. It took about five minutes and when he finished, the only evidence there had been any injury was the blood on the horse's coat. The slashes were completely gone.

Darius reached up and patted Midnight on the neck and said, "Go bring her back."

Without a second's hesitation, Midnight

took off down the hill and disappeared into the night. They could hear his galloping hooves echoing back up the draw to them.

Darius walked to the damaged office and stepped inside and picked up Seth's bedding. As he walked back across the bridge, Seth looked up at him and said, "You son of a bitch."

"Oh? Why?"

"Why didn't you do that for me?" asked Seth, trying to raise his voice, but was too weak to do so.

"Because it doesn't work on us. Only on animals. It's a gift from God, but I guess you could also say it's His joke on us. Apparently, He cares more for the animals than He does for us."

He crouched down and put the bedding around Seth, tucking it in to keep him warm.

"Alright, I need you to get some sleep and rest. Probably should sleep all the way through this coming day. Hopefully, you'll get a good portion of your strength back by tomorrow night."

"You think the wendigo is going to come back, don't you?"

"It's obviously hungry and it knows where there are a couple of tasty meat sacks."

Darius sat down across the fire from the kid and started checking his pistols and rifle, making sure they were ready for the next encounter.

Looking across the pit, he could see Seth was trying to stay awake, but he lost the battle within ten minutes. His head fell forward and his chin rested on his chest.

You should have gone back when I said to.

Their battle with the wendigo was far from over.

10 – And You Brought Her?

Darius woke with a start a couple of hours after sunrise. Some sound had awoken him and it took a few seconds to realize it was the sound of horses. Standing up, he looked down the draw and saw Midnight coming up the hill, followed by Seth's horse.

He smiled, but then his smile faded when he saw the sheriff and Clem behind the front horses. Then his smile turned to an absolute scowl when he saw Anna Marie on a chestnut mare, bringing up the rear.

"Oh, good lord!" said Darius under his breath, causing Seth to come awake.

Sorry, Darius. I couldn't catch her before she reached town.

Stepping across the bridge, he met the small group and stopped them in their tracks.

"Just exactly what are you doing here?" he asked of the group.

The sheriff looked at him and said, "When Lily showed up without Seth and then your horse came galloping in about twenty minutes later, we knew something bad had happened."

Darius took a deep breath and hung his head. Shaking it, he looked back up.

"And you brought Anna Marie."

Clem and the sheriff climbed down from their horses and Clem said, "It wasn't our first choice."

"You should have forbidden her to come."

The sheriff chuckled and said, "Apparently

you don't know Miss Anna Marie as well as you think."

Anna Marie stepped up in front of Darius and looked him in the eye, with a bit of fire in hers.

"I'm here, so live with it."

She glanced past him and saw the destroyed shack.

"Oh, my god! What happened?"

"The wendigo happened," he said, "which is why you shouldn't be here. None of you should."

"Where's Seth?" she cried out, grabbing him by the front of his shirt.

He put a hand on her shoulder and said, "Follow me."

He led the three of them across the bridge and when Anna Marie saw Seth sitting by the fire, bundled under his blankets, she ran to him. Dropping to her knees next to him, she reached forward and cupped the side of his face.

"What happened?"

"Well, like Mr. James said, the wendigo happened."

"Are you hurt?" she asked as Darius crouched down next to them.

He reached forward and took hold of the blanket to show her the wound, but Seth grabbed his hand and stopped him.

"She don't need to see that."

Darius let go and stood up.

"It's not a pretty sight, Anna Marie."

She reached forward to uncover the

shoulder and he stopped her, too.

"Seth Gooden! You remove your hand this instant!"

The young man swallowed and then dropped his hand. She carefully lowered the blanket and with the extent of his injuries exposed, her hand flew to her mouth and she bit her finger, trying to keep from crying out.

He could see the pain in her eyes and said, "It's okay, Anna Marie. It's not as bad as it looks."

She looked at him as a tear streamed down her cheek.

"Have you looked at it?" she asked with some fire in her voice.

"Well, no. During our battle, I kind of got hit and my neck was sore. So I can't see it."

He reached up and wiped the tear from her face. She covered the shoulder and then looked him in the eyes.

"You shouldn't have come up here," she said.

"Hey, I'm still alive."

She raised her voice and said, "Oh yeah?"

Then she punched him on the shoulder, which brought a howl of pain.

"Did you feel that?" she yelled at him.

"Yes," he groaned.

"Good! Then you are still alive."

Then she jumped up and got in Darius' face.

"And you! You should have taken better care of him!"

Darius tried to step back as he stammered,

"I ... um ..."

His stepping back had no effect. She just closed the distance and poked a finger into his chest.

"You what?" she said with her anger fully lit.

The sheriff and Clem stayed back a few feet not wanting to get anywhere near this seething volcano of womanhood. Apparently, they knew Anna Marie all too well. Or maybe it was just her mother. But they didn't want to get caught in the crossfire.

Then a rescue came from the most unlikely source.

"Anna Marie! Knock it off!"

She stopped and turned to see Seth was struggling to stand up.

"It's his fault you're hurt," she said, her voice a little more subdued.

She moved to him and helped steady him as he stood.

"It is not his fault, woman. So lay off him."

She went to say something else, but one of his fingers to her pretty lips put a stop to it.

"To tell you the truth, Anna Marie," said Darius, "if it hadn't been for Seth, we'd both be dead. This brave warrior actually saved my life last night."

"Really?"

She looked at Seth and he had a sheepish grin on his face, unable to make eye contact with her.

"Yes, he did. And in the tradition of when men get stupid and go off to battle and get wounded, it's usually their brave women that nurse them back to health. You seem like one of those brave women I've encountered throughout my life."

She looked at him and bit her lips. Then she looked at Seth and reached up and kissed him on the cheek.

"I'll do whatever I can to help you mend."

Seth's face went a bright red as he tried to figure out what to say. But, as he and Darius had discussed last night, talking to a beautiful woman was a heck of a lot scarier than dealing with a wendigo.

Darius turned and looked at the other two men.

"I appreciate you making sure Midnight got back here safe. Now, as you can see, I am fine, but Seth obviously can't stay here. So, I need the two of you to make sure he and Anna Marie get back to town safely."

Both of them nodded without a word. They had seen the wound on Seth's shoulder and they knew this beast was the real deal. Neither one of them wanted to stay any longer than was necessary. Getting Seth and Anna Marie back to town was the best reason to get off this mountain.

As they moved to help Seth walk down to the bridge, Anna Marie stepped in front of Darius.

"I am sorry for what I said. I never should have doubted you."

He lifted her chin with his finger and said, "You have nothing to be sorry for. Don't apologize."

He looked back to see the three men had reached the other side of the bridge.

Turning back to Anna Marie, he said, "I assume the best place for him to regain his health will be upstairs at your mama's place."

She smiled and said, "Of course. Right where I can keep an eye on him."

Then Darius leaned down and asked softly in her ear, "Were you aware that he can't read or write?"

She jerked back and looked up at him.

"No!"

"Well, seems to me he'll have plenty of time on his hands while he mends and I'm betting you'd be a great schoolmarm to him."

She nodded and said, "Just leave that to me."

He held out his arm and she hooked hers through it and they walked to the bridge and across.

The sheriff and Clem were working out a way to get Seth up on his horse. With his injured shoulder, it was a bit of a struggle, but they got it done. Darius didn't like the way he was going to be sitting up for the entire journey.

"Any of you ever seen an indian travois?"

Anna Marie and the sheriff looked and he could tell they hadn't, but Clem spoke up.

"Yeah, I've seen 'em. Two long poles dragging on the ground behind the horse and able to carry a wounded man between them."

"You might switch to that when you reach

the flats," said Darius. "I don't think he's going to be good for two or three hours in the saddle back to Hell's Gate."

"I'll be just fine," said Seth with a cough.

"You shush," said Anna Marie, which caused him to be quiet.

The three of them climbed into their saddles and looked down at the monster hunter.

"It don't feel right leaving you here by yourself," said the sheriff.

"No, it surely don't," agreed Clem.

"Gentlemen, I have a job to do and that is to kill this beast. You both have a job to do and that's make sure these two get safely back to Hell's Gate."

They both nodded and the sheriff asked, "Any message I should give to Mr. Stalls?"

"Just tell him this should be over in a couple of days. If'n you don't see me by the end of the week, you'll know the wendigo got the best of me."

This brought a sharp gasp from Anna Marie.

He looked directly at her and said, "I ain't never lost to a monster before and I don't intend to start now."

He cast his gaze back and forth across the four faces and then said, "Now, get back to town."

Not needing anymore encouragement, they turned their horses and headed back down the hill. Seth gave him a half-salute as he was turning away. Anna Marie settled her horse right next to his for the journey down the hill.

As he watched them go, he felt a presence behind him.

You know he really didn't save your life.

"She don't know that, nor does she need to."

As the four riders disappeared into the trees, he turned back to Midnight.

"How are you feeling?"

I'm feeling tired. After chasing Lily all the way back to town, I could use a little rest.

"Get some rest. We have all day to wait."

Darius walked back to the ruined shack and sifted through the shattered timbers. He found his pack and bedrolls and then smiled when he found his journal, pen and inkwell intact.

Walking across the bridge, he settled down against a log near the fire and opened the book and started writing.

11 – Mountain Battle

Time seems to pass much more slowly when you have nothing to do, but are waiting for something terrible to happen. This wasn't something new for Darius. He had spent hundreds of years fighting monsters and had learned early on they sometimes took their own sweet time.

He had sent Midnight down the mountain, to the small grassy meadow. Midnight didn't have to be asked twice, but expressed some guilt over leaving. It wasn't very often Darius made sure he was not around when a beast was on the prowl, but this beast had already drawn the horse's blood. Darius wasn't willing to find out if the wendigo would kill Midnight for a late-night snack.

As the sun started heading for the western horizon, Darius started settling in. He picked a spot near the mine's entrance which provided him cover from three different sides.

Of course, he had to take a lantern down the mine tunnel just to make sure the wendigo wasn't hiding in there. Wouldn't be the first time for a monster coming out of the darkness of a tunnel and catching him by surprise. Some vampires hid in just such a place.

As the sun sank behind the mountain, he placed a couple of smaller logs in the fire. Keeping it burning during the night would keep the smell of smoke hanging over the camp. He even sat downwind of the smoke most of the afternoon so his clothes would soak up the smell and cover his own scent.

Then he gathered every weapon he had and moved to the mouth of the mine. Two six-shooters, loaded and ready. One Winchester lever action rifle stuffed with every round he could put in it. Four silver-coated steel spikes in the belt across his chest. And his silver-edged cavalry sword, along with two daggers stuffed in the tops of his boots.

As he hunkered down just inside the mouth of the tunnel, the darkness washed over the camp like a flood. From his vantage point, he could see the fire pit about fifty yards away and had a good view of the bridge. The only thing he didn't have a good view of was the hillside the mine was carved into. If the wendigo came down from that side, he'd have to hear it long before he would see it.

There was a large boulder, still very much a part of the mountain they had cut the mine around. This offered him some protection to the front, but allowed him to hide in the tunnel's darkness. It blocked his direct view of the fire, but that was a good thing. It allowed his night vision to settle in while still being able to see the glow the fire cast.

Wedging himself between the boulder and the side of the tunnel, he set his rifle in a crack where it would be handy. Settling down, he pressed his back against the cave wall. He pulled one of his pistols, cocked it and rested it on his lap.

Then came the waiting.

The darkness moved. Or was it something in the darkness? Whatever it was, it caused the monster hunter's eyes to come open in a flash.

Having stayed awake the whole day, planning his defenses and his attacks, he had neglected to grab some shut eye when he had the chance. So, it wasn't surprising to find he had drifted off to sleep while sitting in the gloom of the tunnel.

It wasn't the movement or the sound that had awakened him. It was the feeling of something dragging across his arm that was nearest the middle of the tunnel. He thanked the Lord he didn't jerk when he awoke.

Looking toward the opening of the tunnel, without moving his head, he couldn't make out any glow from the fire.

Aww Hell! How long have I been asleep?

Figuring it must have been hours for the fire to go out, he was in total darkness. But then the glow of the fire jumped out at him. The beast had moved out of the tunnel and allowed the light of the fire to reach his eyes again.

Son of a bitch, how did it get into the mine?

As he watched the wendigo move slowly down the slope toward the camp, he saw the long, stringy hair hanging from its body and realized that was what he felt drag across his arm. It moved with the stealth of a wolf walking on two legs, casting its snout to the breeze and trying to catch the scent of its prey.

He could see the antlers sprouting from the top of its head and its claws nearly dragging along the ground. He could hear the raspy breathing of the beast and wondered if it was because of the rounds he and Seth had put into it the night before.

After the wendigo moved away from the mouth of the tunnel, Darius got up as quietly as he could. He moved around the boulder and stepped to the opening of the mine and stared at the back of the monster as it stopped and surveyed the camp below.

It was less than twenty feet away and Darius could smell its odor from there. He brought up the cocked pistol, keeping the other one at the ready. He couldn't ready the second pistol, knowing that any click of the hammer going back would sound like a stick of dynamite going off in the quiet of the night.

Aiming at the base of the wendigo's skull, he calmed his breathing and gently squeezed the trigger. The pistol erupted with a flash and the bullet flew straight. When it impacted the back of the monster's skull, it exploded, taking half the head with it.

A short grunt escaped from the wendigo before it crashed face-down to the ground.

Darius stepped forward and aimed his pistol at what was left of the monster's head and began to squeeze the trigger. He stopped when a screech froze the blood in his veins.

Swinging around, he caught a clawed paw across the chest and was sent flying twenty feet through the air. One of his pistols flew from his hand as he crashed into the ground and up against a tree trunk.

He shook his head to clear the fog in his eyes. His mind was working overtime, trying to figure out what just happened. One second he was thinking about how easy it had been to kill the wendigo and the next he was getting his bell rung hard.

It had never occurred to him there might be two of them.

As he struggled to his feet, he could feel a couple of ribs were cracked, if not broken. He could taste blood in the back of his throat as he coughed.

Looking back toward the downed wendigo, he saw another one, much smaller than the first. He guessed it was a female, and she was bent over the body of the other.

A low wail emanated from the throat of the female. She was reaching down, jostling the shoulder of her mate, urging him to get up. Darius could almost imagine her wailing sounded like the cries of sorrow.

Then he felt something deep in his soul he had never felt before. In over four hundred years of hunting, he had never felt sorrow and regret for doing the thing they tasked him with. But there it was, wrapping itself around his heart, making him question if he had done the right thing.

Of course, it was the right thing! I've never

questioned killing a vampire and its mates. This monster was killing indians and had tried to kill Seth. It was no different from a vampire or werewolf.

Be that as it may, it didn't lessen the fact this female was suffering genuine sorrow. Something he had never seen a vampire exhibit, even after he killed their mate.

He looked down and saw the second pistol and picked it up. Shaking the dirt off, he pulled the hammer back and faced the two wendigos.

The female looked up at him from about twenty yards away and made the most mournful sound he had ever heard. It was almost as if she were crying, "Why?" He could see the green-yellow eyes set back in her skull and would have sworn on a stack of Bibles they were the eyes of a crying woman.

She climbed to her feet and looked at him. When she raged at him, he knew he was going to have to end her life, too. Much as the idea had become distasteful to him, it had to be done.

She took a couple of steps toward him and he raised both pistols and fired. Each bullet struck her in the chest, driving her back, but they didn't take her down. The only thing they seemed to do was make her even more determined to get to him and rip his heart out.

As she began advancing toward him, he fired again and again, emptying both pistols into her. The fragmenting bullets didn't seem to do anything to her other than make her angry.

His last shot, aimed at her head, missed as his hand trembled from the pain in his chest.

She closed the gap between them in just a couple of seconds and slammed her paw into his stomach, driving him backwards. Gasping for breath, he dropped both useless pistols into the dirt and pulled his sword.

If he wasn't in such dire straits, he would have laughed at how his bullets were ineffective and now he was going to try a sword. If he wasn't on the verge of being killed, he would have found this situation comical.

As she came at him, he raised his sword and jabbed at her, only to see his blade batted away by her claws. She brought her other clawed paw around to take his head off, but he raised an arm at the last second and all she did was knock him sideways and down a small slope.

He came to rest face-down in the creek, but the cold water was just enough to revive him and drive the fuzziness from his head.

Scrambling to his feet, he realized he had now been relieved of his sword and was left with very few options. He had the silver spikes in his vest belt and his daggers in his boots. Casting his thoughts back to how effective the rest of his weapons had been, he had little faith in his remaining arsenal.

He looked up the hill just as the wendigo lept off a boulder and straight at him. In the blink of an eye, he had one of his spikes in his hand and brought it up just as the beast slammed into him. Though she didn't weigh nearly as much as her mate, she still felt like having a two hundred pound sack of flour dropped on his head.

As they crashed into the edge of the creek bed, his head slammed into a rock and darkness claimed his sight instantly. The last flickering thought he had was, "Well, I hope she enjoys her meal."

A brightness shone around him and he wondered if he had finally made it to Heaven. After all the work he'd done for God, he was sure it was the least He could do. One thing didn't add up, though. If he was in Heaven, what was this disgusting feeling on his face? And if it was Hell, why was it so bright and cool?

Finally able to crack one eye open, he looked up to see a whiskered muzzle and some of the biggest lips he'd ever seen. Then a big, fat tongue came out and slathered across his face.

Feebly reaching up, he pushed the face away and groaned.

"Dammit Midnight, I'm awake!"

I was wondering. Thought I was going to have to go back to town and tell that pretty lady you were dead.

"Her name is Anna Marie."

No, I was thinking of Lily.

Darius pushed himself up and moved his neck back and forth, seeing if everything was still attached and working properly.

"You can get those thoughts out of your head right now. We're not staying long enough for her to bat her pretty brown eyes at you, you big stud."

Says you.

Then Darius' mind cleared instantly and he jumped up and looked around. He was standing ankle deep in the creek, but he and Midnight were the only ones there.

No wendigo.

He looked back toward the mine, but was so far below that ground, he couldn't see up toward the entrance. He checked his vest and found one spike missing.

Looking for something?

"Why am I not dead?"

That seems to be something you wouldn't want to question.

"No, I mean, that second wendigo got the best of me. I should be dead."

Midnight waggled his head and pointed with his nose.

Up the hill.

Darius clambered his way up the hill, struggling for breath through what were surely broken ribs now. When he reached the top of the slope, he saw the two wendigos, one laying across the other.

As he moved toward them, he found his pistols and stuck them into their holsters. Being empty, they were of no use at the moment.

He could feel Midnight stepping slowly behind him, his hot breath on the back of his neck.

Moving cautiously, he stepped over to the wendigos and reached out with the toe of one boot and nudged the female. He didn't get a response, so he reached down and grabbed her by the shoulder and rolled her over.

His silver spike was embedded in her chest.

Then, he saw her chest was rising and falling slightly. He looked into her eyes and could see they were focused on him, but they were very dim. The sound of her shallow breathing told him she didn't have much longer to live.

She raised one of her paws. Her claws weren't nearly as long as her mates', but they were still sharp as thistle thorns. She did not try to use them on him.

He took hold of her paw, wrapping his fingers around her claws and looked into her dying eyes.

"I'm sorry," he whispered. "I truly am."

Her claws squeezed his hand as if she understood what he said. He reached forward with his other hand and ran the back of his fingers across her skull cheek. He heard her whimper at his touch and then her head fell to one side. Her grip on his hand loosened and her arm fell to her side.

She was gone.

Darius hung his head and fought to contain his emotions. He could hear Midnight breathing behind him.

I have never seen you react like this.

"She didn't deserve to die. She was only protecting her mate."

True, but if you didn't kill her, she would have killed you.

"That doesn't make it any better."

It does to me.

Darius looked over his shoulder at the black stallion. Midnight just waggled his head.

If you died, I would probably end up as a plow horse.

Darius forced a smile and stood up. He patted Midnight on the side of the face.

"Being a plow horse is an honorable vocation."

Easy for you to say. You're not the one pulling the plow.

Darius went to chuckle, but then coughed up some blood. As he spit it out, Midnight looked at him.

We need to get you back to town.

"I need to do right by these two first."

Over the next hour, Darius packed his things and then created a travois to carry the two fallen warriors. After getting them situated on the platform of the travois, he started walking down the mountain beside Midnight. Going was slow because using the travois was a little more difficult on the mountain trail.

Midnight wondered why he didn't ride, but then Darius started stacking wood on the travois with the bodies. By the time they reached the flatlands, there was a good stack of wood with the bodies. When they came to a stop, Darius lowered the travois onto four rocks, keeping it raised off the ground. Then he stuffed some of the wood underneath the platform and spread the rest across the two bodies.

Night had fallen by the time he pulled a sack of gunpowder from the saddlebags and poured it over the bodies and into the wood below. Then he pulled a cigar from his vest and struck a match and lit it. Dropping the match into the gunpowder, he watched as the flames took hold.

Within seconds, the flames lit up the surrounding night. He stood near the heads of the two combatants and said a silent prayer for them. He knew they were the monsters he was sworn to get rid of, but this one felt different.

This was the first time he felt genuine sorrow for killing a monster.

As he bowed his head, offering his prayers for them, he heard Midnight nicker behind him. He turned to find they were not alone. Standing next to the black horse was the old medicine man.

The old man looked into his eyes with the understanding of knowing the pain the monster hunter was feeling. He stepped forward and placed a hand on Darius' shoulder.

In his native tongue, he said, "They did not belong in this world. You have sent them back to theirs."

Darius just nodded slightly as the old man's eyes looked into his soul. Then the medicine man patted him on the chest, which brought a bout of pain and a spasm of coughing. When he spit blood, the old man helped him to sit on a rock on the edge of the firelight.

"You have been wounded in battle."

"Wouldn't be the first time," croaked Darius as he tried to catch his breath.

Midnight stepped over and looked over the medicine man's shoulder.

Can you help him?

The old man nodded and said, "Yes, I can mend his injuries."

Darius sat back and looked at the old man.

"You can hear him?"

"Yes. The mind of the horse is easy to hear for my people."

The old medicine man placed a hand on Darius' chest and began his healing process. In a split second, Darius remembered what it felt like when Father Drake found him near death, on the field of battle. He remembered how he would have pissed his pants if he had been wearing any pants.

He could feel ribs moving around underneath his skin and being put back in their rightful places. He reached up and grabbed the old man's shoulder and squeezed. The old man didn't falter for one second, but continued with his healing work.

It took about five minutes before he pulled his hand away, saying he was finished. He patted Darius on the shoulder and then stood up. He walked over to Midnight and pulled the bedroll off the saddle. Laying it out near the rock, he helped the monster hunter down off the rock and onto his back.

"Why did you come back?" asked Darius.

"I heard the voice of the Great Spirit. It said I was needed."

"Thank you for listening."

The old man just smiled and nodded. With experienced hands, he removed Darius' vest with spikes, his belt with sword and pistol holsters and the daggers from his boots. Finally, he pulled his boots off and set them near the fire to dry.

Darius was too weak to say anything or make any move to continue his journey toward Hell's Gate. He saw the old man pull the saddle and blanket off Midnight and turned the horse out to graze on some grass nearby.

The last thing he was conscious of was the medicine man sitting down on the rock next to him and chanting. Within five minutes of laying down on the bedroll, his eyes closed, and he was lost to the land of sleep.

12 – More Vampires Than Thought

Darius awoke the next morning to find the old man gone, Midnight a little way off munching on some grass and the fire completely burned down to ash.

Getting up, he found he wasn't feeling any of the pain he had expected. He had been through many battles and always felt like he was getting way too old to be doing this kind of thing. That was something he didn't feel this morning.

He pulled a small spade from his pack and began digging a hole in the ground near the fire. When it was deep enough, he took the bones of the wendigos, their skulls with antlers and buried them. After filling the hole in, he found three flat rocks and placed them in a stack near the head of the grave. He did not know why he did that. It just felt right.

A couple of hours later they walked into Hell's Gate. The streets were quiet, with only a handful of people out and about. Every person he saw looked like they were rushing to get somewhere and didn't pay any attention to him.

He saw the boy from the telegraph office hurrying down the street and called him over.

"What's going on?"

The boy looked up at him and said, "A deputy got killed last night. It looked like an animal killed him."

"Last night? Do you know which deputy?"

"Yes, sir, the one called Clem."

Darius felt a stab of sorrow in his heart when he heard the name. He closed his eyes and shook his head.

"Some say the vampires are back, but that can't be true," said the boy. "You killed all the vampires, didn't you?"

Darius looked at the boy and mumbled, "I thought I did."

He urged Midnight forward, toward the boardinghouse. After tossing the reins over the rail outside, Darius climbed the steps and walked through the open door. There were just a couple of people in the dining room. When they saw him, they immediately turned back to their meals, ignoring him.

Nothing was said, but the message was clear. They were holding him responsible for the death of the deputy. They tasked him with ridding the town of the vampires and it appeared he had failed.

He walked through to the desk and tapped the bell. The door to the back room opened and Anna Marie walked through. When she saw him, she ran around the desk and threw her arms around him.

"Thank the Lord you're back safely," she cried into his chest.

He didn't know how to handle this woman wrapping her arms around him, so he just put his arms around her shoulders.

"How is Seth doing?"

She pulled back a little and looked up into his eyes.

"He's doing okay. He's upstairs in bed. I think he's going to be fine."

"That's good. I think I'll stop in and see him when I go to my room."

"He's in the first room at the top of the stairs. I'll put you in the room next to his."

Releasing her hold on him, she walked back around the desk and took a key from the rack and handed it to him. As he reached for it, he took her hand and held it.

"I've been told that my work with the vampires may not be finished."

"It was awful," she said. "About midnight, we all heard a scream and it sounded like a man being attacked by some wild animal. I was in my room upstairs and ran to the window. I saw the sheriff run down the street, toward the commotion."

"So, he may have seen what happened?"

"I don't know. He won't talk about it. All I know is Clem was tore up real bad. The sheriff is walking around in a daze now, like he saw something so horrible he can't believe it."

Darius bit his lip and then pulled a dollar from his pocket. He handed it to her and said Midnight needed to be taken to the stables. He was going to seek out the sheriff and find out what happened.

Walking into the sheriff's office, Darius saw a man that look defeated. When he looked into the man's eyes, he could tell this would not be a pleasant conversation. Without a word, he walked over and sat down in a chair and looked across the desk.

Sheriff Jackson said nothing for a few seconds, gathering his thoughts on what he wanted to say.

"I guess you didn't get all the vampires the other day," he finally said.

"I got the ones I knew about," said Darius, trying to keep the conversation from exploding into animosity.

"I'm not really even sure it was a vampire. It could have been a wildcat."

"Anna Marie tells me you might have seen what happened."

"That little lady needs to learn to keep her mouth shut."

"Hey! That's uncalled for," said Darius, raising his voice a little. "If you're going to be angry, be angry with me, not her."

The sheriff took a deep breath and sat back.

"You're right. I'm sorry and shouldn't be angry with anyone, even you. Before we get to what happened last night, how did it go at the mine?"

"The wendigos are dead and the mine is safe again."

"Wendigos?"

"Yes, there were two of them. A male and female."

"And you're sure there are no more?"

"How can a person really be sure? Three days ago I didn't even know there was a wendigo this far south. Now I know there were two of them."

"Aren't you supposed to be the expert in all this monster stuff?"

"Sheriff, this is not an exact science. There are plenty of things we don't know about the monsters in this world and sometimes, we're just learning as we go. We do the best we can."

The sheriff just looked at him and Darius could tell he was seething just under the surface. It would not take much to cause him to become a roaring fire of rage.

Then the sheriff asked, "Why did you ask Seth about Joshua Dalton?"

Darius sucked in a breath. He should have known the sheriff would talk to his deputy about the things the two of them discussed while at the mining camp.

"I had some suspicions about Joshua. I wanted to get a sense from him about what happened to Mr. Dalton."

"And you didn't think it important to tell me about it?" asked the sheriff, his voice rising to a point they could probably hear it in the street.

"Would you have believed me if I told you Joshua Dalton was now a vampire? I didn't really have time to look into it before needing to go off to the mine."

"I've known Clem for more'n twenty years! To see him tore up like that was ..."

The sheriff stopped and Darius waited for a few seconds. He could see the sheriff was struggling to hold it together.

While it was quiet, they could hear the stage come into town and stop across the street at the boardinghouse. Usually, the sheriff would sit in the chair outside the office, just watching to see who got off the stage, but not today.

"I know Clem was your friend. He was a good man, something I could see in the short time I knew him. Now, let's work together to see if we can catch the bastard that killed him."

"I don't know that I want your help!" shouted the sheriff, causing Darius to sit up a little straighter.

As he struggled to figure out what to say to cool the situation, they heard some footsteps outside the office and the door swung open. When Darius looked to see who was coming in, his heart stopped and he just shook his head.

"Sheriff, I believe you're going to want his help."

The sheriff looked at the new arrival and felt all the fire in his temper go out.

"And who are you?" he asked.

"Sheriff Jackson," said Darius, "this is my boss, Father Benedict."

The padre looked at Darius and smiled.

"I should think the good Lord is your boss."

"Well, that's what you keep telling me. There are times, like now, for instance, when I wonder if He really cares."

Father Benedict's smile faded to a frown when he heard that. He'd heard Darius suffer a crisis of faith before, but he never questioned whether God was at the helm.

"I think ...," he started to say, but was interrupted by the sheriff.

"What brings you to town, padre?"

The padre walked over and stood behind Darius, placing his hands on his shoulders.

"I just came to see my favorite demon hunter. It's not very often I get to sit down with him, face-to-face. We mostly talk through telegrams."

"Well," said the sheriff, "I'm very close to telling you to pack him up and get him out of town."

"What did you do this time, Brother James?" asked the padre, giving his shoulders a bit of a squeeze.

Darius went to say something, but the sheriff beat him to it.

"He missed a vampire when he killed three of them a few nights ago and that one came here last night and killed a good man."

Father Benedict's head dropped and he said a silent prayer for the dead man and also asked for strength in dealing with this situation.

Darius was tiring of these two talking about him as if he weren't even there. He went to stand up, but the padre kept his hands on his shoulders and kept his butt planted firmly in the chair.

"Caleb, I know ..."

"How do you know my name?" asked the sheriff.

"The voice of God is in my ear. That and I make it my business to know who I'm going to be dealing with when I come into a new town. I had a quick chat with the marshal over in Sage Springs on the way here."

"You talked to Marshal Thompson?"

"Yes, I did and he had nothing but good things to say about you. Said if there was a monster problem here in Hell's Gate he said you'd be one of the best men to handle it. You need to change that name by the way. "

This took a bit of wind out of the sheriff's sails. He was pretty sure the marshal thought little of him or his little town, but he wasn't about to call the priest a liar.

"He thinks as highly of you as I do of this man right here," he said as he patted Darius' shoulders. "This is the best monster hunter we have in the church."

"And just how many monster hunters does the church have, padre?" asked the sheriff.

"At last count, thirty-eight scattered around the world."

When Darius heard that, he exploded out of the chair and looked at the padre.

"Thirty-eight? Last I heard there were forty!"

"Brother Darius, calm down. We'll talk about it later."

"We'll talk about it now! Who did we lose?"

He looked down at the diminutive priest, who stood a full head shorter than him and his eyes blazed, demanding answers. Father Benedict may have been short, but he more than made up for it with strength. It was easy to see from his broad shoulders he was a powerful man.

"We lost Brother Kendrick and Sister Carroll last month."

"Richard and Sophie are gone?"

The padre just nodded, not wanting to add anymore to what was already said.

"How?"

"Later, Brother Darius."

"No! Not later!" shouted the hunter.

Father Benedict raised himself up to his full five feet, two inches tall and bellowed.

"Brother Darius! Curb your tongue!"

James went to say something, but realized he was overstepping many boundaries and closed his mouth.

The padre took a deep breath and let his anger subside.

"Now, I am famished and would like to get something to eat. They don't serve lunch on the stagecoach. Sheriff, would you like to join Brother Darius and myself across the street? The church is buying lunch, if you like. We can sit and discuss what we are to do about your present problem, but only if we can do it as civilized adults."

The sheriff sighed and stood up, picking up his hat and putting it on.

"I am a bit hungry and if the church is

buying."

"It would be my pleasure," said the padre.

Three somber men sat around the table in the boardinghouse dining room. There were a few other diners in the room, but with the threat of vampire violence starting up again, most people were staying locked up in their homes.

"Okay," said Darius. "I've talked to Seth about Joshua Dalton and he says the same thing Anna Marie said. He went out one night to investigate something and was never seen again. His body has never been found, nor was there any evidence of an attack."

"You think he was turned," said the padre.

"I think we need to consider that possibility."

Then he looked at the sheriff and asked, "Do we know what happened to Joshua's wife and son?"

"We found his wife's body a couple of days after she went missing. Their son is safe here in town now. We keep him busy working at the telegraph office. When he's finished for the day, he comes to my office and sleeps in one of the cells."

"That young'un that delivered my telegrams is Joshua Dalton's son?"

"Yes, he is and don't go getting him riled up. He doesn't know his mama is dead or what happened to his pa. Let's just leave it at that."

The padre looked at the sheriff and asked, "You're keeping that from the boy?"

"What are we supposed to tell him, padre? Your mama is dead from a vampire attack and it might have been your pa that killed her?"

The priest hung his head and said softly, "I understand your reasoning, but eventually the boy is going to need to be told."

The sheriff was about to say something, but Anna Marie walked up with plates and began setting their meals on the table. It had been obvious to them she had been trying to listen to their conversation without actually coming over and taking part.

"Jason needs to be told," she whispered.

"He will be, but it needs to be the right time," said the sheriff, "if there is such a thing."

"Well, no time like the present," she said, looking out the window.

Darius followed her gaze and saw Jason walking down the street, having just delivered a telegram. Standing up, he patted her on the shoulder.

"Keep my plate warm," he said. "I'll be right back."

Without another word, he turned and headed out the front door and hustled across the street.

"Jason, can I have a word with you?"

The boy stopped walking and turned to see

the monster hunter coming toward him.

"Sure, Mr. James."

Darius stopped in front of the boy and realized just how unprepared he was to do this. He reached out and put a hand on the boy's shoulder.

"Let's take a walk down to the livery. I need to check on Midnight and there's something I need to talk to you about."

As they turned and began walking toward the stables, he glanced over his shoulder and could see three faces looking at him through the window of the boardinghouse. The pain was very clear on Anna Marie's face.

"Is it true you can talk to your horse?"

Darius forced a smile and said, "Sure. Don't you talk to yours?"

"Well, I don't have a horse, but if I did, I guess I'd talk to it. But they're saying Midnight can talk back to you and you can hear 'im."

Darius chuckled and said, "Sometimes I wish I couldn't hear him."

They walked into the dark coolness of the livery barn and the man that ran the place just nodded to the two of them. When Darius motioned for him to make himself scarce, the man didn't have to be asked twice. He hustled out the door and around the corner to his office door.

Wish you couldn't hear me, do you?

"There are days, Midnight, when listening to you is a curse."

Jason giggled as they came to a stop just outside Midnight's stall. The coal-black stallion reached his head over the gate and looked down at the boy. Jason reached up and ran his hand over Midnight's face and smiled.

Don't listen to him, boy. He needs me more than he will admit.

Jason jerked his hand back and his eyes went wide.

"I guess I should have told you, anyone can hear Midnight talk to them if he decides they deserve it."

"I can't believe it. I ain't never heard a horse talk before. But it was only in my head."

"Well, it would probably be quite disturbing to most people if they heard a horse talk with its mouth. Besides, I don't think Midnight would lower himself to our level to talk to us with our own words."

You got that right.

Jason laughed and said, "I like him. He has at ... ati ..."

"Attitude?"

"Yes, attitude."

"Yes, he does, by the bushels."

Darius reached over and opened the gate and let Midnight walk out of the stall. He patted the horse on the neck and then turned to Jason.

"I need to talk to you, Jason, man to man."

"Me?"

"Yes. Come over here and sit down."

Darius led him to a bench on the side of the open space and they sat down next to each other. Midnight just moved over and stood in front of them, wondering why he had been let out of his stall.

"What did you want to talk about, Mr. James?"

Darius closed his eyes and took a breath, asking for the strength to do what needed to be done.

"It's about your ma and pa, Jason."

"Do you know where they went? No one is telling me anything."

After staying silent for a few seconds, Darius decided he might as well just get it out there.

"First, your mama has passed away. She was ..."

"No!" yelled Jason as he jumped up from the bench. "You're lying. She went to find pa and will be back."

Darius looked at the boy and could see he was shaking. It wasn't fear that Darius would actually lie to him about something like this. It was the fear that he was telling the truth.

"I wish that was true," said Darius softly.

Jason's knees buckled and he dropped to the ground. His hands were clutching at the straw on the ground as he tried to fight back the tears.

He gasped as something big and soft rubbed against his face. He turned his head to see Midnight was nuzzling his nose against his face.

Be strong, young one.

Jason reached up and put a hand on the side of the horse's face and held it against his.

"It's true, isn't it?" he whispered.

Darius was leaning forward, resting his elbows on his knees. He was just staring down at the dirt between his boots, wondering why he thought he was equipped to tell this boy about his parents.

"It is true," he finally said. "I wish to God it wasn't, but no amount of wishing or praying is going to change it."

Jason dropped his hands to his lap and let his tears fall into the dirt.

"And my pa?" he said, almost so softly no one would hear.

"This is where it gets even worse," said Darius, still staring at the ground.

He looked up and saw Jason was staring into his eyes, trying to control his breathing.

"You know why I came to town?"

"To kill the vampires that were here."

"Yes. There had been several people killed by them before I got here."

"Yes, I know."

"There is a reason your pa's body was never found. It appears he may have been turned."

"Turned?"

"It's when a vampire bites you, but doesn't kill you. Instead of dying, you become a vampire, just like the one that bit your pa."

Jason jumped to his feet, almost colliding with Midnight's chin.

"You're saying my pa is a vampire."

"Might be a vampire. We don't know for sure."

"So, he might not be a vampire," said the

boy defiantly.

"That's entirely possible."

"So how can we find out?"

"We need to find him."

Jason stood there, his face wet from the tears and Darius could see he was thinking.

"Do you think my pa might have killed my mama?"

"That is something we don't know. No one saw what happened to your mama."

"I heard something that night," said Jason.

"What did you hear?"

"It sounded like some kind of animal. It was growling out near our barn. I was standing on the porch of our house and, I guess mama heard it, too. She came out of the house with pa's shotgun and told me to stay in the house."

He went quiet and Darius just waited for him to continue.

"She went out to the barn and a minute later, I heard her yell my pa's name, but it got stopped. You know like if you say something and it gets stuck in your throat? Anyway, then I heard the shotgun go off and ran out onto the porch. Then, it was quiet as a graveyard."

"Did you see anything?"

"No, sir, I didn't. After a few minutes, I went out to the barn and I can tell you, I was scared like I never been before. I found the shotgun on the ground and there was some blood. I figured mama must have shot some animal, but there was nothing there."

Darius continued to stare at the ground, not wanting to look the boy in the eyes. The image of Sebastian kept coming into his mind and he couldn't stop it.

"They found your mama's body about a mile from the house," he mumbled.

"Why didn't they tell me that before?"

"Because, Jason, contrary to what you might believe, adults aren't always brave and don't always do the right thing. The sheriff and the others could not work up the courage to talk to you about it."

"You did."

He looked up and met Jason's eyes.

"I didn't want to. This is one of the hardest things I've ever had to do in my life. But, I thought you deserved to know what happened and it would do no good to keep that from you."

"So, do you think my pa might have killed my mama?"

"That's certainly a possibility. You say you heard her yell his name that night. I think he was there and she saw him."

"But my pa loved my mama. He told her that almost every day and I seen it in the way he treated her. He never would hurt her."

"Jason, there is something you need to hear and you need to listen good. If your pa has been turned into a vampire, he is not the same man you remember. He doesn't even think the same way. So, in truth, your pa didn't kill your mother. The monster he has become killed her."

Midnight stepped forward and hung his head over Jason's shoulder and rubbed his face against the boy's. The suddenly grown-up young man reached up and ran his hand over the horse's face.

"So what are you going to do?"

"There is only one thing I can do. Find the monster your father has become and kill it."

"Do it for my mama."

"And for you," said Darius as he stood up.

He walked over and pulled the door to the stall open and Midnight walked back in. He closed and latched the gate and reached up and patted Midnight on the side of the face.

"Thanks, buddy."

He's hurting. Keep an eye on him.

"I'll do that."

Turning around, he put a hand on Jason's shoulder and led him out of the barn and back down the dusty road Hell's Gate called Main Street.

"The sheriff tells me you're sleeping in one of the jail cells at night."

"Yes. He didn't think I should be out at the farm by myself. Now I know why."

"Go easy on them, Jason. If a grownup has to tell a young man his parents are dead ... well ... sometimes they just don't have the strength to do it, even if they know it's the right thing to do."

Jason nodded and then angled away from Darius and started walking toward the telegraph office.

"You going back to work?"

"I might as well," said the boy. "Got nothin' else to do right now."

"Jason," said Darius, causing the boy to stop and look at him. "You're a good, young man. It's an honor to know you."

Jason tried to force a smile, but it didn't come out the way he hoped. He just nodded and walked away.

13 – Preacher, We Are Going To Have Words

For the next week, the nights were quiet. Most of the townsfolk knew what had happened to Clem and that the vampire nightmare didn't seem to be over. They stayed locked up inside their homes once the sun went down. If anyone had chosen that time to ride through Hell's Gate, they would have been forgiven for thinking this was a ghost town.

Father Benedict got on a stage and headed back to San Francisco, leaving Darius with the charge of cleaning out Hell's Gate, ridding it of all vampires.

Darius stopped in and checked on Seth at least once a day. The young man was healing nicely and would be allowed to get out of bed and get on with his life. The only thing keeping him confined to bed was Anna Marie. Darius was sure it had nothing to do with his injuries. It was about doing everything to take care of his every need.

Seth didn't seem to be complaining at all.

Darius had little to do in the mornings, but sit outside the boardinghouse in his usual seat and watch the world go by.

Darius spent his afternoons sleeping in his room, not wanting to be tired at night. During the darkest hours of the night, the only movement in the town was him, patrolling the one main street and the two small alleys that ran parallel to it.

The alley along the south side of the town was where he found the laundry that did his clothes. It was run by a Chinese man, his wife and two children.

Darius made it a point to stop in each night and talk with them and see how they were doing. They were completely shocked the first night he did that and spoke to them in their native Mandarin tongue. From that night forward, they always had a bowl of soup and some noodles ready for him to sit and enjoy.

Down the northern alley was the one saloon in Hell's Gate. It was a rather seedy place and the people that patronized it weren't any different. He stopped in every night, just to take a quick look and make sure everything was okay.

The owner was usually cordial to him, but most of the customers were quite uncomfortable having him in their midst. It never dawned on them his reason for being in town was to protect them from the monsters that skulked around at night.

Tonight, as he walked the quiet, deserted streets, he looked up and saw the moon was about halfway toward full and his senses became heightened. If ever there was a night for Joshua Dalton to make himself known, it would come soon.

At about five in the morning, just as the sun was lightening the eastern sky, he allowed himself to relax, knowing the night was almost over. One more night of quiet behind him and he could wonder just how long he was going to stay in this little town.

Surely there had to be other monsters raising havoc in other parts of the country. Yes, there were other monster hunters to handle them, but he got the feeling he was being kept out of action for some reason.

His mind drifted back to something Father Benedict said when he came to town. Richard Kendrick and Sophie Carroll were a monster hunting couple that worked the Old Country, in and around Romania. Being the birthplace of a lot of the monsters of our nightmares, they had plenty of work.

He had known the two about a hundred years earlier, before they sent him to the unfamiliar country of America. Back then, this new nation had just come out of a bloody war, having fought to gain its independence from a ruthless king and the old world.

Before coming here, he worked around the Italian peninsula, sometimes venturing north when the need arose. That's when he met Richard and Sophie. They were each a couple hundred years younger than him, but every bit as capable of fighting monsters as him.

He smiled when he thought back to the two of them and how they were inseparable. They constantly acted like a couple of young people who had eyes only for each other. The church tried to split them up, but it was hopeless. They always seemed to gravitate back toward each other and the leaders of Heaven Sent finally gave up and just put them together.

One of the last things Darius did before he left for the New World was attend their wedding. Father Simon had officiated, but kept having to stop when they couldn't stop giggling. This had the unfortunate effect of causing the rest of the gathered to laugh, too. The problem was, if there ever was a man born without a sense of humor, it was Father Simon.

The two of them were lucky. They found each other and would live to be very, very old together. Something Darius hadn't been lucky enough to find himself. All of his wives had been ordinary, mortal women and though he loved each one more than life itself, it wasn't enough to give them the long life he desired for them.

Richard and Sophie's long lives were cut short one night, when they were lured to an abandoned church, searching for a vampire that was terrorizing the small town down the hill. What they found when they got there was not one vampire, but a whole family of them. A family of twenty-three vampires whose sole purpose was to get rid of the two of them.

Richard and Sophie walked right into the trap. They never saw the sunrise the next morning.

According to Father Benedict, a dozen hunters descended on that church the next week and floors were awash with the blood of the vampires. Usually, the hunters would just do their jobs as quietly as possible and fade away.

But not this time.

Twenty-three vampire heads were left mounted on stakes around the inside of the old church sanctuary. Their bodies were piled in the middle of the room and set ablaze. If there were any vampires left in the area, they would quickly get the message their days were numbered.

It was said that Father Simon ventured into the church after the hunters massacred the vampires and walked slowly around the empty hall, spitting on the faces of each vampire. He cursed each one and then left the church, never looking back. They say he had tears streaming down his face, crying over the loss of the two starry-eyed hunters. He would have given his own life to hear the two of them giggling and laughing again.

Darius felt a mixture of sadness and rage in his own heart, knowing he would never hear the two of them laughing again.

As he walked out of one alley and back onto Main Street, he smiled as he saw the sun cresting the hills to the east.

One more night coming to a peaceful end.

Until a horrifying scream of a woman broke the silence of the early morning.

Darius whirled around and looked to the alley where the saloon was situated. Taking off at a run, he ducked between the buildings and came out just in front of the watering hole. There was a woman on her knees in the middle of the alley, covering her face with her hands.

He ran to her and crouched down, placing a hand on her shoulder. He recognized her as one of the working girls from the saloon.

"Alice, what's the matter?"

She looked up at him with terror in her eyes and just pointed. When he followed her finger, he felt the same terror rip into his soul. The sight would have caused any man to fall to his knees in fear.

Ten feet off the ground, staked to the side wall of the saloon, was the body of one of the men that frequented the place. He had been gutted and nailed to the wall, his body placed like Jesus on the cross.

A message was scrawled on the wall in the man's blood. It was a message clearly aimed at him.

*Leave this town and
don't ever come back.*

Darius heard a couple of sets of footsteps coming up behind him and looked to see the bar owner and one of the other girls running toward them. He jumped up and stopped the woman from coming past the edge of the wall and seeing the sight.

He reached down, grabbed Alice by the arm and pulled her up. Putting her into the care of the other woman, he told them to get back inside.

As the two women retreated to the safety of the saloon, the sheriff came hustling around the corner and straight to him and the other man. When he saw the sight, it looked like he was going to retch right there in the dirt.

"That's ol' Ben," said the sheriff. "He never hurt a soul in his entire life!"

Darius walked over to a spot directly in front of the dead man. Looking up, he could see the rivulets of blood had run all the way down the wall and were puddled in the dirt below.

Looking at the words of the message, he could feel his rage growing. If there was one thing the message accomplished, it was to steel his resolve to stay and finish this.

"Looks like the good Lord has punished this wicked town."

Darius and the sheriff turned to see the fire-and-brimstone Baptist preacher standing there, looking at the sight.

Darius took two steps and grabbed the preacher by the throat and drove him against the wall of the building next door. Pushing the man's head up slightly, he made sure the preacher could see the dead man hanging on the wall.

"You see that?" he growled in the man's face. "He was a human being and a good man."

The sheriff grabbed his forearms and said, "Mr. James, let him go!"

He squeezed a little tighter before finally releasing the man, who almost fell to his knees.

As the preacher rubbed his throat, he gasped, "You're the reason this evil has come to Hell's Gate. You're the reason people are dead!"

Before anyone could stop him, Darius had one of his pistols in his hands, pointed right between the eyes of the preacher. He pulled the hammer back and pressed the tip of the barrel against the forehead of the man.

"Do you want to die right now?"

The preacher was trembling and the sheriff was hesitant to grab Darius' arm, thinking it might set the gun off.

"Do you want to die?" roared Darius.

"No," whispered the preacher.

Without lowering his weapon, Darius said, "Then this is what's going to happen. After they take Ben down from the wall and prepare him for burial, you will accompany his body to the cemetery and you will give one of the finest eulogies you have ever given. Am I clear?"

The preacher was still focused on the gun pointed at his head.

"Am I clear?" thundered the hunter.

"Yes ... yes."

Finally, Darius lowered his pistol, softly reset the hammer and put it back in its holster.

"I intend to be there when he is laid to rest. I'll be looking forward to your beautiful words over his grave. Now, I would suggest you head on back to your church and begin writing those words."

Without a second's hesitation, the preacher stumbled away and disappeared around the buildings.

"For a moment there, I thought you were going to shoot Preacher Smythe."

Darius looked at the sheriff and shook his head.

"I've never lost my temper enough to kill a man just for some words that came from his mouth. But today, I came damn close."

They heard a woman squeal in distress and turned to see Anna Marie had come to find out what the commotion was.

"Damn it, Anna Marie!" said the sheriff. "Get on back to the boardinghouse. This is not a sight you need to see!"

She bristled at his words and stood up straighter.

"Sheriff, I already seen it and I can't wash it from my eyes now!"

Darius walked over and put an arm around her shoulders and turned her away from the sight.

"Could you run to the undertaker's office and wake him? He'll need to get some men and equipment over here to get Ben down. Can you do that for me? For Ben?"

She looked up into his eyes and he could see the tears forming in hers. She nodded and then walked away, going in search of the undertaker.

He turned to the sheriff and then to the saloon owner.

"We need to rope this place off to keep others from walking back here and seeing this."

The saloon owner nodded and said he'd go get some rope and take care of it. While he did that, Darius and the sheriff started looking for anything that would point to the killer. It was obvious a vampire had killed the old man, but they were hoping for clues to where they could find this monster.

Within twenty minutes, the undertaker showed up with his wagon and three men. They had to work from the rooftop to get at the body and get it off the wall.

Once they had him down and left the alley, Darius and the sheriff looked at the message on the wall.

"I guess we need to get that washed off," said the sheriff.

"Not just yet," said Darius and he walked over to the wall.

He read the words a couple of times and then reached out and dabbed his fingers in the still wet blood. Working quickly, but deliberately, he wrote his own message.

Not until I kill you.

"You know, that will probably only make him angry," said the sheriff.

"Just how angry do you think he needed to be to kill Ben like that?"

"Point taken. And for the record, I'm glad you're here and staying."

They looked at the wall one last time and then turned and walked out of the alley and back to the boardinghouse.

Neither one of them took notice of the raven perched on the roof of the building next door to the saloon. It appeared to be paying particular attention to the words on the wall before it grunted and flew away, just before the sun would peek over the mountains to the east.

14 – Pigheadedness Is Hard To Argue With

Most of the town attended the funeral for Ben. It surprised Darius to see over two hundred people there that afternoon, especially on such short notice. Due to the nature of the killing and condition of the body, the sheriff and undertaker decided to have him planted before the sun went down.

With a closed coffin.

Word had spread quickly throughout the day about what happened and the saloon owner had to go out and wash the side wall of his building, whether the monster hunter liked it or not. There were just too many people gathering in the alley and it made him uncomfortable.

The people who saw the message left on the wall were aghast at the words Darius had written underneath the original message. About half were ready to ask him to leave and they were sure it was only going to get worse if he didn't get out of town, like the message said. They failed to realize the sender of the message wanted him to leave so he could have free rein over the town.

The other half who read the message were ready to pay him to stay. They knew he was the best chance they had for getting rid of this new monster. If he left town, about half of them were ready to leave, too.

Preacher Smythe did himself proud, extolling the gentle kindness and friendly spirit that was old Ben. Those that heard his eulogy would have been forgiven if they thought the preacher was talking about the wrong man.

Though all of them knew Ben was a good man, they also knew he was far from perfect. He loved to pickle his insides with the cheapest whiskey he could get his hands on. From the sounds of it, the preacher was nominating Ol' Ben for sainthood.

The preacher's adulation was probably more effusive because Darius had taken up a position right behind him. Every now and then the preacher would reach up and rub his neck where Darius had grabbed him. The sheriff had to bite his tongue to keep from laughing at this solemn occasion.

Once the graveside service was completed, the preacher disappeared into the crowd and back to his church without so much as a goodbye. Darius just watched him go.

"I can tell you," said the sheriff, "I've never really liked him. For a man of God, he spends more time condemning the people of this town than he does showing love and compassion."

Darius looked over his shoulder and nodded.

"The good Lord doesn't take kindly to hypocrites that would use His name and teachings to cause fear in the hearts of the people."

He looked down at the simple pine box sitting next to the grave. It sat there quietly, waiting for everyone to leave, so the gravedigger could lower it and fill in the hole.

Darius fished into his pocket and pulled out a dollar coin. Flipping it across the backs of his fingers a couple of times, he took it and slammed it into the top of the box, embedding it like a blade.

In a soft, low voice he said, "Allow me to buy your first round in the next life."

By this time, there were only three left in the cemetery. Him, the sheriff and the gravedigger. One look toward the grubby man leaning on the shovel left no question of the message he was sending.

That dollar gets buried with him.

He and the sheriff called the man over and the three of them lowered the box into the ground and that was it. Darius fished one more dollar from his pocket and gave it to the gravedigger, so he wouldn't be tempted to take the other one.

Turning and walking away, the sheriff and Darius headed down the hill and back to town. Behind them, they could hear the digger stabbing his shovel into the dirt pile and dropping it into the hole.

Looking to the west, they could see they had about an hour before the sun went down. Darius dreaded the coming of night because he was sure this new vampire was done waiting.

"Care for a quick supper, sheriff?"

"Yeah, I guess so. I'm not really hungry, but I know I need to eat something and so do you. I know you haven't eaten anything all day."

They headed straight to the boardinghouse and went straight to Darius' usual table. For some reason, it always seemed to be open when he walked into the dining room, no matter how busy the place was.

Anna Marie came hustling over when they sat down.

"Today's special for you two gentlemen?"

"Sounds good to me, Miss Anna," said the sheriff.

Darius just nodded and she returned to the kitchen.

"So, what is the plan?" asked the sheriff.

"At the moment," said Darius, "I hate to admit I don't have one. We do not know where this new vampire is or who it is."

"But, you're still thinking it might be Joshua Dalton."

"All evidence would seem to point that way. Young Jason said his mama called Joshua's name just before it killed her. Like she was seeing him and knew him."

"That's a damn shame. The Joshua I knew wouldn't have lifted a finger to harm her or Jason."

"Being turned changes a person," said Darius, as Anna Marie walked up with plates heaped with food.

"It turns them into monsters, doesn't it?" she asked softly.

"Yes, it does. People you would never suspect of being capable of evil will cause the greatest harm."

After making sure the men had all they needed, Anna Marie left their table to see to the other guests. Even though neither of them would admit it, both of them found themselves to be starving and ate most of their dinner in silence.

About twenty minutes later Anna Marie stopped by the table to refill their water glasses and see if there was anything else she could get them. As they were talking to her, she looked out the window.

"What in the world?" she said.

Darius looked up and then out the window. The preacher was crawling down the main street in his small wagon, being pulled by one horse. It looked like he had everything he owned, which wasn't much, packed in the back of the buckboard.

He was staring at the boardinghouse and it was clear he was staring right at Darius. He did not have a smile on his face, but according to the sheriff, he had never seen him smile.

Darius pushed back from the table and got up. Walking across the dining room, he stepped out onto the porch just as the wagon came even with him.

"Leaving town, Preacher Smythe?"

"It has come to my attention that this town is beyond redemption. My good works will be better appreciated elsewhere."

"I wouldn't be so sure of that," said Darius. "Nobody likes a hypocrite."

"How dare you speak to a man of God in such a way!"

Darius could feel a presence come up behind him and from the softness of the footsteps he knew it was Anna Marie.

"Look, I don't much care whether you stay or go and from what I understand, there is pretty much nobody that is going to miss you," said Darius who could see the preacher's face getting redder. "But the sun is about to set and it will be dark within half an hour. You can't make it to Sage Springs in that time and it is not a good idea for you to be heading out alone."

"The power of God will watch over me!" thundered the preacher.

"Preacher Smythe," said Anna Marie, "please come inside. I'll get you some dinner and even get you a room. If you are still intent on leaving, you can leave first thing in the morning when the sun comes up."

Smythe looked at her and for a moment, they thought he might take her up on her offer. Then he reached up and touched the brim of his black hat.

"Miss Anna, you are one of the few bright rays in this town. I regretfully must decline your offer. Now, if you'll excuse me, I must be on my way."

He slapped the reins on the backside of the horse and it began pulling the wagon.

"We should stop him," said Anna Marie.

"There are only a couple of ways I can think of to do that and one of them involves shooting his horse."

Anna Marie stepped back from him with a

horrified look on her face.

"Something I am not inclined to do," he said. "Besides, Midnight would never forgive me if I did that."

Just then, the sheriff stepped up to them.

"What's the other way?" she asked.

"Going after him, knocking him on his backside, tying him up and throwing him in a jail cell across the street."

"Those are the only two ideas you can come up with?" she asked.

"Do you have any better ideas? I mean, we already tried talking to him. Me trying to scare the daylights out of him and you trying to be as nice as could be. Neither of us met with much success."

"I could go after him and arrest him," said the sheriff.

"On what charge? Being stupid is not a crime," said Darius.

They looked to the east and watched the preacher's wagon disappear into the gloom. Darius could not shake the feeling that nothing good was going to come of this.

"Damn it!" said Darius.

Turning to the other two, he said, "Anna Marie take the sheriff upstairs to my room and get him the rest of my weapons. Sheriff, bring them to me at the livery."

He turned and stepped down off the porch and headed west to the stables.

"Wake up, Midnight. We have to go rescue an idiot."

You mean there's more than one of you in

this town?

"Now is not the time, buddy."

Sorry. I'm ready to go.

It took about five minutes for the sheriff to show up with his rifle, spikes and sword. He was in the company of Anna Marie. It took about ten more minutes for him and the liveryman to get Midnight saddled and ready to go.

"Get my horse ready to go, too, Hector."

Darius looked at the sheriff and then said, "Ignore him, Hector. Just exactly where do you think you're going, sheriff?"

"I'm going with you."

"No, you are not! You will stay here and make sure the people of this town get off the streets and safely in their homes."

"Darius," said Anna Marie as she put a hand on his arm, "you might need the help."

"Like the help I got from Seth? Look where that got him."

Both the sheriff and Anna Marie looked at him like he was heading to his doom.

"Look, I appreciate what the two of you are saying. I really do, but I have been doing this for over four hundred years and I've killed hundreds of vampires. This one will not get the best of me. Now please, sheriff, stay here and look after your town."

Hector finished with Midnight and stepped back as Darius climbed into the saddle.

"Anna Marie, tell your mama not to wait up for me."

She gasped, her face turning red and he smiled at her.

"Oooo, you are incorrigible, Mr. James!"

He winked at her and said, "That's what I've been told."

Without another word, he turned Midnight and spurred him out the door of the stables and into the darkness.

Anna Marie ran to the doors and stopped, watching him go, her shoulders bobbing up and down as she fought to keep control of her emotions. She felt the sheriff step up behind her and put a hand on her shoulder.

"Don't you fret about him, Miss Anna. Somethin' tells me he's gon' be alright."

She reached up and patted his hand and said, "I hope so."

Together the two of them began walking back to the boardinghouse, him to finish his dinner and her to go upstairs to check on Seth.

15 – You Didn't Deserve This

The darkness that enveloped the land was complete. Within five minutes, the hunter had lost sight of the lights of Hell's Gate. Out here, the only lights were the multitude of stars that covered the night sky over their heads and for illumination, they were sorely lacking.

Being the night of the new moon, there was no glow from that ruler of the night sky. Of course, Darius was happy about that. No full moon meant fewer monsters to worry about.

The horse and rider slowed down to an easy walk because they couldn't see over five feet in front of them. They needed to be extra careful to stay on the wagon trail that ran east to the town of Sage Springs. Not knowing if they were exactly behind the preacher, they had to hope he stayed on the trail.

About twenty minutes later, Midnight got spooked by something and Darius felt it in his heart. Whatever they were feeling, they both knew it wasn't good.

Coming to a stop in the darkness, Darius looked around as best he could. His eyesight was as good as it had ever been, but he still couldn't see in the dark. His other senses alerted him to the potential trouble.

"What is it, buddy?"

I don't know. It's not the preacher.

"Any idea where it is?"

For a moment, Midnight stood still, swinging his head back and forth. Then he started walking off the trail and came to a small depression in the landscape. Just the kind of hole in the ground a small meteor would make.

Darius jumped down from the saddle and walked to the edge of the crater.

There's something down there.

"Great," mumbled Darius as he began picking his way down the sides of the slope.

When the crater flattened out at the bottom, he could barely see he was about ten feet below the rim. As he got closer to the center of the hole, he began to pick up a smell. One that he was quite familiar with.

Dead body.

But it didn't have the sickly, sweet smell of a recent death. This one was days, if not weeks old.

Moving around the floor of the crater, he picked his steps carefully. There were small rocks and bushes and it would have been very easy to trip over any of them. He wished he had stopped to pull his small lantern from this pack, but then remembered his pack was safely in his room back at the boardinghouse.

"Good job, Darius," he mumbled.

As he took another couple of steps, the toe of his boot nudged up against something that didn't feel like rock or sagebrush. He kicked at it a little harder and set off a swarm of blue flies.

Waving his hands in front of his face, he

pulled out a match and struck it against his belt buckle. The flare of light showed him what was on the ground and he wished he hadn't seen it.

Before the match burned out, he walked a few feet away and set one of the small, dry sagebrush on fire. As the flames grew, illuminating the bowl of the crater, he turned back to see the horror he and Midnight had stumbled on.

Spread out on the ground was the body of a man, gutted from waist to neck. His neck was completely ripped open and most of the flesh was gone from his face.

Crouching down, he stared at what was left of the man's face, still frozen in the terror of what was happening to him.

From the look of the body, it had been here at least a couple of weeks, but Darius didn't have any doubts about how long.

"I guess I should apologize for sending you out in the middle of the night. You deserved a lot, but not this, Sully."

He reached down and tried to close the man's eyes, but they were so stiff they wouldn't budge. Shaking his head, he stood up and looked around the crater. The light of the fire was fading as the bush was close to burning out.

It was clear Sully had used the crater as a camp the night he left Hell's Gate and most likely died that night. Looking at the wounds, there was no confusion about what had done this to him. Only one thing would have done this much damage to a man.

A feeding vampire.

It wasn't your fault.

He looked up at Midnight, standing at the edge of the crater.

"It wasn't not my fault, either."

I think we need to go. We need to find the preacher.

For a moment, Darius had forgotten the reason they were out here. He looked one last time at the body and promised to catch the monster that had done this. Turning around, he started back up the side of the crater as the last of the flames in the sagebrush died out.

The sweet smell of sage smoke hung over the area, covering the smell of death that had brought them to the hole in the ground.

Climbing back into the saddle, he turned Midnight back toward the trail and they began their search for the preacher again. This time with a little more urgency.

Once they were back on the trail, Midnight started trotting, hoping to find the preacher sooner. Not that he really cared about the pompous idiot, but he knew Darius would suffer mentally if anything happened to him. He worried Darius got too involved with the victims of the monster attacks. He invested too much of his heart and soul into saving people and it took its toll when bad things happened.

For the next thirty minutes, they hastened through the darkness. Midnight hoped there were no large rocks or holes in the trail that could cause him to set a hoof wrong. Last thing he wanted was to break a leg and have Darius shoot him.

Hear that?

"Nope, what do you hear, buddy?"

Something up ahead. Sounds like some sort of attack.

Midnight picked up his pace and Darius pulled one of his pistols and cocked it, getting ready for just about anything.

As they came over a small rise, Darius could just make out the preacher's buckboard. It was turned on its side and it looked like the horse was dead on the ground. It wasn't the horse making the noise.

It was the preacher, locked in a life or death struggle with a vampire. Smythe, who appeared to be quite strong, had one of his hands around the neck of the vampire, holding it back. In the other hand, he held his crucifix, screaming at the vampire, trying to draw the power of Heaven down to protect him.

The vampire tried to get his fangs in close enough to rip the preacher's throat out, but every time he did, Smythe would press the crucifix to its face, bringing a screech of pain.

"Hey!"

The vampire turned its head just in time to see Darius jump down from his saddle and fire his pistol. All the movement caused the hunter's aim to go wide and the bullet just clipped one of the vampire's ears.

Releasing its hold of the man of the cloth, the vampire turned its attention to James and began prowling around him in a circle. Its fangs were flashing in and out of its mouth while its eyes glowed with an evil red. The monster hissed as Darius took aim for a second shot.

Before he could squeeze the trigger, the vampire lept with more speed than Darius expected and knocked him to the ground. His pistol skittered away in the dirt. He tried to free his other pistol, but the vampire was on him before he cleared leather.

Swiping at him with his clawed fingers, he knocked the other pistol from James' hand and dropped on him. Darius got a hand on the throat of the vampire and held him back, but he knew he was in a serious predicament. Being pinned flat on your back by a monster is never a suitable position to find yourself in.

The vampire stabbed at his shoulder with its claws, causing Darius to grunt in pain. With his free hand, he was trying to get hold of one of his silver spikes, but it seemed like the vampire knew exactly what he was doing. The monster grabbed his wrist and pinned it to the ground.

Darius could feel his strength waning and he called out for help.

Help is on the way.

"You demon from Hell!"

The vampire looked up just in time to see the preacher point one of Darius' guns at his head and saw the flash from the barrel.

The preacher, not being a man of weapons, missed slightly and the bullet grazed across the top of the vampire's head. It was enough to knock it off James and send it rolling across the ground. It came up to its feet and snarled at the two of them.

Deciding they outnumbered it, it lept into the sky, turning into a raven and flying away into the darkness.

James pushed himself up and looked at the preacher. The old man was shaking like crazy and Darius was afraid he was going to shoot himself. He took the pistol from his hand and put it back in its holster. He looked around and found the other pistol and secured it, too.

As he looked back at the preacher, he saw some blood on the man's neck. His hand lashed out, grabbing Smythe by the throat and turning his head to get a closer look at his neck.

"What?" gasped the preacher.

"Did he bite you?" growled Darius.

"No."

"Where did you get this blood?"

The preacher reached forward and patted Darius on the shoulder, bringing a fresh wave of pain.

"Same way you got yours," squeaked the preacher. "His claws got me in the neck."

Darius looked a little closer and couldn't see any bite marks, but in the dark he couldn't be sure.

"If you're lying to me, preacher, I will shoot you between the eyes."

He relaxed his grip on the man and let him go.

As the preacher rubbed his neck, he said, "I may be an ornery, old jackass and not much fun to be around, but one thing I am not is a liar."

Darius could feel himself getting a little weaker from the blood loss. He looked at the buckboard and the dead horse.

"We need to get this wagon back on its wheels and get back to town."

Together, the two men were able to push the wagon back upright and it settled with a small crash in the soft sand.

Looking down at the dead horse, the preacher let out a muted cry.

"Sadie, you were my only friend."

Midnight moved over and butted his shoulder with the side of his face. Smythe looked up at the black stallion and forced a bit of a smile.

Darius pulled all the harnesses off Sadie and then looked at Midnight.

"I hate to ask this of you, but we're going to need your help."

Midnight nodded his head twice and moved to the front of the wagon. Darius removed his saddle and dropped it in the back of the wagon. Then he and Smythe put the harness on the proud horse.

Do not tell anyone about me doing this.

"Wouldn't dream of it, buddy."

Just as they were finishing with the harness, Darius felt dizzy from the blood loss and wobbled on his feet. The preacher grabbed him and helped him into the back of the buckboard.

"Back to Hell's Gate," groaned the hunter as he laid down, his head resting against his saddle.

"After the things I said, I'm not sure I'll be welcome in that town again."

"Swallow your pride, Preacher Smythe. A humble man is welcome anywhere," said Darius just as he passed out.

Smythe walked to the front of the wagon and took one last look at Sadie. Midnight could feel the sorrow he was feeling for his dead friend.

Climbing into the seat of the wagon, he didn't bother with the reins.

"Take us back, Midnight."

Turning in a wide circle, the black horse found his way back onto the trail and set a good pace. He didn't want to be out here any longer than he needed to be. Especially when Darius was in no shape to battle any monsters.

16 – A Change Of Heart

As the coolness brushed across his forehead, Darius found himself relaxing on a shore of a distant ocean. He had just finished a coven of vampires in a small town in southern France. Before his handlers could send him on to his next assignment, he slipped away and spent two weeks just laying on the beach and being tended to by a couple of French beauties.

Nevermind, this was the early 1800s and that kind of thing was still frowned upon. Especially when both of the said beauties were the daughters of a French nobleman. It didn't matter that French society was some of the most decadent on the European continent. They took exception with him kibitzing with the daughters of Napoleon's cousin.

He felt the soft caress of a feminine hand brushing over his shoulder and this brought a smile to his face.

Until a raging pain tore through his body, starting in his shoulder and not stopping until it curled his toes. His eyes flew open and he found himself not looking into the brown eyes of a French beauty, but the blue eyes of an American woman.

Anna Marie, to be exact.

She was sitting on the edge of his bed, running a wet rag over his shoulder and whatever was in the water stunk to high Heaven and burned like crazy.

"What in the world!" he roared as she wiped his shoulder again.

"Oh, you're awake. Good. It's about time."

She laid the wet cloth over his wounded shoulder and he could feel whatever was in the water seeping into his cuts. Reaching up, she lifted the wet cloth from his forehead and dipped it into another water basin and then put it back on his forehead.

He laid back against the pillow in the bed, which was obviously in his room. He glanced over and saw his weapons stored neatly in the corner, along with his shirt and pants.

Realizing he was exposed from the waist up, he looked up at her.

"Excuse me for not being properly attired, Miss Anna."

"Oh pooh, Darius. You would not be the first man I've seen without a shirt on."

There was a light rap on the door.

"Is he awake?"

Anna Marie turned and smiled, saying, "Yes, padre. Come on in."

Darius looked up to see Preacher Smythe walk into the room and pull a chair up to the other side of his bed. He had a bandage on his neck where the vampire had scratched him.

"How's your neck, padre?"

"Much better, thank you. How are you feeling?"

"Well, I believe Anna Marie is trying to kill me with whatever is in the water, but I'll try to survive."

She reached up and clapped her hand on

the cloth on his shoulder, causing a fresh round of pain to shoot through his body.

"What's in this water is saving your life," she said. "At least, that's what John Dark Cloud told us when he was here."

"He was here?"

"When he heard a vampire had injured you, he left the mine and came straight here."

"If you could, would you tell him I'd like to see him when he has a chance?" asked Darius.

"Well," said Anna Marie, "if you want to see him, you'll have to get better and go to the mine. He left here and went back a couple days ago."

"What? How long have I been here?"

"Coming up on three days now," she said.

"Three days?" he bellowed as he tried to sit up. Finding himself still a little weak, she put a hand on his good shoulder and pushed him back down.

"You're not going anywhere just yet," she said. "Doc said to keep you in bed at least until tomorrow. But that was only if you woke up."

"I thought I heard voices over here."

They all looked at the door to see Seth standing there. He was dressed in a robe and barefoot and Darius could see the bandage still on his shoulder.

"How are you feeling, Seth?" asked Darius.

"Much better, thanks to you. I should be up and out of here by tomorrow if the mean nurse will let me out."

"Keep talking like that and you're never getting out of here. Did you finish your lessons for the day?"

"Yes, mother," he said with a grin.

"Oh, you men are so exasperating sometimes," she said as she stood up and took the water basin and set it on the chest of drawers.

"I'm going downstairs to see about getting you two something to eat. Padre, would you like something, too. A sandwich, maybe?"

"I would like that very much. Thank you, sweet lady."

She smiled at him and turned and whisked out the door. Seth stepped in and took a seat on a trunk near the wall.

"Before we talk and before she gets back," said Darius, "padre, there is a dead man about five miles east of town. Do you know of the meteor crater?"

"Yes, I know of it," said Smythe.

"A vampire killed him, but no one ever found him until I happened on him the other night. His body should be retrieved and taken care of."

The padre nodded and said, "I'll take care of that."

Darius looked toward the small window in the room and could tell it was late in the afternoon.

"Wait until tomorrow. I don't want anyone out there in the dark. He's been out there for a while, one more night will not change things for him."

He looked at the two of them and asked, "What's been going on here in town for the past three days?"

"It's been pretty quiet," said Smythe.

"No vampire attacks?"

"None that we're aware of."

"Okay, I want you to think hard, padre. That vampire we fought the other night. His face may have changed, but ... did you recognize him? Did he seem familiar to you?"

The padre took a breath and bit his lips. After a few seconds, he nodded.

"I would swear that it was Joshua Dalton. But that can't be true, can it?"

"I am sorry to say that it can be true. My worst fears seem to be coming true, that he's been turned."

The padre dropped his head and mumbled, "That poor boy."

"What?"

"Oh, I was just thinking of Jason Dalton. To lose his mother and father in this manner. I can't even imagine."

They all went quiet for a few minutes, realizing there was a twelve-year-old orphan who now seemed to be the charge of the town. Darius had no doubts Jason would be well taken care of.

Just then, Anna Marie came bustling in with a platter of sandwiches and a pitcher of water. When everyone was silent for a few seconds, she looked around.

"Don't stop talking on account of me."

"I was just getting caught up on the events around here for the past three days and I guess it's been pretty quiet."

"It has been quiet," she said. "You know there's that quiet moment before the big storm hits? It feels like that."

"Well, hopefully it stays quiet for at least one more night," said Darius. "I want to be well rested and ready by tomorrow."

"You will not push yourself, Darius," said Anna Marie. "It won't do you any good to get up too soon and aggravate that shoulder."

Darius looked down at his shoulder and lifted the cloth to take a look. It was easy to see he truly had been in bed for three days because the wound was healing over nicely. He figured it had something to do with whatever salve the medicine man had conjured up. Much as he didn't like the smell, he couldn't argue with its effectiveness.

"Well," said the padre as he stood up and picked up a sandwich, "if there is nothing else for me here, I shall return to my church and begin preparing for this Sunday's sermon."

"Thank you, padre," said Darius, "and oh, it's good to have you back."

For the first time in many years, a smile adorned the face of the preacher. It was a small one, but it was there just the same. He nodded to the other three and left the room. They could hear him stepping down the stairs and heading for the front door.

Anna Marie looked at Darius and cocked her head.

"I wonder just what happened out there the other night. He seems to be a completely changed man."

Darius nodded and said, "Coming face-to-face with a vampire can effect a change on any man. He's a good man. He was just a little wayward in the past."

Anna Marie held out a hand to Seth and said, "Time for you to get back to bed. By this time tomorrow, I'm sure the doctor will allow you to be up and about."

Seth took her hand and stood up. He looked at Darius and grinned.

"She really does have a motherly streak in her," he said.

Darius laughed and said, "Or wifely."

The smile faded from Seth's face as he thought of the implications of what the hunter had just said. As Anna Marie turned him out the door, she glanced back at Darius, smiled and gave him a wink.

As she pulled his door closed, he laid his head back and closed his eyes.

Three days of quiet in this little town. It was exactly what Hell's Gate needed, but he knew it wouldn't last. Somewhere out there, in the hills surrounding the town, evil eyes watched and a mouth craved. It craved the blood of innocents and Darius knew he needed to get up tomorrow and put an end to the terror.

17 – Two To Become One

Sitting in his customary chair outside the boardinghouse, Darius leaned back and put a boot on the rail. It had been a chore for him to get out of bed that morning and take a quick bath. He knew he couldn't lie around any longer. There was a vampire that needed killing and he was the man for the job.

He still could not get his head around having been unconscious for three days. He was still feeling weak from the blood loss, but he was feeling his strength returning.

As he sat and enjoyed the cool morning breeze, Anna Marie was back to her usual job of making sure he had a fresh glass of water at all times. She would duck in and out of the dining room to make sure he was feeling okay and he always tried to impress upon her he was feeling fine.

Just after ten, the doctor came strolling down the street and stopped in front of Darius.

"I was thinking you'd still be in bed, Mr. James."

"I can't lie around on my backside forever, doc."

"Maybe not, but I'd like to see that you don't push yourself too soon."

"I'll be fine. As you can see, I'm taking it quite easy right now."

The doctor went to say something, but looked to the east. There was a wagon coming toward town with what looked like two men riding on the seat.

Darius saw the same thing and turned to the doctor.

"Are you also here to see Seth?"

The doctor took his eyes off the approaching wagon and said, "Why yes, I am. I think he'll be able to get up and out of bed today."

"That's good," said Darius, without taking his eyes off the wagon. "Could you do me a favor? Go inside and up to see Seth, but make sure you take Anna Marie with you."

"Take Miss Anna upstairs with me?"

"Doc, something is coming into town right now and I'd appreciate it if she didn't see it."

The doctor looked at the wagon, being less than a quarter of a mile from where he stood and would be there in just a minute.

"Understood," he said as he walked into the boardinghouse.

Darius heard him call to Anna Marie and ask for her help in examining Seth. He heard the two of them walk up the stairs and nodded to himself.

A minute later, the wagon with the undertaker and preacher rolled past him. Neither man had a smile on their faces as they looked at him. The preacher nodded as they rolled by, heading to the western edge of the town and the funeral parlor.

In the back of the undertaker's wagon was a simple pine box. It looked like they had nailed the lid on securely, like they had no plans to open it again. Ever.

As they were going by, the sheriff walked out of his office across the dusty street and watched them. After they passed, he walked across the street and straight to the monster hunter.

"Any idea who they just brought in?"

"Yes, I do, sheriff, but if I tell you, you need to swear on the grave of your sweet mama that you will not say a word of this to Anna Marie."

"Given."

"It was the body of a Mr. Sully."

"Sully? I was wondering what happened to him. Haven't seen him around for nigh on a week now."

"He left here back before I went to the mine, heading to Sage Springs, I suppose. Stopped at the meteor crater to camp one night and I guess a vampire got into him."

"Good lord. You found him when you went looking for the preacher."

Darius nodded and said, "Yes, I did."

"And why does this need to be kept from Anna Marie?"

Darius hung his head and took a deep breath. Then he told the sheriff the story of how Sully came to be out there in the desert, in the middle of the night.

The sheriff sat back against the rail and just shook his head.

"Rumor has it Sully was one to take advantage of many women. If I had known what happened upstairs, I'd have stuck him in jail for a few days and then chased him out of town. Can't say I'm going to shed any tears for him."

"No, sheriff, no tears, but he didn't deserve to go out like that. No man does, no matter how dark his character may be."

They looked to the west and could see the undertaker pull his wagon around the back of his funeral parlor. This got them out of sight of anyone walking down the street.

A few minutes later, the preacher came out the front door of the funeral parlor and walked back to the boardinghouse.

"We are going to lay him to rest this evening, just before the sun goes down. I assume we should keep this gathering as small as possible."

"That would be best," said Darius. "I'll be there to pay my respects."

"I'll be there, too," said the sheriff.

"Let's not make this a big deal," said Darius. "I'm serious when I say I'd like to keep this from Anna Marie."

"Absolutely," said Smythe. "I'm heading back to the church to take care of a couple of items and prepare for his interment."

Without waiting for a response, he turned and headed toward his small church just past the funeral parlor.

"If you want, the doctor is upstairs right now with your deputy. You can go up and check on him. I think Seth is going to be back on his feet today."

"Yes, I think I'll go up and see how he's doing," said the sheriff as he walked to the doors and into the boardinghouse. He stopped and reaching in, pushed the swinging door open.

"Miss Anna Marie, how are you doing this fine day?"

"Sheriff Jackson, I am doing wonderfully. The doctor has released Seth just now just and he should be down any minute."

She stepped through the door he held open for her and Darius could see she had another glass of cold water for him. Draining the last couple of swallows from the glass in his hand, he exchanged it for the fresh one.

"The doctor is giving Seth a clean bill of health?"

"Yes, he is," said Anna Marie, "and I have you to thank for that."

"I didn't do much."

"You knew enough to take that hot poker to his wounds to keep him from bleeding out. The doctor said that if you hadn't done that Seth would have died within the hour."

"Well, I knew if he had died I'd have had to come back here and explain it to you. I did not want to see that kind of pain in your eyes."

She sat down in the chair next to him and patted him on the hand.

"You mean like finding out that Mr. Sully is dead and I had something to do with it?"

"Anna Marie!" bellowed an exasperated Darius.

"What? You think Seth is going to be able to keep a secret like that from me? I could tell he was holding something back and didn't give him no rest until he let it out."

Darius just shook his head and said, "Yep, you two are made for each other. He's going to be the perfect husband for you, not being able to keep any secrets from you."

"I don't need protecting from news like that," she blurted out.

"Really? Because I think you do."

"Why? Am I some shrinking violet to be protected?"

"Yes! You just took blame for his death and it was not your fault."

They sat in silence for a moment and then Darius said softly, "If there is any blame to be placed, it will be on me."

"If either of us had known there was still a vampire around, we never would have sent him away like that."

She squeezed his hand and he could feel the warmth and kindness radiating from her soul.

"You trying to make time with my best girl?"

They both looked up to see Seth standing in the doorway, smiling at them.

"Well, Seth," said Darius, "if you'd get over your blasted fear of beautiful women and just ask this sweet lady to be your wife, that would take me right out of the picture."

Seth's face got bright red and he mumbled, "I don't figure we know each other well enough for me to ask her that."

Darius felt Anna Marie squeeze his hand and he said, "Gol' darnit Seth! She likes you,

you are completely enamored with her. What in the world else is there to know? Tie the damned knot with her and work it out from there. I'm sure you two will figure it out."

Seth walked over and leaned against the railing and looked at the two of them. They were both staring at him, daring him to say something. Darius had seen that frightened look in the eyes of many a man when it came to women.

"I don't ... I just ...," he stammered, trying to find the words.

"Oh, good grief!" said Anna Marie as she stood up.

She stepped in front of Seth and put a hand on his chest.

"Seth, do you want me to be your wife?"

"Well, yes, I do."

"Good!" she said. "That settles it. Now was that so hard?"

He looked at her, still at a complete loss for words, so she just leaned up and planted a kiss right on his quivering lips. As she pulled away, he looked like he was going to pass out again, probably from the blood rushing from his head.

"Now," she said, "I'm going to tell mama I'm getting married."

Without another word, she turned and floated through the doors and was gone. Seth watched her go and then looked at Darius, with eyes as wide as saucers.

Darius started laughing and said, "I thought I was going to have to get Midnight out here to drag those words out of you."

Seth walked over and plopped down in the recently vacated chair and just stared straight ahead.

"I'm getting married," gasped Seth.

"Yes, you are."

The deputy turned his head and looked at Darius. Then an enormous grin broke across his face.

"I'm getting married!"

Darius laughed and punched him in the shoulder, which brought a quick cry of pain from the younger man.

"Oh, sorry. Forgot that was your bad shoulder."

He reached up and gave the deputy a friendly pat on the shoulder.

"Just never do anything to break her heart."

Seth looked into his eyes and said, "Never in a million years."

Then he sat back in the chair and looked straight ahead. He took a deep breath and let it out slowly, letting the full weight of what had just happened wash over him.

As they sat there, enjoying the morning breeze, neither one paid any attention to the black raven sitting on the scraggly juniper tree just outside of town.

18 – Ramping Up His Game

There were only five people in the graveyard later that afternoon. Seth and Anna Marie, standing next to each other and holding hands. Darius, Sheriff Jackson and the preacher stood on the other side of the grave.

The gravedigger had already done his thing and the pine box was already at the bottom of the hole.

The preacher kept his remarks short. His words weren't of the caliber that had been said over Ben's grave, but he still asked the Lord to allow Mr. Sully into His kingdom if there was anyway it could be done.

Darius asked forgiveness for sending him out into the dark that night and Anna Marie did the same. She said she held no ill will toward him and hoped he was now walking the streets of Heaven.

As the brief graveside service finished, they started walking back toward town. Their quiet reverie was interrupted by the guttural croak of a raven in a tree about a hundred yards away.

No one seemed to notice except Darius. He was walking at the back of the group and came to a stop, looking across the expanse between him and the bird. Even from that distance, he could feel the true nature of the bird.

The sheriff realized he had stopped and turned back to see what was happening when he saw Darius pull one of his pistols, cock it and fire in one smooth motion. The blast of the gun shocked the other three into turning around.

They looked to where the gun was pointing and could see the raven taking to the skies, flying away from them.

Anna Marie stepped up to him and gripped his arm.

"That was him, wasn't it?"

The hunter twirled his pistol a couple of times and slid it back into its holster.

"I believe it was," he said.

"You couldn't have hit him from this distance," said the sheriff.

"No, but now he knows I'm on to him."

As the five of them watched the black bird get smaller and smaller in the distance, each of them felt the terror in their souls taking hold.

"I think we should get inside," said the sheriff.

It took a few seconds, but the rest of them followed his lead and began moving back to town. This time with a little more haste in their steps.

Darius looked back and could see the gravedigger was just filling in the hole and he turned back to the cemetery.

"You four go ahead. I'll be along shortly," he said as he began walking back up the hill.

He would not leave anymore men alone as the darkness of night was falling.

As Darius sat and ate his supper, he looked out the window. Darkness had fallen and with it, the town outside had grown quiet.

This was one of the worst times for him. Sitting around, waiting for the monsters to strike. He would much rather take the fight to them, but over the centuries had learned the monsters were very good at hiding themselves when they wanted to.

Anna Marie kept coming by his table and checking on him, but he could tell she was as nervous as could be. Seth was back on the job and had taken the night shift at the jail so the sheriff could get some rest. Every now and then, they would see the deputy making his rounds.

"I just don't know if I'm cut out to be the wife of a deputy."

Darius turned from the window to see Anna Marie standing next to him, watching Seth walk by.

"Don't think like that, Anna Marie," said Darius.

"It's awfully hard not to think that way with all that's going on."

"And that's what you need to remember. Once I take care of this vampire problem, things will go back to being normal. Think about it, if you didn't have this vampire problem and things were the same as they were say, a couple of years ago, would you be saying the same things?"

She thought about it for a second and then said, "I suppose not."

"There you go."

He reached over and gave her hand a squeeze.

"You just be patient and this will all work out."

"Hopefully," she said in nearly a whisper, "with no one else being hurt by the vampire."

"I pray for that, too."

She bit her lip and then asked, "Is there anything else I can get you? Mama is getting ready to close the kitchen."

"No, I think I'm good. You tell your mama this supper was excellent, as always."

She smiled and said she would. She could see Seth had made the turnaround at the end of the street and was coming back, so she walked across the dining room and stepped out onto the porch.

Darius could hear her as she said, "Good evening, future husband of mine."

Seth stopped and bowed to her.

"And good evening to you, my future queen."

She stepped down off the porch and leaned up and kissed him.

Darius, watching from the window felt a pang of sorrow drift across his soul. He remembered all too well the times he lost his heart to a beautiful woman and becoming attached to them. Those were the best times of his long life, but they were always destined to end in heartbreak.

Four times he had stood over the grave of a loved wife and he felt like he couldn't do it anymore. Fighting monsters and getting wounded by them didn't hurt nearly as bad as holding the hand of a dying woman that you loved, knowing that you couldn't go with her to the other side of the veil.

He had discussed this with the seven different padres that oversaw Heaven Sent, but never felt like they understood. How could they understand? They were sworn to vows of celibacy, never knowing what it was to love a woman.

One thing that always pained him was how Richard and Sophie had made a life together. They lived for over two hundred years together and would have gone much further if the vampires didn't cut them down. But they had grown up together and were inseparable, leaving the church with no choice but to take both of them.

His thoughts came back to the present as he looked back through the window and saw Anna Marie standing with her head resting on Seth's chest and his arms wrapped around her shoulders.

Seth glanced over and saw the monster hunter looking at them and smiled slightly. Darius just returned his smile with a nod.

Feeling a bit like he was intruding, he got up from the table and headed up the stairs. It had been a long day and he was definitely ready for a good night's sleep.

After getting undressed and crawling under his covers, he reached up and snuffed out the candle with his fingers and closed his eyes.

Three miles outside of town, Jenny and Cal Tompkins were doing the same thing. They were an elderly couple, having raised four children on their small farm and watched them leave the nest and start lives of their own.

As they laid down in their double bed, Jenny's head resting on her husband's shoulder, they heard a rustling sound. It sounded like the wings of a hundred birds, all taking flight at the same time.

Jenny sat up, wondering what was happening, but before she could ask, the door to the small farmhouse flew off its hinges. As the wood broke apart and scattered across the room, she screamed. Cal jumped from the bed, dressed in nothing but his long-johns and reached for the rifle he kept near the bed.

As the dust cleared, they saw a dark figure standing in the doorway, just barely outlined by the light of the crescent new moon. Cal levered one round into the chamber, brought the rifle up and fired immediately. Cal knew he was an excellent shot with the rifle, but the bullet didn't seem to have any effect on the person standing in the door.

"You spawn of the devil!" roared Cal as he fired again and again.

In the blink of an eye, the dark figure swept across the room and slammed its clawed hand into the chest of the farmer, driving him back against the wall.

"Run, Jen," gasped Cal as he tried to hold the demon back by the throat.

Jenny jumped off the bed and ran out the door in her nightclothes and barefoot. Crying, she ran into the darkness, but did not know where to go. Town was three miles away and she knew she'd never get there and find help in time.

A scream of pain cut through the night and she stopped and looked back at the house. She could hear Cal trying to put up a fight, but it was clear it was a losing battle. The vampire roared, shaking the night with its terror.

She turned and began running again. Cal was giving his life so she could save hers and she didn't want that sacrifice to be in vain.

She only got another hundred yards before she heard the fluttering of cloth in the wind and looked over her shoulder to see the vampire descending from the sky toward her. Without watching where she was going, she tripped over a low sagebrush and fell, feeling something snap.

Trying to get to her feet, it was clear she had broken her shoulder and couldn't push herself up. She ended up falling back down and rolling onto her back.

The vampire floated down out of the night sky and alighted next to her. Looking up, she could just barely make out his face in the pale light of the moon. What she saw terrified her.

"Joshua, why are you doing this?" she cried.

Reaching down, he grabbed her by the throat and lifted her off the ground. As her feet left the ground, she could feel her neck stretching to the point of breaking.

"The hunter decided not to leave like I told him to. So, I will bathe this valley with the blood of the people who live here."

She gurgled as his fingers squeezed even harder. With her last breath, she snarled through clenched teeth.

"I hope he kills you slowly."

He stopped squeezing and looked into her defiant eyes.

"That is an excellent idea," he growled in her face.

He released her throat, grabbed the back of her head and yanked it back, exposing her neck. Leaning forward, he slowly bit into her skin and began ripping small pieces away, one by one.

With every bite, she screamed in pain. As the blood spurted from her neck, the vampire continued to lap at it and enjoyed the taste. He kept from killing her quickly, let her heart pump the life-bearing fluid from her body.

It took Jenny a full ten minutes to die and the vampire relished every minute. When her heart finally stopped, he licked the last of the blood from her throat. Then he dropped her dead body to the dirt, discarding her like a soiled tissue.

Looking down, he gazed upon her body and felt a sense of ecstasy as her blood found its way into his veins. Having fed on two this night, he knew he wouldn't hunger again for days.

Pulling a handkerchief from his pocket, he wiped his mouth and dropped it onto her body.

Hunger or not, he wasn't finished and any killing over the next few days would be simply for sport.

19 – The Aftermath

The next morning, Darius sat at his usual table and visited with the sheriff while they enjoyed one of Abbie's substantial breakfasts. Neither one had any idea what had happened the night before, just outside of town.

"How are we supposed to look after all the people that live around here?" asked the sheriff. "We have people spread all over the area and there is no way we can protect them all."

Darius took a bite of his eggs and thought about it for a moment.

"Sheriff, I hate to say it, but we can't protect everyone. We can only protect those that live inside the town limits."

"That didn't seem to help old Ben."

"True, but we didn't realize we still had a vampire problem. Now we know."

"Tell me, why did you take a shot at that raven the other day? You had to know you probably wouldn't hit it."

"Like I said, I wanted to let it know I was on to it. I want it to know it won't be as easy as it thinks to do its thing."

"It may just go into hiding until you give up and leave."

"I don't think so. Vampires are the ultimate apex predator."

"What does that mean?"

"It means nothing hunts it, but it hunts

everything. Well, nothing hunts it, but me."

The sheriff took another bite.

"Aren't vampires supposed to be afraid of the daylight?"

"Yes. Not just afraid, but deathly afraid. Direct sunlight can kill them."

"Yet, we saw that raven during the day."

"We saw it just after the sun had gone down," said Darius. "The time after the sun goes down and before it comes up in the morning is the realm of the vampire."

The sheriff was about to say something, but Seth came racing into town from the west. His horse looked like they had been in an all-out race from wherever they came from. They skidded to a stop outside the sheriff's office and Seth jumped down and ran through the door of the office. He didn't even bother to tie his horse up to the hitching post.

A few seconds later, he came out of the office and looked around and the sheriff waved at him through the window.

"I don't like the look on his face," said Darius.

"Me neither."

Seth came through the doors to the dining room and they could see he was trying to remain calm and not attract any attention.

He leaned over and said quietly, "We need to go. It happened again."

The sheriff nodded and stood up. Darius stood up and leaned in to the deputy.

"A bad one?" he asked quietly.

"Worse than anything I've ever seen,"

whispered Seth.

"Let's go," said the sheriff.

The three of them walked out the door and the sheriff told Seth to go alert, Simon Cuthbridge, the undertaker and also the preacher. Then he and Darius headed for the livery to get their horses.

Darius felt his stomach churning. As they walked, the sheriff didn't say a word. He could tell the old man was trying to keep his temper under control.

After saddling up, they headed to the west, meeting Seth just outside of town.

"Where are we going?" asked the sheriff.

"The Tompkins place."

"Jenny and Cal?"

"Yes, sir."

The sheriff just closed his eyes and shook his head. Darius could feel the rage boiling off him. He had felt this kind of thing many times before and he knew it wouldn't be long before the sheriff turned on him. When you're the legendary Darius James, monster hunter, they expect a lot from you. Whether or not he liked it.

Miracles were expected, even though Darius felt far from being a miracle worker.

"This is exactly what I was talking about," said the sheriff. "Three miles outside of town and we can't protect them."

A few minutes later, the undertaker and preacher rolled up in a wagon and they all headed out across the desert to the site of the latest massacre.

About thirty minutes later, Seth brought them to the body of Jenny Tompkins. She had been placed on a fence post near the barn, her arms extended out from her side and wrapped under the barbed wire. Her feet were placed, one on top of the other and her head was cocked backwards, her face toward the sky.

It was clear the vampire had been trying to evoke the image of Jesus on the cross and that is exactly what all five men thought of when they saw her body.

Her lifeless blue eyes stared toward the heavens and her face still bore the look of terror she had been feeling at the time of her death.

Darius climbed down from Midnight and stood in front of the body. After examining the wound on her neck, he came to a conclusion that sent an icy shiver up and down his back.

She had been killed for sport. Drinking her blood was just done as a matter of habit. The vampire could have just as easily ripped her throat out and left her to bleed out in the dirt.

Reaching up, he closed her eyes and then placed a hand on her forehead. Images flooded into his brain, images showing her last horrifying moments. One face loomed in front of her as she struggled to get free. With her dying breath, she uttered the proof he and the others had been looking for.

Joshua, why are you doing this?

"Joshua," Darius said softly, but not softly enough. The other men heard him say it.

Then he smiled as he heard her gather her courage and pray for a slow, painful death for the vampire.

"You find something amusing?" asked the sheriff.

"Not amusing, sheriff. Just gratifying. She was a fighter right to the end."

He leaned down and whispered in her ear, "Rest easy, Jenny Tompkins. I will make him pay for what he did here."

Standing up, he turned to face the others and the sheriff said, "So, I guess we can now be sure it truly is Joshua Dalton."

Darius nodded.

The sheriff turned to Seth and asked, "Cal?"

"He's in the house, sheriff."

"Okay, can you stay here and help Simon and Preacher Smythe with her body? Mr. James and I will go to the house."

"Sure thing, sheriff. And just so as you know, when I said earlier this was the worst thing I've ever seen, I wasn't talking about Jenny."

Sheriff Jackson stared at him for a moment, then turned and headed for the farmhouse.

"Prepare yourself, sheriff," said Darius.

"What is that supposed to mean?" asked the sheriff through gritted teeth.

"All I'm saying is, I've seen what these monsters can do to a person. If Seth is spooked, I'm guessing this vampire tore Cal up worse than anything you've ever seen."

The sheriff stopped walking and turned to Darius.

"Let's get one thing straight, Mr. James. He

isn't *this vampire*. He has a name and his name is Joshua Dalton! And he was a friend of mine. I'll thank you to remember that."

Darius reached out and put a hand on his shoulder and could feel him bristle underneath it.

"Okay, now let me get one thing straight with you. Joshua Dalton is no longer with us. He ceased to exist when he became a vampire. He is no longer your friend and will rip your throat out just as easily as he did to Jenny, Cal and Clem."

"And Ben," said the sheriff, with a bit of fire in his eyes.

"Believe me, I haven't forgotten one soul that these vampires have killed. Not the ones that were your friends or the multitudes of names and faces from the four hundred years I've been doing this. It is the curse I bear."

The sheriff took a deep breath and let it out slowly. He was trying to push all the anger he felt out of his body.

In a much softer tone, he said, "Let's see to Cal,"

Darius squeezed his shoulder and the two of them turned and walked the last few yards to the porch. As they got closer, the sickening smell of bloody iron in the air assaulted their noses.

They could see the door to the house was destroyed, knocked off its hinges. Without even stepping through the door, they could see the blood splattered all over the walls. And the floor. And the ceiling.

When they walked through the door, the sheriff immediately turned around, bolted off the porch and puked in the dirt. It took him a few seconds to regain his composure. Standing up, he pulled his handkerchief and wiped his mouth, spitting out the sour taste.

He turned back around and saw that Darius was still standing just inside the door, not having moved one step. He stepped back up, just behind him.

"What in the Hell kind of monster would do something like this?"

He didn't hear an answer and looked up into the hunter's face. Darius had his eyes closed and was breathing slowly.

He bowed his head and said faintly, "The kind of monster that is sending a message."

"What kind of message could you possibly get from this?"

"He wants me to leave town and never look back."

"Maybe that's not such a bad idea," mumbled the sheriff.

"Sheriff Jackson, make no mistake about it. He wants me to leave so he can freely kill you and everyone in this valley."

For a moment, they stood there, surveying the scene in front of them. Cal Tompkins had been torn into many pieces, his entrails scattered around the room and his body parts hung on the walls.

The most horrifying part of the scene was Cal's head. It was impaled on one bedpost and its dead eyes were staring straight at them.

"I guess you're right about one thing," said the sheriff quietly.

"What's that?"

"Joshua Dalton is truly dead. The man I knew would never have done something like this."

Darius just nodded. After a few seconds, he reached up and put a hand on the sheriff's shoulder and squeezed.

"Let's get out of here. Both of us have seen enough."

He turned and walked out of the farmhouse. The sheriff followed him to a spot about twenty yards away. This was how far they had to go to get away from the smell.

Looking back near the barn, they could see the preacher and undertaker were just finishing up with Jenny's body. They had sealed her into her pine box and were sliding it into the back of the wagon.

Midnight started walking across the distance toward the two men and the sheriff's horse just followed along.

This is getting worse, isn't it?

Darius reached up and ran a hand over the side of Midnight's face.

"Nothing we haven't seen before, but this is beginning to pain me more than most."

I think it's because you're beginning to care about these people and this town more than any other time.

"Father Drake warned me about that."

Based on the conflict I feel in your soul, I would say you would be well served to heed his warning.

As the wagon rolled past them to the house, Darius put his forehead against Midnight's and whispered, "Thanks buddy."

It took about half an hour for the five of them to clear the house of Cal's remains and nail the lid on his coffin.

They sealed both pine boxes tight because the undertaker didn't feel there was going to be any need to prepare the bodies for burial. All of them agreed it would be better just to get them in the ground as quickly as possible.

As they finished up, the sheriff looked at the house and said, "I doubt anyone is going to want to live in this house again."

"We can't just leave it like this," said Darius. "It will attract other vampires and become a nest for them."

He reached into his saddlebag and pulled out a bag of gunpowder and walked into the house. He poured a thick line of black powder on the floor and folded the empty bag and put it in his pocket.

Striking a match, he looked around at the gruesome scene for a moment. He could feel the evil that had invaded the home hanging in the air. One thing he never would admit to the sheriff or the others was this was worse than anything he'd ever seen before.

This vampire was taunting him.

He dropped the match into the gunpowder and it flared to life and spread quickly through the dry wooden planks of the floor. Turning around, he walked out the shattered door and straight to Midnight.

Climbing into the saddle, he sat and watched, along with the others, as the flames consumed the house. No one moved until the roof and all four walls fell in on themselves.

They turned around and began the slow walk back to town. When they got there, the preacher and undertaker went directly to the back of the funeral parlor, hoping to stay away from the watchful eyes of the town.

The other three went straight down the middle of the street, heading for the boardinghouse and the office.

All of them were dismayed when they saw Anna Marie step off the porch and into the street, directly in front of them. They could see from the look on her face she knew something bad had happened.

As they all stopped in front of her and climbed down, she took the reins for all three horses. While she waited for the men to pull their rifles and saddlebags off, she looked into the distance.

Seth could see she was looking at the hazy cloud of black smoke in the distance. He moved to her and could see the tears forming in her eyes.

"Who was it?" she asked softly.

"Jenny and Cal," was all he could say.

"Oh my God," she cried.

Once the men had taken their things from the horses, she turned and began leading them toward the livery. She was having a hard time walking in a straight line because her eyes were filled with tears.

She felt something soft and warm and realized Midnight was nuzzling his nose against her face. She reached up and ran a hand over the side of his face. As the three horses followed her, she tried hard not to lose control.

Be not sad, sweet Anna. They are both in the arms of the Lord now.

"I know," she whispered through her tears. "It's just hard to know how they came to make that journey."

After turning the horses over to the stableman, she walked out of town a couple hundred yards. There was a hill behind the stables, covered with a small copse of trees. They surrounded a tiny spring that supplied the town with its water. There was a stone bench in the shade of the trees, placed there because it was such a beautiful, quiet place to sit and look out over the town.

She could see the people of Hell's Gate walking around below, most of them not knowing what had happened yet.

Then she leaned forward and buried her face in her hands and began crying. She had known Jenny and Cal most of her life, having grown up with their kids. Jenny had been the schoolmarm during Anna Marie's school days.

As she tried to fight the tears back, she heard footsteps and looked up with blurry eyes. She could just barely make out Seth walking toward her. He sat down on the bench next to her and put an arm around her shoulders.

"I can't believe they're gone," she lamented.

Seth didn't say a word. He just held her tighter as he stared at the water bubbling up from the ground.

Without warning, she turned and buried her face in his neck and sobbed even harder. As she cried, he wondered if he really had it in him to be her husband, or husband to any woman. He quickly found that he didn't like to see a woman in tears. It tore at his heart and made him swear to himself that he would never cause such pain to Anna Marie.

They sat there for about an hour before making their way back down the hill, her with an arm around his waist and him with an arm around her shoulders.

"I love you, Anna Marie," he said softly.

She stopped and looked up at him, still with tears in her eyes.

"That's the first time you've ever said that."

"And I regret waiting this long to tell you."

He took the sides of her face in his hands and looked into her eyes.

"If I fail to tell you that each day, make sure you correct me for my errors."

A pained smile crossed her lips and she put her arms around his neck and kissed him.

"I love you, too," she whispered.

Somewhere in an evil place, the monster

that used to be Joshua Dalton laid in blissful sleep. A faint smile curved the ends of his evil lips as he dreamed of streets awash with blood.

In his dream, one man stood out. Impaled on a high pole overlooking the town, Darius James was helpless to do anything but watch as the monster destroyed the lives of every person in Hell's Gate. The monster laughed each time the hunter screamed in anguish as he witnessed another human being torn to pieces.

20 – Stirrings Best Ignored

The night was especially dark, with black clouds hanging low over the town. It blotted every trace of the moon out and there wasn't even a slight breeze to stir things up.

Darius walked from one end of the street to the other, checking all the dark corners evil might hide in. Midnight plodded alongside him, walking easily without saddle or halter. On nights like this, Darius liked to have him along because of his ability to sense danger.

It was well after midnight, closing in on four-thirty in the morning and neither of them had felt any danger lurking about.

Darius felt completely helpless, knowing the vampire could stay outside the town for days or weeks. There were plenty of potential victims outside the protection of the hunter and the monster didn't need to be in any hurry.

Maybe it's time to send for help.

"I was just thinking the same thing," said Darius. "I'm just not sure there are any other hunters close enough to help."

You won't know if you don't ask.

As they reached the center of town on their twentieth, or fiftieth, round, someone stepped out of the boardinghouse and stood on the porch. As they got closer, they saw it was Anna Marie dressed in a long robe and slippers.

She stepped down off the porch and handed Darius a glass of cool water and pulled an apple from her pocket for Midnight. As the horse munched on the treat, she looked up at Darius.

"I worry about the two of you out here by yourselves."

Don't worry, sweet Anna, I'm looking after him.

She giggled when she heard that and then realized it was the first time since that afternoon she had laughed. Since seeing her two friends being buried in the cemetery.

"I take it Midnight has decided you are worthy of hearing him speak," said Darius.

"Yes, he has. I can tell you, it is strange to hear the thoughts of an animal, even one so majestic as Midnight."

Darius smiled and said, "Please don't say things like that about him. He already has an over-inflated opinion of himself."

Midnight swung his head and hit Darius on the shoulder, almost knocking him off his feet and causing him to spill all of his water. Anna Marie laughed again, stepped up and kissed the horse on the nose.

"Don't you listen to him, Midnight. I think you're amazing."

Darius regained his footing and stood there, staring at the two of them.

"Oh, I see how it is. The two of you ganging up on the poor, defenseless hunter."

Midnight just bobbed his head up and down.

Darius started walking again, saying, "Come on, you old nag. We still have work to do."

Did he just call you an old nag?

"He must have because he certainly wasn't referring to you," said Anna Marie with a look of feigned shock on her face.

The hunter stopped dead in his tracks and turned around and faced the two co-conspirators. His mind was racing as he tried to find some words. With Anna Marie standing there, with her hands on her hips and staring at him, he could not see an escape from his mistake.

"I ... umm ... I was just referring to ..."

He stopped talking because he knew anything he said would just dig the hole a little deeper. It had always been like this for him. He poked fun at Seth for being unable to talk to a pretty woman, but if the truth were known, he was even worse at times.

She cocked her head to one side, raised an eyebrow and said, "Well?"

As he continued to struggle with something to say, Midnight stepped forward and hung his head over Anna Marie's shoulder and focused his black eyes on his rider.

Then, Anna Marie's shoulders bobbed up and down and he was sure she was about to cry. But the sound that came from her mouth was definitely not crying.

She started laughing and almost doubled over, holding her stomach.

"You should see the look on your face, Darius," she struggled to say.

He took a breath and let it out. The look on

his face said he was struggling to find any humor at all in the situation.

"Oh, come on," she said as she jumped forward and wrapped her arms around one of his. "We're just funnin' with you."

Then her eyes closed and she had a pained look on her face.

"Darn it!" she squealed.

"What?"

Without opening her eyes, she moaned, "I just stepped in an enormous pile of horse poo."

This time it was Darius' turn to laugh. As he laughed loud enough to wake half the town, Anna Marie tried to scuff her slippers back and forth in the dirt to get the offending stuff off her feet.

"Midnight! Did you leave that little gift there for Miss Anna Marie to find?"

For the first time since he'd known him, the horse could not continue with any kind of repartee. Midnight's eyes were wide open and he looked back and forth from Darius to Anna Marie.

Then Midnight jerked his head back and looked at Darius.

You know very well I would never do something like that in the middle of the street.

Darius was still chuckling softly when Anna Marie looked up at him.

"You knew it was there!" she exclaimed. Then her eyes narrowed. "You are not a very good protector of women, Mr. James."

He laughed again, put a hand on hers and turned to continue his walk down the street. As she walked along beside him, she squeezed his arm.

For the first time in over a hundred years, he felt something and he knew he had to fight it. It wasn't the love he felt for Anna Marie. He'd already succumbed to that from the first moment he laid eyes on her.

It was jealousy. He was jealous of the fact that Seth had captured her heart and would be the one to marry her. It took every ounce of strength of spirit to knock that feeling down and subdue it. Buried underneath the jealousy was the absolute joy he felt that the two of them had finally found each other and would soon seal their futures together.

Be careful with your feelings, Darius.

The hunter just nodded slightly, knowing Midnight had directed that thought to him and him alone.

When they reached the end of the street near the livery, Darius put Midnight back in his stall and closed the gate.

"Get some rest," he said as he patted the horse on the side of the face.

He and Anna Marie walked out of the stables, heading back to the middle of town as the sun was lightening the eastern sky.

"So, what are you going to do, Darius?"

He remained silent for a moment, wondering if what he planned was really the best course of action.

"I need to talk to Jason later."

21 – Entering The Vampire's Den

Darius sat in the dark telegraph office, letting his eyes adjust to the gloom. It appeared the telegraph operator liked it dark and didn't bother to open any shutters or the door to let some light in.

The telegraph operator was noticeably absent, having been sent to get some breakfast by the hunter. Only two occupied the small shack sitting at the base of the final telegraph pole near the edge of town.

"Do you really believe my pa is a monster now?"

Darius just nodded in the darkened room as he sat knee-to-knee with the boy. Jason had been hoping that his father wasn't the vampire everyone feared now, but in the back of his mind he knew it was true.

"I know that's hard to hear," said Darius. "I'm sure the last time you saw your pa, he was the kind of man that would hurt no one. But Jason, that man is gone. He has been replaced with something that will kill every man, woman and child in this valley and then he will move on to some place new."

Jason looked down, scuffing his toe in the dust on the floor. It was finally sinking in that he was truly alone in this world.

Looking up, he asked, "Why did you come to me?"

"Because I need to know if there is some

place your pa liked to go? You know, to be alone with his thoughts. Some place he would be alone and would see no one else."

Jason thought for a second and then said, "There's a cave in the hills just west of our farm. I liked going there because it was cool, even on the hottest days of the summer. I think pa used to like going there, too."

The boy thought for a moment and then asked, "Do you think he would go there?"

"I think he would go to some place familiar, some place he felt was safe. Can you draw me a map to this cave?"

Jason got up and went to the small desk and picked up a pencil and paper. In a couple of minutes, he had drawn an accurate map that left Darius with no questions about the cave's location.

As there was nothing else to say, Darius stood up and patted the boy on the shoulder. As he stepped out of the shack, he looked up to see the sun was not quite halfway across the sky, but he knew he had plenty of time to make the trip.

He headed for the boardinghouse to get his weapons and make sure he was prepared for this. As he was putting things together in his room, he heard a voice behind him.

"So, did he tell you anything useful?"

He turned to see Anna Marie standing there. The look of fear on her face was easy to discern.

"Yes, he did and if it works out the way I hope it does, this will all be over by this evening."

As he continued to pack, she sat down on the edge of his bed.

"It must be hard for Jason to turn on his father like that. I can't imagine what's that like for him."

Darius stopped for a second and looked at her. He was actually tiring of trying to explain to people that Joshua Dalton was dead and gone. The vampire was no more Jason's pa than he was Midnight.

"Yes, I'm sure it was," he whispered as he put the last of his arsenal together.

He went to say something else, but the sound of a horse galloping past the boardinghouse interrupted him. Whoever was flogging that horse was in a serious hurry to get somewhere.

Stepping to the window, he looked out, but could only see the settling dust of the passing horse. Something tickled at the back of his mind and he picked up his bags and rifle and headed for the door.

Anna Marie followed him out, pulling the door closed behind her. She nearly had to run to catch up to him as he rushed down the stairs and out into the street.

Darius stopped and looked to the west, but couldn't see anything. That itching in his head was getting more and more insistent. He turned and headed to the livery as fast as he could walk, with Anna Marie shadowing his every step.

"Darius, what's wrong?"

He said nothing. He just kept walking until he stepped into the cool air of the stables. The livery man came walking around a corner.

"You needing your horse, too, Mr. James?"

"Who else needed a horse?" he asked.

"That Dalton boy. He came in here and said he needed to borrow a horse and even paid me for it. I let him use Clem's old horse."

Darius hung his head and closed his eyes.

"You don't think he's going ..."

He looked at Anna Marie.

"Yes, I think that's exactly where he's going."

Turning back to the stableman, he said, "Get my horse ready to go! Now!"

"Yes, sir!" exclaimed the man as he jumped to get it done.

"You can get mine ready, too," said Anna Marie.

"No!" stormed Darius. "You are not coming!"

"Don't you even presume to tell me what I can and can't do, Mr. James!"

Without warning, Darius grabbed her by the arm and hauled her over to one of the posts. He reached up and pulled a length of rawhide from a hook and tied one end around one of her wrists. She struggled against him, but he was much too powerful for her to fight back.

He pressed her back against the post and tied her other wrist behind her. When he looked, he saw the stableman was just staring at the two of them.

"Is my horse ready?" he bellowed.

"Oh, no, sorry," said the man as he went about getting the saddle ready for Midnight's back.

The whole time the two of them worked to get Midnight ready to go, Anna Marie struggled and pulled against the strap holding her wrists. She was ready to spit fire and Darius could feel the heat.

"You can struggle all you want, Anna Marie, but I've asked the powers of Heaven to keep you bound here. Save your strength."

When she heard that she stopped pulling at the bindings. How could she possibly break the bonds being strengthened by Heaven?

As Darius climbed into the saddle, Midnight looked at Anna Marie.

It's best if you just stay here. We will bring the boy back safely.

Darius looked at the stableman and said, "Under no circumstances are you to let her loose. You can get her some water and can put a bucket down for her if she needs to take care of business. But do not cut her loose."

"I hate you!" yelled Anna Marie.

"No, you don't. You're just madder than a wounded wildcat right now. You'll get over it."

Without another word, he spurred Midnight out the doors of the stables and headed west as fast as the horse could run.

You know there is no such thing as the powers of Heaven for holding her.

"I know that, but she doesn't."

If Darius didn't know better, he could have

sworn he heard Midnight laughing.

It took about an hour for them to find the path leading to the cave. It was easy to find because Clem's horse was standing near the end of the path, tied to a tree. Darius looked up and could see the path was too steep for Midnight to make it up safely.

"Stay here and keep each other company."

Checking all of his weapons, he pulled the rifle from its scabbard and turned, heading up the hill. He wasn't sure how far he had to go, but he was sure he would not like what he found there.

Every step of the way, he couldn't get the image of Carlos out of his head. He was under no illusion that Jason was here to kill the vampire. Finding his father and proving he wasn't the monster everyone thought he was seemed to be the plan.

Darius knew it was a plan destined to fail and if he didn't get there soon, it would result in the death of another boy. His conscience would not allow for that again.

It took about twenty minutes for him to reach the cave. Rounding a small curve in the path, he felt the icy fingers of danger gripping his soul and then, seeing the mouth of the cave removed all doubt he had found the right place.

The roof of the cave appeared to be just over eight feet in height at the opening. There was a cool dampness that engulfed him as he moved into the darkness.

Moving deeper, the cave turned a couple of times to the right and left. By the time he'd made a couple of turns, the light from outside had completely disappeared and he had to stop to light his small lantern and hang it on his belt.

The roof of the cave was sloping downward, making it harder to move. He moved another ten yards into the darkness and had to crouch to move forward.

The lantern couldn't shine forward unless he took it off his belt and held it out in front of him. He didn't like that because it meant he had to use his rifle one-handed. Deciding on a different course of action, he set the rifle down in a corner and pulled one of his pistols.

He moved a few more yards and came to a stop. Not because he couldn't move any further. Advancing into the cave wasn't the problem. The problem was he had reached his goal.

Laying on a stone bed, in a state of torpor, he saw the vampire. As he raised his gun and took aim at the head, a hand reached out of the darkness and settled on his shoulder. Never had he jumped so hard, almost slamming his head into the roof of the cave.

He swung the pistol around and aimed at his attacker, only to find he was aiming right between Jason's eyes. The boy gasped when he saw the large barrel of the gun pointed right at his head.

"I'm sorry, Mr. James," whispered Jason.

Darius lowered the gun and almost felt like punching the boy in the face. But that would have awakened the vampire, so he held back.

"You and me are going to have some words later," he hissed at the boy.

"I'm sorry. I thought," he whispered as he looked at the sleeping vampire, "that was my pa, but that isn't him. It looks like him, but it ain't."

"Why does no one believe me when I say Joshua Dalton is dead and gone?" he asked quietly. "Jason, your pa is dead. That monster used to be your pa, but it is not anymore."

"I'm scared. What should we do?"

"What *we* should do is get *you* out of this cave and back into the sunlight."

Jason hesitated and Darius turned him around and pushed him back toward the cave entrance. As they began moving back toward the light, they heard a low growl coming from behind them.

"Move it!" ordered Darius.

They both started scrambling down the tunnel, heading toward the increasing light in front of them. Darius could almost feel the danger coming up behind them and he urged Jason to move even faster. He grabbed his rifle as they ran past it.

Rounding the last turn in the tunnel, the bright daylight flooded in and they ran as fast as they could. Again, Darius felt something right behind him. Just as he shoved Jason out of the cave and into the sunlight, he felt a stabbing pain in the back of his right shoulder.

Something tried to grab him and pull him back, but he was able to wrench himself free and fall into the sunlight. He almost landed on top of Jason.

He rolled and brought the pistol to bear on the cave opening, but couldn't see any target. All he could see was the darkness inside the cave.

He squeezed the trigger and from the gun erupted a bullet that flew into the dark mouth of the cave. He kept his pistol trained on the cave, but couldn't see anything.

He also felt dizzy from the wound he had just taken in the back. He didn't know what the vampire had done, but it felt like some sort of poison was working its way into his body. His hand was trembling and his eyesight was getting fuzzy.

"Mr. James!" yelled Jason as he knelt down behind the hunter and tried to steady him.

"Jason, come to me, my son."

They both looked at the darkness, but still couldn't see anything.

"You belong here at my side," came the voice from the cave. "Together, we will rule this valley and then beyond."

"Who are you?" asked Jason cautiously.

Darius was struggling to keep his arm raised and the gun pointed at the cave. It horrified him to see a man walk to the edge of the darkness and stand there, looking at them.

"I am your father, Jason. Do you not recognize me?"

The hunter tried to fire again, but didn't have the strength to pull the trigger. The pistol fell from his hand to the dirt. He began coughing as he tried to catch his breath.

"Tell him to step into the sunlight so you can get a better look at him," wheezed Darius.

Jason looked at the figure at the cave entrance. He could see the resemblance to his pa, but the soft kindness of the face he remembered was gone. His skin was a grotesque shade of ashy gray, his ears had grown pointed and the fangs extending beyond his lips were frightening.

"Step out of the cave so I can see you, pa."

The vampire stepped a little closer to the light, but stopped short of actually setting foot in the sunlight.

"You can't step out of the cave, can you?" said Jason as he felt Darius slump back against him.

The vampire's head dropped and his eyes slanted as he stared at the hunter and the boy, sitting on the ground, just out of his reach.

"Come to me!"

Before anyone could stop him, Jason reached forward and grabbed the pistol off the ground and pointed it and fired. The roar of the explosion echoed across the valley landscape as the bullet flew at the monster.

Because he was still a young boy, the pistol jumped from Jason's hand and flew ten feet behind him. The bullet slammed harmlessly into the wall of the cave next to where the vampire stood.

"So, you have chosen," growled the vampire. "When darkness comes, I shall rip the flesh from your bones and devour your blood."

Jason trembled as he heard the voice of the vampire and then became truly terrified as he watched it fade backward into the darkness of the cave.

He cried out, "Come on, Mr. James. We need to get out of here."

He could feel Darius' dead weight leaning back against him and there was no movement other than his chest moving up and down as he struggled to breathe.

"Mr. James?"

He shook the hunter, trying to get a response from him.

"Please wake up," he pleaded.

He knew he had to get him up and down the hill before darkness fell, but he was still too small to lift a full grown man. Shifting himself backward, he let the hunter's body lay back on the ground with his head resting on his lap.

He looked up through the trees at the sky and could tell they had about four hours before the sun would set. Four hours before the monster could leave the cave and slaughter both of them.

"I'm sorry, Mr. James," he blubbered. "This is all my fault."

He sat there, rocking back and forth, knowing he would never leave Darius' side, but also knowing the hunter would yell at him to get away from the hill.

He reached down and pulled the other

pistol from the hunter's holster and held it up. He tried to will himself to hold it steady and not let it waver. His hands shook under the weight of the heavy gun and he asked the heavens for strength to hold it steady.

As the first hour passed, he would raise the gun every few minutes and point it at the cave. He was hoping each time he lifted it his arm would become stronger. To his surprise, that's exactly what happened. Each time he raised the gun, he could feel his strength grow and the shaking lessened.

As the second hour passed, he kept trying to wake Darius, pleading with him to get up and leave this mountain. As he looked up, he could see the sun was getting closer to the tops of the trees to the west and it wouldn't be much longer until the shadows grew.

Then he thought he was imagining things. Somewhere down the hill, he could hear someone walking up the path. Not only could he hear them walking, he could also hear them singing.

O, I wish I was in the land of cotton

Whoever it was, they had a terrible singing voice, but to Jason, it was one of the sweetest sounds he had ever heard.

Old times there are not forgotten
Look away! Look away!
Look away! Dixie Land.

He kept his eyes on the trail down the hill, but he also kept his hand firmly on the pistol. The sound of this man singing might have been soothing, but he didn't recognize it and wasn't ready to trust anything or anyone.

In Dixie Land where I was born in
Early on one frosty mornin'

After a few more seconds, he saw a head come into view below him. The man still hadn't looked and didn't see the boy pointing the gun at him. He just kept stepping up the path, getting closer to the two outside the cave.

Look away! Look away!
Look away! Dixie Land.

As the man got about ten yards away he said, without looking up from under his hat, "Boy, do you intend to shoot me or can I come closer?"

"I ain't quite decided."

The man stopped and raised his head and Jason finally got a look at him under the brim of his hat. He was an older man, with snow-white whiskers on his face, leathery tanned skin and blue eyes that sparkled like stars.

The thing that got him to lower the gun was when the man smiled at him. The man stepped closer and stood over the two of them. He looked down and nudged the hunter with the toe of his boot.

"Darius, what the hell did you do now?"

"You know Mr. James?"

"Of course, we're both part of the same brotherhood. Uhh ... and sisterhood. Don't tell any of the lady hunters I said that. They can get furious if we leave them out."

The old man looked at the cave and it was plain he could feel the evil coming from the gloom.

"So, what happened, boy? What's your name, by the way? Can't keep calling you boy."

"My name is Jason Dalton. I went into the cave because I thought my pa was in there. Mr. James tried to tell me my pa was dead and turned into a vampire, but I was stupid and din' listen."

The old man crouched down and put a hand on Jason's shoulder.

"Well, I wouldn't call you stupid. Just a little confused."

He reached down and put a hand on Darius' forehead and closed his eyes. After a couple of minutes, he pulled his hand away and stood up. Walking toward the cave, he stopped just short of stepping out of the remaining sunlight.

"Are you going to go in there and get the vampire?" asked Jason.

"Oh no, I don't have a wish to die anytime soon. Going into a vampire's lair in the daytime and waking it up is a very foolish thing to do. I'd rather get stuck in a dark room with an angry bobcat."

"Mr. James went in there," whispered Jason.

The old man turned and looked at him and smiled.

"I'm sure he went in there to get you, not to fight the vampire."

"We need to get Mr. James down off this hill and away from here before it gets dark."

"Yes, we certainly do," said the old man as he stepped back to their side. "Help me get him up."

He reached down and took Darius by the arm and lifted him into a sitting position. Then he and Jason got him up and over the new hunter's shoulder.

"You know how to shoot that gun, Jason?"

"Not very well."

"Okay, you keep it in your hands and if we end up having to fight our way out of here, try not to shoot me."

"Yes, sir."

Then Jason started looking around on the ground, searching for something.

"What are you looking for?"

"His other gun. I lost hold of it when I fired it earlier and ... there it is."

He ran over and picked it up off the ground and now had a gun in each hand. As he turned back to face the old man, he saw him laugh.

"Damned if you don't look like a little hunter, Jason. Let's go."

The boy felt a swell of pride as he realized what the old man had said.

As they made their way back down the hill, Jason asked, "What is your name, sir?"

"My name is Marcus Decimus Aurelius."

"That is a funny name. How did you get it?"

"Why, the same way you got yours, Jason. From my mother and father when I was born back in Rome."

"Rome? Where is Rome?"

"You are kidding with me, right? You don't know of Rome? The Roman Empire?"

"Sorry," said Jason as he stepped along behind Marcus.

"What are they teaching children these days?" wondered the old man.

As they continued making their way down the hill, the old man gave Jason the shortened version of the Roman Empire. By the time they reached the bottom of the hill, Jason had learned Marcus was the son of one of the last Roman emperors. There was a rumor his mother was a god and oh, he was over one thousand, four hundred years old.

After laying Darius over Midnight's saddle and tying him down like a sack of wheat, they got on their horses and began their swift journey back to Hell's Gate. A name Marcus suggested should be changed as soon as possible.

22 – Help Comes While You Sleep

There was no passage of time in the mind of Darius as he lay in the bed in the boardinghouse. The poison from the claws of the vampire had worked its way through his system, causing him to venture into lands he would just as soon not.

He had fleeting images of being taken off the hill and placed over the back of Midnight. For some reason, he felt as if the way he returned to town should embarrass him, but in his current state of mind, he wasn't feeling much of anything.

While he was in his dreamland, it was a constant battle with vampires, werewolves, wendigos and every other type of monster his mind could conjure up. Sometimes he won those battles and sometimes he lost.

Now, he was feeling something wet and cool on his brow and even in his dream-like state; he knew it had to be Anna Marie tending to him. Try as he might, he couldn't open his eyes and bring the nightmares to an end.

He did not know how long he was out, but if it was anything like the last time, it would be about three days.

"How's he doing today?"

"Seems about the same," he heard Anna Marie say.

Who in the world is she talking to? I know that voice.

"Well, let me know if there is any change. I'm going to get back outside and keep an eye on things."

"Alright, Marcus."

Marcus? No! What the hell is he doing here?

His ears picked up the sound of Marcus going down the stairs just outside his room. He heard Abbie ask if there was any change to which he answered, "None."

Darius fought with every fiber of his soul to open his eyes, but just couldn't do it. Now that he knew Marcus Decimus Aurelius was here, flashes came back to him about what happened in the cave. And how he had come back to Hell's Gate draped over the back of Midnight like a dead body. As a matter of fact, he seemed to remember Anna Marie screaming when she saw him, fearing him to be dead.

Probably was mad I was dead because it meant she couldn't kill me herself.

Slowly, he sank back into the darkness, even though he tried to stay above it. Back down to the battles with the monsters again. Back to hoping this wasn't to be his fate for the rest of eternity.

It took a full seven days for Darius to open his eyes and the first thing he saw was the grizzled face of Marcus. The door to his room was open so he could hear the goings on downstairs. It must have been mealtime because it sounded like a full house.

The old man was sitting in an armchair that had been brought into his room. He had a ragged copy of the Bible, giggling at something he was reading.

"What could possibly be funny in the Bible, old man?"

Marcus looked up from the book and smiled.

"Well, Revelations is quite funny if you read it correctly."

"Revelations? Revelations is a horror story, worse than anything we ever face," croaked Darius.

"I guess that depends on how you look at it."

Marcus pushed himself up and moved over and sat on the edge of the bed.

"How are you feeling, boy?"

"Boy?" whispered Darius. "I'm four hundred and thirty-seven years old. Hardly a boy."

"And I'm a thousand years older than that. So, you're a boy to me. Especially after that stunt you pulled in the cave last week."

"I admit, it wasn't my finest h ... last week? How long have I been out?"

"Today is the eighth day since your misadventure."

"Eight days?"

Darius took a deep breath and relaxed.

"Why are you here, Marcus?"

"You don't seem thrilled to see me."

"Oh, don't get me wrong. I am very glad to

see you, especially since I've been out of action for more than a week. If there was anyone who could look after this town while I was down, it would be you. But, I never sent for you."

Marcus smiled and said, "You know we never need to send for anyone and our orders come with no warning to us."

"Father Benedict?"

Marcus just nodded.

"I guess he felt you needed some help this time. That's why he sent us."

Darius relaxed back against the pillow and rested his head as much as he could.

"Wait, us?"

Before Marcus could answer, they heard someone come in downstairs and walk across the floor to the desk.

"Why, Miss Anna Marie. You look positively beautiful. I dare say, each time I see you, you get prettier."

Darius recognized the British voice immediately and wanted to hide in the nearest closet. Or town. Or parallel dimension.

"Thank you, kind sir," they could hear Anna Marie say, "but need I remind you, I am engaged to be married?"

"But," laughed the other voice with its thick, London accent, "you're not married yet, so I still have hope."

"Tell me he's not here," groaned Darius.

"Are all hunters as incorrigible as you, Mr. Bartles?" they heard Anna Marie ask.

"No, beautiful lady. Only the very best of us."

Anna Marie giggled and then they heard some footsteps coming up the stairs and Darius wanted to jump out of the bed and bolt the door. If he had the strength to do it, he would have.

Then his biggest nightmare stepped into the doorway.

"Well, good afternoon, chap. We were quite concerned you might never wake up."

Standing in the doorway, at just over six feet tall, was the most dapper looking gentleman to ever grace the boardinghouse. A three-piece suit, tie and a bowler hat left no doubt who had arrived.

"Willoughby Bartles," groaned Darius.

"The third," said Willoughby with a smile.

"Just when I thought it couldn't get any worse."

Willoughby walked over and sat down in the chair and looked at him.

"Come now, chap. We were told you had a vampire problem that you couldn't handle by yourself. Marcus and I rushed halfway across the country to your aid. Well, I did. Marcus was just over in the next god-forsaken state."

Darius looked at Marcus, who nodded.

"I was over in Texas dealing with a werewolf problem when I got the telegram."

"And I was in Boston. They seemed to have a slasher on the loose there. We never caught the bugger and rumor has it he fled back to the Old World."

Darius pushed himself up and leaned back against the wall.

"So the great Willoughby Bartles couldn't catch an ordinary murderer?"

"Hardly ordinary. This fiend preyed on the lovely ladies of the evening, ripping their bodies from waist to neck. It was really quite gruesome."

Darius wanted to continue talking about the failure of this hunter to catch the murderer, but he knew he was in the same situation. Also, from the sound of it, making light of the events in Boston didn't seem to be the right thing to do.

"So, what's happened since you two came to town."

"Not a lot," said Marcus. "Seems your vampire knows well enough to stay away from town."

"That's the problem. He's attacking people outside of town where we can't protect them."

"Which is why we've pulled all citizens into town," said Willoughby. "Well, all those that would come."

"Where are they being housed?"

"We have some tents the Army sent over," said Marcus. "There's a right nice little tent village on the edge of town. Willoughby and I are sharing a very nice, larger tent."

"You have my condolences," said Darius.

Before Willoughby could reply, Anna Marie came bustling into the room and went straight to Darius and checked his condition. Her cool hand on his forehead to check his temperature felt like the touch of an angel.

"How are you feeling?"

"Much better now."

"Good, because you and I are going to have words."

Darius' eyes opened wide and he could see the fire in hers. Then he looked at the other two men.

"Gentlemen, do not leave me alone with this woman."

"And why, pray tell, do we need to protect you from this incredibly gorgeous creature?" asked Willoughby.

"Because," she said, "to keep me from following him to the cave, he used the power of Heaven to bind me."

Darius looked back and forth between the two men and begged with his eyes for them to not give him up.

Marcus couldn't do it. He busted out laughing so hard he almost fell off the bed.

"The power of Heaven?" asked Willoughby.

"Yes, he said no matter how hard I tried to break loose, the power of Heaven would keep me bound."

This time it was Willoughby's turn to laugh.

"And you believed him?"

Anna Marie jumped up and looked at the two men.

"What?"

"Miss Anna Marie," said Willoughby with a big smile on his face, "there is no power of Heaven that would keep you bound, unless you were a monster. I find it hard to believe that a fine woman, such as yourself, would be a monster."

Anna Marie turned and looked at the injured hunter through squinted eyes.

"Darius James! You are a rogue and a scoundrel! I stood there for over two hours before Seth came to rescue me!"

Darius looked at her, this woman about to erupt like a bomb, and he tried really hard, but couldn't keep from breaking down and laughing along with the other men.

"A rogue and a scoundrel?" he mused. "I guess that's not the worst thing someone has called me during my life."

"Oooo!" exclaimed Anna Marie.

Then she stormed to the door. She stopped long enough to tell the new hunters she would have lunch ready for them when they came downstairs.

Before going out the door, she looked at Darius with raging anger in her eyes.

"I don't know if you're going to get anything to eat today!"

Then she was gone, stomping down the stairs, her anger expressed with every step.

Willoughby and Marcus stood up, ready to head downstairs.

Marcus looked at him and said, "I'll try to sneak a little something up here for you to eat."

"Don't bother, Marcus. I'm going to get up, put some clothes on and join you in a few minutes."

After they pulled the door closed, he struggled to sit up and reach for his clothes on the trunk next to the bed. It took every bit of strength he had to pull on his trousers and throw a shirt around his shoulders.

He stopped long enough to look in the mirror at the back of his shoulder and see how bad it looked. To his surprise, there were just a few scars where the vampire had clawed him.

He realized his healing was most likely because of Marcus. He made a note to thank the old man when he got downstairs.

Pulling his boots on was one of the biggest struggles he'd ever faced in his life and by the time he was finished, he was ready to lie back down and get some rest.

He looked at his weapons hanging from the hooks on the far wall and considered them for a moment. Then, he decided with two hunters downstairs, he could forego his guns just this one time.

He opened his door quietly and cautiously looked out, to make sure there was no crazy woman about to gut him. He heard her voice downstairs, conversing with some of the other diners, so he knew he was safe for the time being.

Hobbling down the stairs, he found the other hunters sitting at his usual table and slid into the corner chair. For some reason, he didn't feel safe having his back to the dining room while Anna Marie was on the warpath.

Him being unarmed and all.

After they finished their meals, including Darius, the three of them took a walk to the edge of town. They walked into a cluster of Army tents that numbered close to fifty. The women had set up a kitchen area and were preparing the evening meal, while the men and boys were busy with manufacturing.

Darius looked over the shoulders of a couple of men working at a table and saw they were making bullets.

"We decided we might need an additional source for these bullets," said Marcus, "and these fine people were more than willing to help."

As he looked closer, Darius could see they were making the bullets he and the other hunters were accustomed to using. Six-part, fragmenting bullets in various calibers. He picked up a couple and examined them, finding their craftsmanship was impeccable.

He looked at Marcus and said, "Make sure they make a lot of these, so they can have some for themselves."

"Most of these people are not fighters, Darius," said Willoughby. "Most of them have nothing except a rifle."

"Threaten their families and I guarantee you they would fight."

One man looked up from his work and just nodded.

"Well," said Willoughby, "there's only one vampire, so I say we rid the town of him and be done with it."

"One vampire that we know of," said

Marcus.

After finishing their impromptu tour of the bullet-making tent, they walked out to the far edge of the tent settlement. They found six men stationed at various intervals, keeping their eyes peeled for anything they didn't like. Darius mentioned how remote the chance was the vampire would attack during the day, but neither of the other two said anything to lessen the men's resolve to protect their town.

After seeing the edge of town was sufficiently guarded, the three hunters headed back to the boardinghouse to plan their next move. As they walked down the street, the sheriff came out of his office and joined them.

"Perhaps we should include Seth in this meeting," said Darius.

"Seth is getting some sleep so he can be ready to take over during the night," said the sheriff.

"Okay," said Darius, "there is something I think needs to be made clear here. There is literally no chance the vampire will attack during the daylight hours."

"What are you getting at?" asked the sheriff.

"What I'm saying is you should also get some shut eye right now, so you can also be awake during the night. I am going to get some sleep this afternoon and I'm sure Marcus and Willoughby will do the same. We want every able-bodied man awake and alert after the sun goes down."

The sheriff looked at Marcus, who just

shrugged.

"He makes a fair point," said the old hunter. "We're just wasting energy during daylight hours."

As they all sat down, Anna Marie came over with a pot of coffee and some cups. She gave Darius the stink-eye, but she was starting to get over it.

As she walked away, the sheriff looked at Darius and asked, "How are you feeling? Are you going to be ready for nightfall?"

"I'm still a bit stiff and sore, but I'll be ready to do what's needed."

He looked at the other two.

"Has anyone gone back to the cave while I was off my feet?"

"Yes," said Marcus. "We both went out there. He's gone. I'm sure he lit out of there as soon as the sun went down."

"Oh, I haven't even asked," said Darius. "How's Jason?"

Nobody wanted to say anything. They suddenly found their cups of coffee to be very interesting.

"He's not hurt, is he?"

Finally, the sheriff spoke up, "No, Mr. James, he's actually fine. Physically. But, I don't think he's right in his head."

"What do you mean?"

"He's taken what happened to you real bad. Blames himself for you getting hurt and all."

"I don't blame him. It wasn't his fault."

"He don't see it that way."

"Is he still sleeping in the jail?"

The sheriff just nodded and said, "Won't even come out of the cell. Anna Marie has to run food over to him and sit and make sure he eats it."

Darius stood up and said, "Gentlemen, go ahead and make plans for this evening. I'll go with anything y'all decide. I'm going across the road to see a young man."

The back of the jail was dark, with just one small window, high on the back wall. As he walked into the darkness, Darius could see the shape of the young boy laying on the cot inside the open cell. He was curled up with his back to the door.

Darius walked into the cell and sat down on the edge of the cot. He could feel Jason stir slightly, so he knew he wasn't asleep.

"I know it's hard for you to believe this right now, but I'm sure your father loved you very much. If he had been able to fight the first vampire off, he would have done that to save you and your ma."

For a moment, Jason just laid there without making a sound. Then he rolled onto his back and looked up at the hunter. Darius could see his eyes were red and puffy, but he had long since cried out all his tears.

"When he looked at me, it was like he didn't even know me, Mr. James."

He reached forward and took one of the

boy's hands and held it.

"Jason, he didn't know you. The mind of that monster is no longer that of your father. Your father is dead and gone to be with your mother. What you saw last week was nothing more than a monster with no more humanity in it than that beetle over there on the floor."

Jason looked across the cell and saw a black beetle crawling lazily along the far wall. He pushed himself up and sat next to Darius. The two of them just stared at the bug.

"I have no one left in this world," mumbled Jason.

"That's not really true. You may not have any blood relatives, but you have an entire town that cares about you and will look out for you."

Jason leaned over and Darius put an arm around his shoulders and hugged him close. They sat quietly for a few more minutes.

"I don't know about you, Jason, but I'm hungry. How about you and I go across the road and have ourselves something to eat?"

Jason pulled his boots on and stood up. He looked at Darius for a second.

"How do you feel, Mr. James?"

Darius laughed and said, "Like I'm getting too old for this job."

"Isn't Mr. Aurelius older than you?"

"Yeah, by a few ... centuries."

They walked out of the jail and back to the boardinghouse. When they entered the dining room, Darius guided him to a table near where Willoughby and Marcus were sitting with the sheriff. The two of them sat down to eat by themselves.

Anna Marie walked over and smiled at the boy.

"You hungry, Jason?"

"Yes, ma'am. Very."

"You, too, Darius?"

"Very."

"I'll be right back," she said as she turned and headed for the kitchen.

Darius looked at the other two hunters and Marcus smiled and nodded. The sheriff said he needed to get back out to the tent settlement and make sure things were being handled. He stopped to give Jason a pat on the shoulder and then headed out the door.

A few minutes later, the other two hunters got up and said they were heading for their tent to get some sleep before nightfall. They told Darius to come find them after dark.

After they left and before Anna Marie came back with their food, Jason asked Darius to tell him how he became a hunter. As they ate their meal, Darius told him the tale of Father Drake and being found bare ass naked on the field of battle.

He told him the complete truth, including how he had not been an honorable man before the padre found him. That becoming a hunter was the deal he made with God to keep from being sent to the fires of Hell.

"How long do you think you'll have to do this?" asked Jason ask he chewed on a piece of steak.

"Well, I suppose until the good Lord decides I've done enough to make it into Heaven. Now, Marcus is over a thousand years older than me and even he doesn't know how long he'll be doing this."

"Was he a wicked man, too?"

"He'll say yes, but I have my doubts. Marcus is one of the kindest men I've ever known. Kind of surprising how good of a hunter he is. He was a Roman soldier right near the end of the Roman Empire."

"I know. He told me that. He said he used to stand by while Christians were tortured and killed. Said he hated every second, but he couldn't put a stop to it."

As they finished their meal, Darius looked outside and could see they had about five hours before the sun would set. He told Jason to go get some sleep and the two of them would walk the streets of Hell's Gate together that night, keeping an eye on things.

After he walked out the door and headed across the street, Anna Marie came up to Darius as he was getting ready to head up the stairs. She leaned up and gave him a kiss on the cheek.

"I'm sorry I was so angry with you," she said.

"Don't be sorry. You have every right to be. Just know I will never allow you to go into a situation like that. If that means tying you up, I'll do it. I'd rather have you spittin' fire at me than see you get hurt."

He pulled out his watch and looked at it.

"Can you come up and knock on my door in about four hours?"

"Yes, I can."

He leaned over and kissed her on the forehead and headed up the stairs to get some much needed sleep. He was sound asleep within five minutes of his head hitting the pillow.

A few miles away, in a small hole in the ground, a black rat tossed and turned in its sleep. Having been chased out of its much larger cave, the vampire was having to make do with what he could find.

Tonight, he intended to change that. Tonight, he would join with the others and rain terror down on this town.

23 – On Becoming A Squire

Darius and Jason walked into the tent settlement, with the boy carrying the hunter's lever-action rifle across his body. It impressed the hunter how the boy kept the rifle from pointing at any person as they walked between the tents.

They found Marcus on the outside of the ring of tents, looking to the west as the sun was setting. Darius stepped up next to him and looked at the red sunset. He couldn't shake the feeling that it looked like the sky was bleeding red blood over the landscape.

"It's going to be a clear night," said the old man, "and a full moon. Good in some ways, bad in others."

"Yes, it is."

The old man pulled a small pouch off his belt and handed it to Darius.

"These are for you."

Darius shook the pouch and could tell it was filled with bullets.

"For both types of weapons?" asked Darius.

"Yes, but they may be mixed up somewhat."

"Here you go, Jason," he said, handing the pouch to the boy. "Go through this and separate the rifle bullets out. Load the rifle completely and then put the rest in your pocket. Then give the rest back to me."

"Yes, sir."

He sat down on the ground and laid the rifle across his lap. Then he pulled a handkerchief from his pocket, laid it on the ground and then poured the bullets out. Going through the pile of bullets, he pulled out the longer ones and pushed them one-by-one into the slot on the side of the rifle until no more could go in.

He put the rest of the rifle bullets in his pocket and the pistol bullets back into the pouch and handed it to Darius.

"Looks like you got yourself a great little squire there," said Marcus.

"What's a squire?" asked Jason.

Before Darius could answer, Marcus said, "A squire was one of the most important people on the field of battle during the time of the knights in the old world. They would assist the knights in everything they did. They made sure their weapons were clean and ready, took care of their horses and armor and anything else the knights needed to do their jobs."

Jason looked at Darius and said, "I want to be your squire."

"Jason, it would honor me to have you as my squire."

He handed the pouch back to the boy and told him to tie it to his belt. If he needed to have his pistols reloaded, he would hand them to him and it was his job to do it quickly.

"You know how to load a pistol?"

"Absolutely. My pa taught ..."

He stopped talking when he thought about

how his pa would teach him how to clean and load his pistol. How his pa would hold his arms steady when he taught him how to shoot.

Darius looked down at him, knowing what he was feeling.

"Your pa was a good man."

Darius gazed back at the western sky, noting how the sky had grown darker and the red was now a dark purple color.

"We're going to take a stroll to the other end of town to check on things and try to keep the townsfolk calm."

He and Jason headed back through the tents and back into town. Most of the windows in the buildings were aglow with lantern and candlelight. There were just a few people on the street and they were moving in a hurry to get inside and lock the doors.

As they walked past the boardinghouse, Anna Marie was standing in the doorway. She gave them a cautious smile. As she did, Seth came walking out the door behind her, gave her a quick kiss on the cheek and then joined the two of them as they ambled toward the eastern side of town.

When they reached the livery stables, they found a contingent of men scattered in a line. They also found the sheriff and Willoughby moving along the line, giving encouragement to the men there.

Darius looked back to the west, seeing the last of the twilight disappearing behind the hills. The full moon was just rising in the east, its huge orange ball casting plenty of light over the town. He felt like it was a blanket of fear that was being thrown over Hell's Gate.

He knew tonight was going to be the night. It was just going to be a waiting game now.

The night stayed calm. The only sound being those of the night critters in the sagebrush. Around two in the morning, Darius had hope they would go another night without incident.

His hope came crashing down when a shot tore the silence of the night apart, followed by a half a dozen more shots. They were coming from the area along the southern part of the town. The area near the Chang family's laundry.

Darius took off, yelling at Willoughby to stay put in case it was a distraction. Jason followed along behind the hunter, keeping the rifle at the ready.

As they rounded the corner into the alley, James saw three men laying on the ground and none of them were moving. Each was laying in a growing pool of blood.

A fourth man, Conrad Stevens, was struggling with the vampire, trying to keep his claws away from his neck. Conrad was a large man, having worked in the mines most of his life. He was built like a bull and probably just as strong.

Darius leveled one of his pistols, but was afraid to fire, knowing the big guy was in danger of being hit, as well. When the vampire swept his feet out from under him and took him down, that gave Darius the chance he was looking for. He fired, hitting the vampire in the back, knocking him off Conrad.

The vampire came up snarling and Darius fired again and the bullet tore the top of the vampire's head off. The beast toppled backwards like a tree being felled.

Conrad scrambled away from the dead monster, picking up his gun from the dirt and pointing it.

"We never saw 'im coming," bellowed Conrad. "He just dropped down on top of us from the sky."

Darius pulled his sword and made quick work of the vampire's neck. As the head rolled free, Conrad booted it up against the wall of a building. As it rebounded off the wall, Darius stuck his boot out and stopped its roll.

"Are you okay, Mr. Stevens?" asked Jason.

"Yeah, son. He didn't get me."

They looked at the other three men on the ground and could tell all of them were dead. Darius walked to each one and rolled them onto their backs and checked to make sure, but he knew before he even looked.

As he was doing this, Jason walked over and looked down at the head of the vampire. He studied it for a moment, looking at the right cheek, near the mouth.

"It's missing the scar," he said in almost a whisper.

Darius looked over at him.

"What?"

Jason looked at him and shook his head.

"My pa had a scar on his face, near his mouth. It was from when a mean horse kicked him. I saw it last week when we was at the cave."

He looked closer at the face of the vampire and then looked at the hunter.

"This ain't my pa."

24 – More Pine Boxes

The attack near the laundry wasn't the only one that night. But the other attack had occurred so quietly no one knew it had happened.

While it had occupied Darius with the southern part of town, two men watching the northern edge were killed. The attack on them had been so sudden, not a single shot was fired. The other men in the area didn't even know it had happened until they went to check on the men, not having heard from them for awhile.

That night, before the sun came up, eight children were left fatherless and three women became widows. As the morning got brighter, the men began filtering toward the cluster of tents and the dead were brought there for the undertaker to get them ready for burial.

As he and Willoughby walked into the area, he could feel the tension coming from those around them. The looks they were getting were something Darius had felt before.

When you are built up to be a legendary monster hunter and then have a night like this, people wonder if all the stories were just that. Stories. He knew they were going to be blaming him and the other two hunters.

Walking into the dining tent, they saw Marcus sitting by himself, his head in his hands. When they sat down across from him, he looked up at them and they could tell he was feeling every bit as bad as they were. Jason sat down at the end of the table, leaning the rifle against his chair.

"What did we miss, Marcus?" asked Darius.

Marcus just shook his head.

"We missed nothing. We're just spread too thin here and those blood-suckers know it. They can take their time and pick us off one-by-one."

Willoughby just stared at a spot on the table in front of him.

"Well, gentlemen, we had better figure it out and do so quickly. Another night like this and we'll be run out of town on a rail."

Darius looked across the table and saw Jason resting his head on his folded arms on the table.

"Jason."

The boy sat up and looked at him.

"Hey, let me have that rifle and then you head on down to the jail and get some sleep."

"Aren't you going to need me?"

"Not until tonight," said Darius. "What I need from you is to be well rested. Come on by the boardinghouse about five and we'll get you some supper."

Jason got up and they could tell he was shaky. Darius hoped it was just because he was tired. The boy handed him the rifle and headed out the door of the tent, passing the sheriff and Seth on the way out.

The two newcomers sat down with the

hunters and said nothing at first. Then the sheriff broke the silence.

"I guess we could say it wasn't a good night, last night."

"No, sheriff, it most assuredly was not," said Willoughby.

"Our biggest problem is we don't know where these monsters are." said Darius. "If we knew that, we could take the fight to them."

There was silence around the table for a moment and Darius could tell there was something being held back. Looking at the sheriff, he could see the man just staring at the table in front of him.

"What's the problem, sheriff?"

The sheriff sat back in his chair and looked around the table.

"I guess I don't need to tell you there is a growing sentiment in this town that you hunters are the reason for what's going on. That if we run you out of town the trouble will stop."

Marcus looked at him and asked, "Tell me, Caleb, did this trouble start before or after Darius came to town?"

"You know the answer to that question as well as I do. It started a month or so before he got here."

"So, do you think the trouble will end if we pack up and leave?"

"Hey, don't get me wrong. I don't blame Darius or you two for what is happening. I'm just telling you what the mood is in town right now."

Willoughby asked, "And if the town asks us to leave, what will be your position?"

"To stand against them," said the sheriff with some fire in his eyes.

"We can't have that," said Darius. "You are the law here and if you stand against the town, your authority will be called into question."

"What good is my authority when I know what the town is asking is wrong?"

"Still," said Marcus, "you can't be seen taking sides against the town you are sworn to protect."

"So, where does that leave us?" asked Seth.

"Same place we've always been," said Marcus. "Not knowing where the vampires are or when they will attack again."

Anna Marie walked up behind Seth and put both hands on his shoulders. She looked around the table at the others.

"It's about that time," she said.

Never had Darius seen a grayer day. The sky was overcast from horizon-to-horizon, not letting any sunlight through.

However, that wasn't the only thing that contributed to the gloom of the day. Emotions were quite dark everywhere the hunters looked.

It was all brought into a clear focus after lunch, when nearly the entire town gathered in the cemetery to lay five men to rest. This gathering dwarfed even that of Clem.

The hunters could tell it wasn't just the

mood of the graveside services that darkened the emotions of the people. There was a lot of animosity directed at the hunters themselves and if you were to ask the three of them, they would have agreed they deserved it.

The legends had grown up over the years, about the hunters and how they had saved entire towns and cities from these monsters. And no legend was greater than that of Darius James.

His name was better known than that of the president. Every man, woman and child over the age of five had heard of the exploits of the great Darius James. According to legend, every monster he fought was worse than Satan himself and Darius always prevailed.

The five pine boxes lined up near the five graves were a testament to the fact that the hunters didn't win every time. The three sobbing widows and eight crying children illuminated the failure of the hunters to keep Hell's Gate safe.

The three hunters stood away from the gathered crowd, not wanting to intrude on the sorrow that hung over the graveyard.

Jason stood with them, even though Darius had told him it would be best if he stood with the rest of the townsfolk. He didn't want to and the hunter figured it was because he still felt like he was alone in the world.

The truth was, Jason was feeling every ounce of guilt in the killings, knowing his father was now a vampire and probably killed some of these men. No matter how much

Darius tried to get through to him, the boy couldn't shake the feeling of shame over this.

Once the service concluded and the people finished filtering out of the cemetery, the hunters moved forward and paid their respects.

Conrad Stevens stepped up beside them, silently looking down into one grave.

"He was just a boy," said the man, barely able to keep the sorrow from his voice.

"Who was he?" asked Marcus.

Conrad looked up, his eyes brimming with tears.

"He was my nephew, son of my brother. His name was Charlie and he's been living with me and the missus since ..."

He couldn't say anymore and turned and walked out of the graveyard, leaving the hunters to stare after him.

"Charlie's pa was killed in the war about fifteen years ago," mumbled Jason. "His ma died just after that when he was only four years old."

"A lot of good people died in that war," said Willoughby softly.

"When Mr. Stevens heard what happened, he went as fast as he could, back to Ohio and got Charlie and brought him back here. Him and Mrs. Stevens raised him like they raised their own kids."

They stood silently for a few minutes. Then Marcus and Willoughby looked across the open graves at Darius. He crouched down and picked up a hand of dirt and dropped it on the box in the grave. He did it to the other four boxes as well. After doing the fifth one, he stood up and looked at the others.

"Gentlemen, we need to end this."

"This is a lot worse than we originally thought," said Marcus.

"Come on, old man," said Darius, looking him directly in the eyes. "You and me have dealt with much worse. And I hate to admit it, but Willoughby could probably handle the entire nest by himself."

Willoughby crouched down and pulled the flower from his lapel and dropped it on Charlie's coffin.

"Probably could if I knew where to look," mumbled the dapper hunter.

He looked across the grave at Jason, who was standing next to Darius.

"Young man, do you have any ideas where a large number of vampires could hide during the daytime? Someplace where they wouldn't be disturbed, like that cave,"

Jason just shook his head.

"I don't. I only knew about that cave because I knew my pa liked to go there when he wanted some alone time."

"Time to be away from your mother?" asked Marcus with a questioning look on his face.

"No, sir. Time to be alone to talk to God."

"I am sorry," said Marcus. "Please accept my apologies for thinking badly of your father for a moment."

Jason bit his lips and nodded.

"Well," said Darius, "somehow, some way, we need to find out where they are."

Marcus said, "You know there's only one way that's going to happen and I'm sure it will result in more graves in this cemetery."

"Not if we're lucky," said Darius.

Willoughby stood up and looked at him.

"Brother James, luck has not been much of a friend to us lately."

"Then it's about time that changed."

He put his hat on, patted Jason on the shoulder and turned and headed for the gate, his squire following close behind him. Willoughby followed along after them, leaving Marcus standing at the graves.

The undertaker stepped out of his cemetery shack and walked toward him. Before he got there, the old man dropped to his knees and pulled a rosary from inside his shirt. Closing his eyes, he began a whispered prayer, asking for Heaven to look after these men. He also asked for help in putting an end to this reign of terror.

When Marcus stood up and wiped his eyes, the undertaker asked, "Do you really think Heaven is going to help us?"

Marcus looked at him and forced a smile.

"Sir, I believe the days of the vampires here in Hell's Gate are fast coming to an end. You mark my words. By this time next week, you will walk the street safely after dark once again."

The undertaker nodded and said, "I look forward to that day and I look forward to not having to bury so many people in such a short time."

Marcus reached out and put a hand on the man's shoulder. Then he looked to the west and then back at the shovel in the man's hand. Without a word, he walked over to the shack and pulled out another shovel.

"You're going to need some help to get these filled in before it gets dark," he said.

Without another word, the two of them began finishing the job of laying the five men to rest. They finished with the sun still a good way up in the sky and Marcus walked alongside the undertaker, heading back to town.

Walking into the boardinghouse, Marcus noticed how quiet it was. Though there were easily two dozen people there, it was as quiet as a church at midnight.

Walking over to the corner table, he took a seat across from the sheriff. Seth was sitting just behind him and Anna Marie was standing by him, with her hands on his shoulders.

He looked around at the faces of the others and could tell something was up.

"Out with it," he said. "What's going on?"

"We are being asked to vacate the town," said Willoughby.

"No, you are not," said Anna Marie.

"Okay, that is correct. We are being asked by a portion of the populace to leave town."

Marcus looked at the sheriff.

"Have you changed your position on this matter?"

"I have not," said the sheriff emphatically. "I have to wonder though, how much longer we can go on like this."

Seth asked, "Is it true that if the town asks you to leave, then you would?"

"Who told you that?"

"I'm afraid I may have let that slip," said Willoughby.

Marcus just closed his eyes and shook his head.

"Don't get me wrong, sir," said Seth. "I do not want the three of you to leave under any circumstances until this problem is taken care of. But there is a growing mood in this town that it would be best if you left."

Marcus took a deep breath and looked over his shoulder at the rest of the people gathered in the dining room. It was easy to read their faces and see they were of the group that wanted the hunters to go.

He stood up and walked to the middle of the room and looked at them.

"Is that what you really want?"

One man in the back said, "We can't see having you here has done much good."

There was a murmur of agreement through the group.

Abbie came out from behind the counter and walked over to the old hunter.

"Don't you listen to a word these cowards say," she said as her eyes swept across the crowd.

He gave her a smile and put an arm around her shoulders. Facing the crowd, he did his best to keep his emotions in check.

"Miss Abbie, everyone has the right to be heard and I do not consider these fine people to be cowards. Scared, but not cowards."

He gave her shoulders a quick squeeze and asked, "Could you get me a tall, cool glass of water? I'm a bit parched."

She nodded and headed for the kitchen.

"Now, ladies and gentlemen," said Marcus to the crowd. "I'm going to tell you a little story and after I'm finished, if you still want us to leave ... well ... we'll have no choice, but to abandon this town."

Abbie came back with his glass of water and he took a few seconds to wet his throat. Having worked, filling in the graves, had dried him out something fierce.

He set the glass down on the nearest table and clapped his hands together, making sure everyone was paying attention.

"I know you may look at me and see a handsome, young man."

He saw a few faint smiles, which was what he wanted.

"But, I have lived longer than anyone in this room, As a matter of fact, I dare say I've walked this earth longer than all of you put together. I am over one thousand, four hundred years old and have spent most of that time fighting the very monsters we are faced with now. Yes, they have been around longer than you can imagine."

He looked from face-to-face, seeing that everyone was listening.

"I want to tell you a story of a little town about a hundred miles south of Paris, France."

"Uhh, Marcus," said Darius from behind him, "I don't think that's a good idea."

Marcus looked at him with a look that got the younger hunter to pipe down.

"What my younger friend is saying," he said, turning back to the crowd, "is this is not a cheerful story. It is one of the saddest stories you will ever hear."

"That little town had the same problem Hell's Gate has, but this was just over two hundred years ago. Darius and I were sent by the church to that town to get rid of the vampires. By the time we got there, the vampires had killed fifty people. Others had tried to leave, but were chased back to the town, corralled like a bunch of cattle."

"My young friend and I were able to kill a couple of vampires quickly and it seemed like we were going to get the problem taken care of. Just as we thought we might win that fight, the vampires struck fast, killing fifteen people in one night."

He heard some gasps from the women in the room and some rumbling from the men.

"The next morning, there was a gathering of the townsfolk and they demanded we leave, just as you're doing right now. We tried to reason with them, assuring them that our leaving would not save the town. But, they wouldn't hear it and like my British friend alluded to earlier, if we are asked to leave, we have no choice but to go. The church would demand we leave where we are not wanted."

"So what happened?" asked one woman meekly.

"We left."

They could see Darius drop his head and close his eyes.

"One of the darkest days of my life," he mumbled as Willoughby reached over and patted him on the shoulder.

"You left?" asked the woman again.

"Yes," said Marcus. "We will not stay where we are not welcome. God will not have us where the people feel like they would be better off without us, even though we know it isn't true."

He reached over and picked up his glass of water and drained it. Abbie stepped over and took it from him and went back behind the counter.

"To our everlasting shame, we left," he mumbled.

Then he looked at the crowd and said, "Two weeks later, our leaders sent a couple of other hunters to the town to see if they had softened to the idea of having us there."

He stopped talking for a moment, closing his eyes and gathering his strength.

"What they found when they arrived was a horror beyond imagination. The vampires had slaughtered every man, woman and child. Even the animals had been slain. There was not one breathing person or animal in the town except for the insects and even those were unusually quiet."

Abbie walked back over with another glass of water, which he gratefully accepted to have a few seconds without talking.

"When we got word, Darius and I returned to that town and joined those other two hunters and we went looking for that nest."

"Did you find them?" asked one of the other women.

"Yes, m'lady, we did. We spent that entire day killing each one of those monsters. By the time we were finished, we counted over a hundred and fifty of them. By the time night fell, we stacked vampire bodies five feet high in a pile that would stretch across the street outside. We set fire to the lot of them."

"If you ask us to leave, we will, but you can count on meeting the same fate as Courville. A town that no longer exists and is not even on any maps. No one will live there because they think the ground is cursed. I would have to agree with them."

He looked at each person and then turned and walked back to the table and sat down. Looking out the window, he could see the sun was close to setting and it would be dark within the next hour.

As Abbie and Anna Marie brought them some sandwiches, they could hear the other people getting up and leave the boardinghouse. It looked like Marcus's story had opened their eyes to what lay in store if the hunters left.

"Let's eat quickly and get out there," said the sheriff. "Maybe tonight we get lucky."

25 – The Bait Is Taken

As he walked the length of town, Darius shifted the rifle from one arm to the other. He didn't have Jason to carry it for him tonight. The boy had skipped getting some sleep during the day. By the time night fell, he was dragging, nearly falling asleep on his feet.

When he tried to send Jason to the jail to get some sleep, the boy tried to argue. Darius was having none of it. Anna Marie put an arm around his shoulders and led him across the street and made sure he laid down. He made her promise to come and wake him at midnight so he could do his fair share.

She promised.

He was sound asleep before she left the cell and headed out the door. Coming back to wake him at midnight was a promise she had no intention of keeping.

She saw Darius walking by and joined him for the short walk to the stables.

"Anna Marie, get inside and lock the doors."

"Excuse me!"

"I'm sorry for being abrupt, but I don't want you out here in danger."

"Noted, Mr. James. I will return here and lock myself in momentarily," she said. "I want to check on Seth and I will join you on your return through town."

Darius knew there was no arguing with her so he allowed her to tag along. He figured it would be just as safe for her to be with him than in the boardinghouse. As they walked through the stables, Anna Marie pulled an apple from her pocket and gave it to Midnight.

"You keep treating him like that and I won't be able to convince him it's time to go later."

"Someone has to treat him nice," she said with a smile.

Right!

"You hush," said Darius to the horse, while Anna Marie giggled, though it didn't sound right considering the pall that hung over the town.

While she spent a few seconds with Midnight, Darius went out the back doors and found the men that were guarding this part of the town. Seth and the stable man were standing together, searching the skies for any kind of movement.

"You gentlemen doing okay?" he asked.

"Yes, Mr. James," said the stableman. "Scared to death, though."

"You'd be a fool not to be scared," he said as he patted the man on the shoulder.

Anna Marie came out a minute later and went directly to Seth, who was standing a few yards away with Willoughby. When she stepped up beside him, he put an arm around her waist and hugged her.

"Miss Anna Marie," said Willoughby, "you lend a treasure's amount of beauty to any setting, even one as dire as this one."

"Why thank you, Mr. Bartles," she said. "It warms a woman's heart to hear such words now and then."

She poked Seth in the ribs as she said it.

"Sorry, sweetheart," stammered Seth. "I just don't have the sweet, honey-drenched words Willoughby has."

She giggled and leaned up and kissed him on the cheek.

"It takes a lot more than sweet words to win my heart, Seth."

They watched as Darius walked up and down the line of men, checking on them and giving them words of encouragement.

As he came back to them, Seth asked, "What are you telling them?"

"Same thing I'll tell you, if Willoughby hasn't told you. Don't hesitate to shoot. Make sure of your target and then pull the trigger. Any hesitation can prove deadly."

"I just hope I can be as fast as I need to be."

Darius looked at him and said, "Just look at it this way. Any vampire you don't kill might cause harm to your lovely bride-to-be."

Seth drew in a deep breath, straightened his back even more than usual and hugged Anna Marie closer to his body. She was not complaining. No more words needed to be spoken. The message was obvious to her.

After he walked Anna Marie back to the boardinghouse and made sure she was secure, Darius continued on his walk to the other end of town. He found Marcus standing watch next to the preacher and a couple of other men.

"It feels all wrong tonight," said the preacher.

"What do you mean?" asked Darius.

"It's just that I don't feel the sense of impending doom I felt the other night. I don't know, I can't explain it."

Marcus looked at Darius and said, "I agree with him. Something just doesn't feel right. It feels too quiet."

"Quiet is good," said one man nearby.

Darius looked at him and said, "Quiet is not good. Not when you know the enemy is out there, just waiting for us to drop our guard."

He looked back at Marcus and the preacher.

"I wish you two would figure it out. We can't fight something if we can't even tell we have a problem."

The next couple of hours passed just as the first part of the night. Quietly. At about four in the morning, the hunters began to think they might escape this night without incident.

Darius and Marcus walked to the boardinghouse to see if there was any chance of some sandwiches for the men, but Anna Marie and Abbie had already beat them to it. When they knocked on the doors, Abbie opened it and had two large baskets full of wrapped sandwiches ready to go.

As Marcus took one basket and headed back to the tent village, Anna Marie said she was going to go across the road and see if Jason was hungry. She dreaded it a little, knowing she had broken her promise to wake him, but she was sure he would forgive her.

Darius told her to get back to the boardinghouse as soon as she could and then took the other basket and headed for the stables. He said he'd be back in a few minutes to get some more sandwiches for the men to the south and then the north.

As he was walking to the east side of town, he heard it. It was enough to chill the blood in his veins.

"Darius!"

Without thinking, he dropped the basket to the ground and began running back the way he'd come. The sound of Anna Marie screaming his name caused the hairs on the back of his neck to stand up.

"Darius!" she screamed again.

He ran straight to the jail. Before he got there, he saw Abbie standing on the porch of the boardinghouse, clutching her hands in front of her.

"Get back inside, Abbie!" he yelled as he bounded up the step and through the door of the jail. He had both pistols in his hands, cocked and ready to fire at whatever danger was confronting Anna Marie.

As he rushed through the door, he found her on her knees, crying her heart out. It only took a couple seconds for him to see what the problem was.

There was a huge hole in the jail's roof, allowing him to look straight up and see the stars overhead. But that wasn't what terrified her the most.

He moved to the cell Jason was sleeping in. The bed was overturned, with the bedding scattered across the floor. There was some blood on the sheet and blanket. There was only one thing missing.

A certain twelve-year-old boy.

His hands fell to his sides as he felt the terror of despair wash over him. The pistols felt like lead weights in his hands as his eyes scanned the empty cell.

He heard some feet stomping across the boards outside the jail and turned to see the sheriff and Seth come rushing in. They stopped when they saw the roof.

Seth crouched down behind Anna Marie and put his arms around her shoulders.

"C'mon, sweetheart. Let's get you back across the street," he said as he lifted her to her feet.

She was reluctant to go, but let him lead her out of the jail and back to the boardinghouse. Abbie took charge of her and ushered her inside, while Seth went back to the jail. By this time, a small crowd was forming outside.

"Gentlemen, ladies," he said, "please don't let your duties to watch the town's borders fall. We'll let you know what happened here when we find out ourselves."

The crowd broke up and drifted back to their assigned places around the town.

"How the hell did this happen?" stormed

the sheriff as Seth walked back into the jail. "How in the hell did they tear through the roof like that with no one hearing it?"

Darius walked out of the jail and around the back. There was a set of rickety stairs that went up the backside of the building to the roof.

Climbing the stairs, he stepped over the short wall and onto the roof. As he studied the edges of the hole, he could see the roof was made of sturdy materials. The beams were at least six inches thick and the wood and stucco surface was thick and solid as granite.

As he looked around, he could see the three-foot wall around the roof would have hidden anyone up there from the view of anyone below.

He looked back down through the hole and could see the two men looking up at him.

"If they worked quietly," he said, "no one would have even known they were here."

"You need to come down here," said the sheriff. "There's something you should see."

After climbing down from the roof and walking back through the door, the sheriff pointed to the floor. Underneath where the bedding had been was a message that was obviously aimed at Darius.

Written in blood.

Benson
Come alone

"What is that supposed to mean?" he

asked.

"I suppose it means the old Benson place," said Seth. "It's a farm about five miles south of town. No one has been living there for about ten years, though."

"So, it's abandoned," said Darius. "Just the kind of place a nest of vampires would love."

"What are you going to do?" asked Seth.

"Well, it would be rude of me to turn down their invitation."

"You can't be serious," said the sheriff.

"Very serious, Caleb."

"But why? There is no good reason for you to go out there alone, like the message says."

"Aren't you forgetting something?"

The sheriff looked at him and cocked his head.

"I'm going to get Jason back," said Darius.

"You can't even be sure he's still alive!"

"I can't be sure he's dead either, but there's a good chance he still lives."

"What makes you think that?"

"The fact the vampires left a message. If they had killed him, there would be no reason for me to go out there alone, now would there?"

"But you don't know that," stammered the sheriff.

"No, I don't. And I won't know until I get there. But one thing is for certain, if he's still alive, I'm bringing him home. If he's dead, I'll make every one of those monsters wish they hadn't killed him."

He looked up through the hole in the roof

and saw the sky was beginning to lighten.

"I have less than an hour before daylight," said Darius, "so I need to get on the trail."

"I'm coming with you," said Seth.

"No, you're not! Or have you forgotten what happened to you with the wendigo? These vampires will make that beast seem like an unruly child."

"I can't just let you go out there alone," said the deputy.

"You can and you will. Let me put it this way. You go across the road and ask Anna Marie if it's alright with her for you to accompany me. See what she says."

"Don't use her as a shield," growled Seth.

"I'm not using her to protect myself. I'm using her to protect you."

Just then, the sheriff reached out and grabbed Seth by the back of his collar and dragged him backwards across the jail and flung him into an empty cell. Then he slammed the door closed and locked it.

"Let me out of here!" bellowed Seth as he rattled the bars.

The sheriff just ignored him and walked back over to Darius. He had to raise his voice to be heard over the yelling deputy.

"Something is itchin' at the back of my brain to throw you in the cell right next to him."

Darius forced a smile and said, "Caleb, I've been alive for over four hundred years and have battled hundreds of vampires. I'll be fine."

"That's what you said about going after

Jason last week. Then you came back to town, draped over Midnight with your ass in the air like a sack of 'taters."

"He got the jump on me last week. Won't happen this time."

"At least take Marcus or Willoughby, or both of them."

"Nope, leaving them here to watch over the town."

"What's wrong with you, boy? You got a head full of rocks or something?"

Darius laughed and said, "My horse would agree with you."

He turned and walked out the door and the sheriff followed him. As they stepped onto the boardwalk outside, they could see Anna Marie standing on the porch of the boardinghouse, looking at the two of them.

"Why is Seth raisin' such a ruckus?" she asked, her eyes squinting at them.

Darius turned and said to the sheriff, "Do not let him out, no matter what she says."

"She can be a real handful when she wants something."

"Lock her up if you have to."

"Oh, good lord. Locking up Seth is bad enough. Locking up the two of them might be the end of me."

"Lock them in the same cell. That should quiet them down."

The sheriff's mouth curled up in a smile and Darius turned around.

And ran right into Anna Marie.

"What are you doing?" she scowled at him.

"I'm going to find Jason."

"Take Seth with you."

"Now that's an unexpected thing for you to say. You realize I'm heading into a nest of vampires, right?"

She gasped and backed up. After thinking for a second, she said, "Take Marcus and Willoughby."

"I'm leaving them here to protect the town."

"Oooo ... you men! Why do you always think you need to face these dangerous things like this?"

Darius reached up and gently grabbed her chin between his thumb and forefinger.

"Because, deep down inside, you women expect it of us and we wouldn't have it any other way."

Then, before she knew what was happening, he dipped his head forward and kissed her. On the lips. Causing her to squeal softly.

When they came apart, she looked up at him with fire in her eyes and said, "You scoundrel."

Darius laughed and said, "You already called me that."

Then he turned and headed for the stables. Over his shoulder he said, "Stay here and calm Seth down."

As he walked into the stables, Midnight was standing at the gate to his stall, just staring at him when he walked in.

We're going somewhere?

"Yes, we are, buddy. We have to go rescue Jason."

Again?

"Yes, seems that boy is always at the center of the trouble around here."

Sounds like someone else I know.

Darius moved quickly, saddling Midnight and checking his saddlebags for extra ammunition. He walked around the corner of the last stall and looked at some boxes that were stored there. Walking over, he lifted the lid on the top box and smiled.

Reaching in, he pulled out six sticks of dynamite. They were already fused up and ready to go. He took them back to Midnight and stuck them in the saddlebags.

Planning on raising Hell or something?

"I plan to send these monsters out with a bang."

Well, those should do it.

After climbing into the saddle, the two of them moved quietly out of the livery and headed back toward the center of town. Before reaching the center of town and the jail, they cut left and down the alley.

Crossing the southern parallel dusty track, they moved between a couple of buildings and headed south, away from the town. Midnight walked up to a couple of men who were watching the southern area.

"Mr. James?"

"Just going for a bit of a night ride," he said. "Either of you know exactly how to get to the old Benson place?"

"Sure thing," said one man. He turned and pointed toward a distant mountain and said, "Just head straight at that mountain peak. About five miles. Can't miss it. It's the only thing out there."

"Thank you. You gentlemen get some sleep so you're ready for this evening."

Then he nudged Midnight on and they headed south at a trot.

He knew he had a good half hour to set his mind to the task ahead, so Darius settled into the saddle and let his mind call out to the heavens for all the help they could send down.

He ran through every scenario he could think of, but the one that kept coming up was finding Jason already dead.

Or worse.

Turned.

26 – The Underground

Just as the sun rose above the mountains to the east, Darius brought Midnight to a stop in a dip between two small hills. He had seen the farm in the distance and didn't want to take Midnight any closer than necessary.

After tying the horse to a scraggly sagebrush, near a small patch of green grass, he crept to the top of the hill and studied the layout of the farm below.

There was the main house, which looked like a tornado had sideswiped it. Most of its roof was missing. All the windows were broken and the doors were off their hinges. Not exactly the ideal place for some vampires to hide during the daylight hours.

There was the barn a few yards from the house, but it didn't look any better off. All of its roof was gone and there were a lot of side boards missing on the walls. Again, not a place vampires were going to find much protection from the rays of the sun.

Those were the only two structures below except for a loafing shed and its three walls offered no protection from the sun as its open wall faced to the east.

There was no activity visible below. Not a single animal, human or vampire moved about. Darius was wondering if he had gotten lost and ended up in the wrong place.

As the sun crested the horizon to the east,

he stood up and surveyed the situation a little closer. Nothing caught his eye. There were some tattered curtains that fluttered in the broken windows, but that was the only movement he could see.

Pulling one of his pistols, he began walking down the hill. He only had a couple hundred yards to make it to the edge of the property, marked by a corral of cross-post fencing. The loafing shed was placed up against the edge of the corral and offered him some protection from being seen.

He crept up to the edge of the shed and crouched down. Leaning forward, he peered around the corner of the dilapidated shed and still concluded the place was completely deserted.

The slight breeze brought the smell of sage to his nose as his eyes swung back and forth across the open yard between him and the house. He could see through the broken door of the house, straight through to one wall and could see desert landscape beyond.

"There's no way those monsters are here," he said to himself.

Standing up, he moved out from behind the shed and to the center of the yard, between the house and the barn. He had never seen such a deserted place in his long life.

He was thinking the message on the floor of the jail had been nothing more than a way to get him out of town. Looking back to the north, he could just barely make out the smoke from the morning fires in Hell's Gate. He could almost taste the morning meals that were being prepared.

He stepped up onto the porch of the house and through the door. The place was completely deserted and it was clear no one had lived there for over ten years. No furnishings, no dishes or pots or anything else to signal someone had once called this place home.

He moved quietly and slowly through the house, checking the two back rooms that had once been bedrooms. They were as empty as the rest of the property.

Giving up on the house, he walked back through and out to the porch. The barn sat about twenty yards away and he didn't have any hope he'd find anything different there, but he had to check.

The main doors to the barn were hanging off their hinges and it wouldn't be much longer before they would fall to the ground. The floor of the barn was bare, compacted dirt. There wasn't even any dry straw in any of the four stalls. The sun was shining on the tops of the walls and within a couple of hours, it would shine directly down and into the barn.

He turned a full circle, trying to see if there was something he was missing. There were no rafters with there being no roof. No place for the vampires to be hanging from to drop on him. There were no dark closets for them to be hiding in.

Pushing his pistol back down in his holster, he was ready to give up. As he turned to leave, an image crashed into his head so hard it almost knocked him to his knees. In the distance, he could hear Midnight screech in terror. Whatever the scene was, his horse was seeing it, too.

Pressing the palms of his hands to his eyes, he tried to drive the face of many vampires from his head. They were swaying back and forth in front of his eyes, baring their fangs and their hot breath stung his face.

He's here!

"Where, damn it!" groaned Darius through the fog of pain that rolled across his brain.

Someplace dark.

"Midnight, there is no dark place out here!"

Then he realized he wasn't seeing a vision of the vampires through his eyes. He was seeing them through Jason's eyes. The terror he and Midnight were feeling wasn't theirs. It was the boy's.

Someplace dark!

"Damn it, Midnight! I can see that just like you can, but there is no place out here that's dark!"

One vampire in the vision reached out, its long, sharp claws drawing near Jason's face. When the point of one of them touched the boy's face, the monster began dragging it down over his cheek.

Darius could feel the sharp claw cutting through the skin of Jason's face and apparently, Midnight could feel it, too.

Find him. Darius!

If he didn't know his horse better, he could have sworn Midnight was on the verge of crying.

He pulled his hands away from his eyes and squinted at the bright sun coming through a gap in the wall. Running out of the barn, he stopped in the empty space and turned around and around.

There was no place that would be dark on this farm. The buildings were in such awful shape neither of them could keep the sunlight out.

He began walking around the barn, checking the outside walls to see if he had missed anything. There was nothing. It was just more of the same dead landscape.

Heading across the yard, he started walking around the house, not having any hope he'd find anything different.

Then he found it.

Sitting about five yards from the west side of the house was the well. It was a stacked ring of stones and topped with a frame to lower the bucket to the water below. The frame was in such disrepair it was close to falling over. There was no rope or bucket attached to the rusty pulley wheel.

Stepping over to it cautiously, Darius leaned over and peered into the darkness below. The bottom of the well was far enough down he couldn't see the bottom and didn't see any reflection of water. Picking up a small stone, he dropped it and listened.

It took over a second for him to hear the

stone thud into the sand at the bottom. Obviously, this was a well that had dried up a long time ago. He figured the bottom had to be at least fifty feet down, much too far to jump or attempt climbing down the sides.

"Hey, buddy, I need you over here."

A few seconds later, he heard Midnight trotting across the empty farm yard. He turned to see him dragging the sagebrush along. After removing the bush from the reins, he got into his pack and pulled out a rope.

Tying one end of the rope to the horn on his saddle, he lowered the other end to the bottom of the well. He fed the rope slowly, trying to figure out how deep this hole was. When he felt it touch the bottom, he felt he was right. Somewhere around fifty-three feet.

Midnight moved over and looked down into the well.

I don't like this.

"What's to like, friend? Climbing down into a dark hole where there are possibly some vampires waiting for me? Should be fun."

You have a very strange idea of fun.

"I've heard that before," he said with a smile. "Now, it's time to put this well-laid plan into action."

Midnight just snorted at him.

He pulled his miner's lantern from the pack and made sure he had plenty of kerosene and some matches. He lit it and hung it off his chest belt. Then he pulled some sticks of dynamite and stuffed them in his boots.

Climbing up onto the edge of the well, he

looked down and wondered if Midnight was the smarter of the two of them. He knew there was no question there. The horse was obviously smarter.

He had Midnight back up about fifty feet, pulling the rope back up and then he wrapped the rope around his wrist. Pulling one of his pistols, he cocked it and peered into the darkness.

"Okay, let's get this done."

He slipped off the edge of the well and placed his boots against the far wall.

"Down nice and slow."

Midnight started inching toward the well and watched as Darius disappeared from view. It took a couple of minutes before he felt the line go slack and knew Darius was at the bottom of the well.

How are you doing down there?

"I'm doing great. How about you? How's the family?"

Would you take this a little more seriously?

"Buddy, I just lowered myself into a dark hole, which is probably home to a nest of vampires, looking for a twelve-year-old boy who may or may not be dead. If I take this too seriously, I might just shoot myself in the head. This lantern leaves a lot to be desired, by the way."

I think we can assume Jason is still alive. We both saw through his eyes.

"Which begs the question, how the hell did we do that?"

Don't know. What do you see down there?

"A long tunnel leading away from the well. Looks like the groundwater that used to be here wore its way through the underground. The bottom of the well collapsed into it. Stay alert up there. I'm going off the rope and having a look."

Darius.

"Yes?"

Please be careful.

"Hey, you know me."

Yeah, I do.

Darius let go of the rope and shined the lantern down the dark tunnel. It was flat, just like water would do if it washed its way through the sandstone.

The lantern didn't reach over twenty feet into the darkness and even then it was very weak. Pulling his other pistol, he checked both directions. The water tunnel came in to the bottom of the well from the south and exited to the north.

He tried to reach out with his senses to the south, but got nothing. There was no reason to think the vampires would only inhabit one direction from the well, but he got the strong impression south wasn't it.

Turning to the north, he began moving forward. The roof of the tunnel was only four feet high in most places, so he had to crouch as he side-stepped his way through the gloom.

After a couple of minutes, he'd move about fifty yards and felt the slope of the ground beneath him angle downward. He could see the walls of the tunnel were moving in on him, but they still allowed him to pass through as long as he moved sideways.

As he tried to control his breathing, he could feel his mind wandering. It started asking questions about his sanity and why he would put himself in these kinds of situations. He smiled to himself when he had to admit he was just like Father Drake had said. He had left home looking for adventure and had found a life with more adventure than any sane man would want.

"You still with me, buddy?"

Now, where else would I be?

"I don't know. I saw you making eyes at Seth's little filly. Thought you might run off with her and have a couple of little ones. You know, start a family."

While I would say that idea holds a certain appeal, I am here to take care of you. Besides, I don't think she likes me.

"What? Are you kidding? She bats her eyes at you every time you come around. She's playing hard to get."

Would you pay attention to what you're supposed to be doing right now.

"Yes, mother."

Darius moved further into the tunnel and caught an odor that had become familiar to him over the centuries. Vampires in an enclosed space holds its own special scent and it is not a pleasant one. Kind of a mix of human waste and rotting, dead bodies.

He moved forward another few feet and then came to a dead stop. His lantern had stopped shining.

Or so he thought. He looked down at it as it hung from his chest and could see it was still burning as it always had been. But he couldn't see anything in front of him anymore.

Shielding his eyes from the glow of the lantern, he squinted, trying to focus on something in front of him, but it was a total black void in front of him.

Then his eyes focused a little more and he just about screamed in terror.

The reason the lantern couldn't illuminate the space in front of him was because he had come into a cavern. It had been washed out by millions of years of water rushing through and the entire floor of the space had collapsed downward.

He found himself standing on the edge of a drop off where one more step would have had him falling twenty feet to the rocks below. The cavern was easily a hundred feet across and just as wide.

But it wasn't the cavern that caused his feelings of horror. It was the two dozen vampires lying around, getting some much needed rest from their nighttime activities.

If he wasn't so set on rescuing Jason, he would drop his dynamite into the cave and let it collapse in on itself.

"We got a big problem down here, Midnight."

How big?

"You remember Callisto, Nebraska?"

Get out of there now!

"Can't, I'm sure the boy is in here somewhere."

He pulled the lantern from his belt and shined it down in front of him. There was a narrow ledge that led downward to the bottom of that cavern and it looked like he could inch his way down.

The lantern was killing his night vision, but he couldn't just put it out. So he set it down on the ground, shining into the cavern. He knew as he moved farther away from it, his eyesight could pick out his surroundings.

Moving off the cliff and onto the ledge, he began side-stepping his way down toward the floor of the cave. He had both guns in his hands, cocked and ready to fire.

"Let's see, two pistols with six bullets each. That's enough for about half the vampires down here."

Maybe you can get them to line up and shoot through them.

"You know, most of the time I appreciate your input on these matters. This is not one of those times."

He took a few more steps, leaving him still about ten feet above the floor of the cave. If he had to, he could jump from there. The soft glow from the lantern above him showed him a floor littered with small boulders, so jumping was out of the question.

He gazed across the open space and could see the vampires were still sleeping. Most of them were resting on the sands that the eons of water had deposited. There was one though, sleeping on a flat rock in the middle of the space. It looked to Darius like it was occupying a place of importance and he knew this had to be the leader.

Joshua.

Then he saw something that tore at his heart.

Jason was tied up and bound to the rock his former father was sleeping on. One thing he could see was the boy was looking right at him. He could read the terror in his eyes, even from forty feet away.

He held up his finger to his lips and Jason just nodded slightly.

He continued his slow walk to the side and found himself on the flat floor of the cavern. He had to pick his steps carefully because of the rocks on the ground. One misstep and he'd stumble or fall.

He stepped cautiously through the sleeping vampires, making his way slowly toward Jason. He did not know what he was going to do when he got to him, but those kinds of things were best left for the spur of the moment.

It took him five minutes to carefully step his way across the vampire bedroom and when he crouched down in front of the boy, he could see the tears streaming down his cheeks.

"Let's get you out of here," he whispered.

He pulled a knife from his belt and cut through the rope quite easily. He was always thankful when he remembered to sharpen and clean his knife.

Once he finished, he lifted Jason to his feet. He checked the boy over quickly to make sure he was okay. Then they started stepping back across the cavern floor, picking their steps carefully.

When they got to the ledge, Darius had Jason go first, intending to protect their retreat if they needed it.

About halfway up, Jason dislodged a small stone that was on the ledge and sent it to the rocks below. He gasped and Darius held his breath as they listened to it clatter among the rocks.

They froze in place and watched to see if it alerted any of the vampires to their presence. Other than a couple rolling over, the stone hadn't disturbed their slumber.

"Sorry," whispered Jason as he started moving again. Darius just fell in behind him and in a couple of minutes they reached the cliff where the lantern was sitting.

As he picked up the lantern, Darius said softly, "Let's get out of here."

Five minutes later they emerged to the space directly under the well and they could see the light of mid-day directly overhead.

Darius took the rope and tied it around Jason's chest, under his arms. Once the rope was secure, he told Midnight to pull him up.

As he stood and watched the boy move upward, he started hearing some sounds coming from the tunnel they had just come out of.

"We got trouble down here," he said.

What kind of trouble?

"Vampires waking up kind of trouble."

Midnight pulled back faster, drawing Jason up at a hastier rate. When he got to the top, the boy clambered over the edge of the well and into the sunlight.

Get the rope off quickly, Jason. Then drop it down the well!

It took a few seconds for him to get the rope untied and then he dropped the entire length down the hole, watching it disappear into the darkness.

He could just barely make out the lantern that hung on Darius' chest and could see him grabbing the rope and wrapping it around his wrist.

"Let's go!" yelled Darius.

Midnight started pulling back and lifting the hunter off the ground, but then his effort came to a stop.

There was some screeching coming from the well and Jason screamed as he looked down. The sound of gunshots echoed up from the darkness and Midnight tried to pull again.

The rope wouldn't budge. As a matter of fact, it inched back over the edge of the well and downward.

Jason could see half a dozen vampires had grabbed hold of the rope and were pulling it back down. They were attempting to pull the horse down into the well and they appeared to be strong enough to do it.

One thing Jason couldn't see was Darius. It was too dark to see the hunter and he couldn't tell if he was still on the rope.

Then another shot rang out and one vampire screeched as the bullet found its mark.

Then another shot.

Jason had to duck out of the way when the bullet came ricocheting off the sides of the well and up towards him.

Midnight was struggling to keep his place, but was getting dragged back toward the well. Jason jumped on the rope and tried to help him, not wanting to see the black horse pulled down.

He heard another shot and then another.

The last shot found its mark.

The rope snapped, sending Jason falling to the ground and Midnight floundering backward, trying to keep his feet.

Above the sounds of the vampires at the bottom of the well, Midnight and Jason heard one thing.

"Run!"

27 – What's He Done Now?

Seth and the sheriff were busy cleaning up the mess in the jail, trying to scrub the bloody message off the floor and right the bed. They needed to get finished and get across the road to lunch. Marcus and Willoughby were at the boardinghouse and expecting them.

No one knew where Darius had gotten off to, but the sheriff had a pretty good idea. He had wiped away the message before anyone else could see it, but he and Seth knew the hunter was most likely headed for the old Benson place.

Nothing to do now, but wait.

Seth was still seething, threatening to get his horse and follow Darius. The sheriff told him that would be hard to do with a bullet in his leg.

Seth calmed down.

When they finished, they looked up at the hole in the roof and tried to figure out how they were going to fix it, but lunch was a more important matter at the moment. Neither one had eaten anything since supper the night before.

As they walked into the dining room, they saw the two hunters were in their usual spot and joined them.

"Any word from Darius yet?" asked Marcus. "Where did that boy get off to?"

Seth and the sheriff looked at each other,

knowing that Darius hadn't told the other hunters where he was going.

"Alright, Caleb," said Willoughby, "spill it."

The sheriff looked at him and just shook his head.

"Darius wouldn't like it if I told you."

"I'll tell you where that fool went off to," said Seth

The sheriff kicked him under the table, causing the deputy to jump.

"Keep quiet, Seth," said the sheriff.

Just then, Anna Marie walked up with a pot of coffee.

"You going to kick me, too?" she asked.

"If I have to."

"My enchantress," said Willoughby, "Tell us where that rascal went."

Anna Marie opened her mouth to lay bare the plan of Darius, but was interrupted by the sound of a horse at full gallop. They could hear it coming from a couple hundred yards away. All of them stopped talking and looked through the window, out onto the street.

A few seconds later, Midnight came bursting out from between a couple of buildings and headed straight for the boardinghouse. They could see Jason was clinging to the saddle with every ounce of energy he could muster.

"Oh, my god!" cried Anna Marie.

Willoughby pushed back from the table so fast his chair went tumbling behind him. The five of them rushed out the door and Marcus was able to grab Midnight's reins and get him stopped.

Jason fell off the horse, into Seth's arms, who carried him to a bench on the porch and set him down. They could see the cuts to his face and arms, with the dried blood there and on his shirt.

"What happened?" he asked. "Where's Darius?"

Jason was trying to get some words out, but he was sobbing so hard he couldn't form any.

The sheriff stepped up and grabbed the boy by the top of his head and pushed it back until he was looking him in the eyes.

"Get hold of yourself, boy! What happened out there?" he yelled.

Anna Marie stepped forward and slapped his hand away and sat down on the bench next to the boy. She wrapped her arms around him and held him close.

"What happened, Jason?" she asked softly.

Jason took a couple of deep breaths and looked up into her blue eyes.

"Vampires," he croaked through his tears. "Lots of 'em."

Marcus crouched down in front of the two and put a hand on Jason's knee.

"Jason, what happened to Darius?"

The boy looked the old hunter in the eyes and shook his head.

"They got 'im."

The five grown-ups felt a stab of fear cut through all their hearts.

"At the Benson place?" asked Seth.

Jason nodded and said, "They were down in the well. That's where they took me. They wanted to use me to catch him."

Jason collapsed into a sobbing mess and Anna Marie cradled him to her chest.

She looked up at the men and asked, "What are we going to do?"

"We ... will not do anything," said Marcus. "Willoughby and I will go out there and see what's what."

"I'm coming with you," said Seth.

"I am, too," said the sheriff.

"Gentlemen," said Marcus, "we can make no assurances for your safety."

"And neither one of us is asking for that," said Seth, which brought a small gasp from Anna Marie.

The stableman, who had been in the dining room and heard everything, rushed to the stables and set about getting four horses ready to travel. He hauled all the saddles out of the tack room and began putting blankets on each horse.

A minute later, the small group came bursting into the livery and began pulling their saddlebags and packs from the tack room. They cleaned out the livery's supply of dynamite. The sheriff pulled out his shotgun and slung a belt over his body that had a dozen rounds of birdshot.

"Do you think that shotgun is going to be of any use?" Willoughby asked. "It probably won't have much effect on a vampire."

"Them vampires turn into birds, don't they?"

"Well, yes, I suppose some of them do."

Marcus looked at the shotgun and said, "You bring whatever you're comfortable with, sheriff. Those rounds may not kill the vampires, but they will slow them down."

"Good to know," said the sheriff.

Anna Marie was trying to put up a brave front as she helped Seth get his things together. Her hands were shaking so badly she could hardly hold on to anything.

Once the four horses were saddled and the men climbed up, Marcus looked at Jason.

"About how many vampires would you say were in the cave, Jason?"

"Twenty-seven."

Anna Marie squealed, but then choked her anguish back. She looked like she was ready to pull Seth off his horse and throw him back in the jail cell.

"You counted them?" asked Willoughby.

"Yes, sir. Had nothing else to do when they had me tied up."

"Well, gentlemen," said Marcus, "looks like we have a busy day ahead of us."

He spurred his horse out of the barn and was followed by the other three. In all the commotion of getting the horses ready, everyone forgot about Midnight. When the riders burst out of the barn and headed south, Midnight fell right in beside them.

"And where do you think you're going?" asked Marcus.

Much as I'd like to let him walk back to town for letting himself get captured, he may need a ride.

"You may be bringing back a dead body," mused Willoughby.

Do you really believe that?

"No, I suppose I don't."

They raced on in relative silence from that point, each of them worried about what they were going to find.

It took them less than twenty minutes to reach the Benson farm and stand around the well, looking down into the darkness. The gloom was as black as anything any of them had ever seen and each of them could feel the terror reaching out and wrapping itself about their hearts.

"Well," said Marcus, "no sense standing here looking at a hole in the ground. Shall we go see what that young pup has got himself into this time?"

All of them went to their saddlebags and got ropes and secured them to their saddles. Then, one by one they began to lower themselves into the darkness. Midnight coached each horse in what to do.

If the truth were told, he was as worried as anyone about what had happened to Darius.

28 – Like Shooting Vampires In A Barrel

It took five minutes for the four of them to reach the bottom of the well. They could see the footprints of a lot of vampires in the sand. Scattered among those tracks were the unmistakable prints of a pair of boots. They also found a handful of spent shells from Darius' guns.

One thing that brought a small smile to their faces was the dead bodies of three vampires. All three bodies were missing their heads, showing Darius had had enough time to do a complete job of killing them.

Marcus looked at the others and said softly, "Twenty-four to go. I'll try to leave some for you, young man."

Willoughby bristled at the term *young man*. He was older than Darius, but still not as old as Marcus. Sometimes he thought the old man relished the idea of being the oldest hunter in the organization and loved to rub it in whenever he could.

"Just try to keep up, grandpa," he said as he brushed past the older hunter.

All four men had lanterns and even then, the light still did little to illuminate their way. They crouched and side-stepped their way down the washed-out tunnel, looking for the cliff Jason had told them about.

When they had moved forward for about ten minutes, they heard a commotion in front of them. There were angry voices, screeches and growls coming from the darkness.

They were quite sure they had found the right place.

When they reached the edge of the cliff, they silently took up positions along the drop off and surveyed the situation below.

Twenty-four vampires were ranging about the center of the cave and the object of their disdain was situated right in the middle.

Darius was tied up and laying on the flat rock that had served as Joshua's resting place. They had stripped him of his outer clothes, leaving nothing but his longjohns. They could see his guns and sword were laying off to the side of the cavern.

"Are we tiring of being hunted by these so-called soldiers of God?" bellowed Joshua.

A roar came from the gathered vampires. A couple of them tried to get at Darius, but some of the older ones kept everyone back. Marcus and Willoughby could feel the evil that emanated from the cavern. They could also feel the dread experienced by the sheriff and Seth.

How you doing, boy?

Darius rolled his head to the side and looked up at the top of the cliff. He could see the four men crouched in the darkness above.

Oh, you know. Just lying around trying to get some rest. Can't get much sleep with all this noise, though.

Well, I'm sure Anna Marie will be happy to get you a room once we get back to town.

Sounds good.

Marcus set his lantern down and pulled his second pistol and the others followed suit. With a few hand motions, he divided up the cave for each man and then took careful aim.

At the sound of his gun going off, the other three began firing as quickly and as accurately as they could. But they found they weren't nearly as fast as they needed to be.

Their first few shots took down about half a dozen vampires, but the others scattered and began turning into various animals and birds. The vampires were quick when they were in their true form, but they were even faster when they changed into rats and birds.

That's when the sheriff pulled his shotgun off his back and started blasting shot into the air. His aim proved to be every bit as deadly as the two hunters. Within one minute, he downed eight birds and that was having to reload after every two shots. The vampire birds were no match for his onslaught, sending them flapping to the ground below.

A couple of vampires thought they would be safe if they turned into rats. Little did they know Willoughby practiced his marksmanship at the city dump outside Boston. There wasn't a rat that was safe from his deadly aim and he dispatched two of them in the gloomy light. Within another minute, the odds were definitely turning to their favor when there were less than a dozen vampires remaining upright.

The four men began moving down the slanted ledge to the bottom of the cave. Two braver vampires tried to rush them and got nothing but a bullet through their heads for their efforts.

When they reached the floor of the cavern, Marcus signaled to Seth to free Darius from the ropes holding him. He pulled a knife from his boot and sliced through the ropes holding Darius' wrists and then turned the knife over to him to finish the job. He wanted to get back to the fight.

As Darius cut through the bindings around his ankles, he heard Seth firing as fast as he could and looked up to see one of the larger vampires rushing at him.

"The head, Seth!"

Before Seth could get another shot off, the vampire skewered him through the sides with its claws. Everyone could hear the wind get knocked out of the deputy's lungs.

"Excuse me, sir!"

The vampire looked over his shoulder and right down the barrel of a large pistol. The kind the hunters liked to carry. It was held by a well-dressed man, wearing a bowler hat and the last thing the vampire saw was the flash just before the bullet cleaved his head down the middle.

Willoughby reached down and grabbed Seth by the back of his collar and dragged him to the side of the cavern. He didn't have time to check on his condition with the fight still raging around them. He just made sure Seth was propped up against the wall so no vampire could get behind him and had both of his pistols.

One thing he had a hard time doing was shutting out the sound of Seth trying to draw a breath. He hoped the young man was going to make it out of the cavern alive because he definitely didn't want to see Anna Marie break down in tears.

Darius had finally rolled off the flat rock and scrambled his way to his weapons. He pulled both pistols and could tell just by their weight they were both empty. Dropping them into the dirt, he pulled his sword and one of his silver spikes. Then he swung around to find his nearest target.

He didn't have to look very long.

There were only six vampires left alive and two of them were heading straight for him. He windmilled the blade and cut off the hand of the nearest vampires and then drove his spike into the second one. Two quick slashes with the sword and two vampire heads rolled across the floor.

As he started moving around the floor of the cavern, he felt like he was going to be sick when he realized the wet mud squishing up between his bare toes was made with vampire blood. Usually that sort of thing wouldn't bother him, but when you're fighting for your life, dressed in nothing but your underwear, it can play games with your head.

Three of the remaining vampires were doing their best to protect Joshua, who was obviously the leader of this nest. He looked at Marcus and saw some blood running down one of his arms. One vampire had some minor success in slashing the old man across the shoulder.

Willoughby was trying to get the old man to back off and let him handle these last few, but Marcus was having none of that. Neither man had their pistols in their hands and Darius assumed it meant they were out of bullets. Each one had their swords and spikes ready to finish the job.

One vampire lunged at Marcus, seeing that he was already wounded and weaker. As the old man went to bring his sword up, another sword snaked past his left ear and drove straight through the face of the vampire.

"Damn it, Darius! He was mine!"

Darius laughed and said, "Are we keeping count now?"

Marcus laughed and said, "Don't we always?"

"Why don't you back up so you don't get hurt some more?"

"Why don't you mind your own business? And put some clothes on, for God's sake! It's embarrassing to be seen with you."

"I seem to remember I came into Heaven Sent with even less clothes on my body."

"Hey!" yelled Willoughby. "Are you two going to stop conversing and start fighting again?"

The two hunters looked at him and he had two vampires trying to get at him. He had a genuine look of concern on his face.

"Oh, for Hell's sake, Willie," said Darius. "Just kill the bastards."

Darius slashed his sword past the ear of Willoughby and beheaded one vampire. As its head bounced off the ground and rolled across Willoughby's boot, the other vampire screeched and lunged at the two hunters, driving them back and away from Joshua.

Just as the vampire jumped, Joshua disappeared in a cloud of smoke and when the hunters looked for him, they couldn't see him anywhere. That just left the five vampires in the cavern and Seth took care of one of them.

Firing from his seated position near the side of the cave, his bullet tore through the head of one vampire and Marcus finished him with his sword.

Darius felt a little under-dressed as he continued battling with a couple of blood suckers and all he had in his hands were his sword and one spike. He skewered one vampire and he stabbed at the other with the spike, but the monster was too fast for him.

He swept the legs out from under the vampire that was impaled on his sword and took him to the ground. Leaving his sword where it was, he came back up with the spike and found himself in the claws of the other vampire. As its claws wrapped around his throat, he looked out the sides of his eyes, wondering how the others were doing.

They were already occupied with other vampires, with Willoughby looking like he'd drawn the largest vampire any of them had ever seen.

Seth was trying to draw a bead on that

vampire's head, but he was quickly losing strength and his hand was getting shaky. He decided not to shoot, worried that he might hit someone else.

Marcus was locked in a fierce battle with a female vampire and she was acting like anything but a lady. The old hunter was one to give lots of respect to the womenfolk, but he had his limits. With one quick swish of his sword, he sliced her across the leg, just above the knee.

As she screamed in pain, he twirled the sword and slashed across her other leg, driving her to her knees.

"How could you attack a woman like that?" she screeched at him.

"Oh, I'm sorry, m'lady. Let me see what I can do to ease your pain."

Another slash of the sword and it caught her a couple of inches below the ear, slicing cleanly through her neck.

Her head bounced over the floor of the cave and rolled up against the boot of the vampire that had hold of Darius. When he looked down, he screeched in a pain of his own.

"You killed my wife!" he roared at Marcus.

Just as he turned back to finish Darius, a silver-plated spike slammed through his right eye and embedded into his brain. His entire body went stiff and he released his hold on Darius, but the hunter didn't release the spike. Instead, he pushed it even further into his attacker's head and ground it around.

"Let me see what I can do to reunite you with your lovely bride," growled Darius as he got right in the vampire's face.

As the vampire fell backward, Darius just rode him down and drove a knee into the monster's gut. He reached over and pulled a knife from Marcus' boot and set about to removing the vampire's head.

Slowly.

While he was sawing away on the neck of the vampire, the other one that was still impaled on Darius' sword just rolled his head and watched, horrified at what it was seeing. Darius looked at him and smiled.

"You're next," he said with a gleam in his eyes.

It took a couple minutes for Darius to finish the vampire, but before he could move to the other one, Marcus sliced its head clean off.

"Damn it, Marcus! That one was mine!"

"You can have the next one," said the old hunter, pointing at the one that was giving Willoughby a hard time.

Darius scrambled to his feet and pulled his sword from the dead vampire and started moving across the cave. Willoughby was doing everything he could to drive the large vampire back, but he couldn't seem to land any effective blows.

"Stand back!" yelled Willoughby. "No one kills this monster but me."

Darius and Marcus looked around and realized there were no other vampires in the cavern, so they backed off.

Darius walked over to where his clothes had been thrown and began getting dressed. He was cursing up a storm about how the vampires had put several holes in his shirt and pants.

While he did that, Marcus sat down on the flat rock Darius had been tied to just a few brief minutes before. He looked over and saw the sheriff was tending to Seth and he hoped the young man would survive his wounds. Last thing he wanted to see was Anna Marie crying over the loss of her beau.

As he sat there, Willoughby was struggling to get any kind of edge on the big vampire, who appeared to be about as dumb as a box of rocks. Apparently, it didn't realize it was alone in a cave with three vampire hunters and there was no way it was going to walk out of there alive.

Well ... undead, as the vampires were already dead.

Marcus decided he'd seen enough and when the two combatants got close enough, he reached out with his sword and jabbed the vampire in the back of one knee.

Screeching in pain, the vampire hobbled as it tried to find some advantage. But the wound Marcus had inflicted was caused by a silver-edged blade and was one thing the vampires would definitely feel.

Seeing the tide of the fight had turned in his favor, Willoughby stabbed the vampire through the chest. It drove the monster to its knees and the hunter, in one smooth motion, pulled his sword and sliced the vampire's head off. Its head rolled across the floor and came to rest under the sole of Marcus' boot.

As it snarled and gnashed at Marcus, Willoughby stepped forward and drove his sword through the head and lifted it off the ground and looked at it. It was still trying to put up a fight, but found it nearly impossible without a body.

"You are rather ugly, old chap," said Willoughby. "I believe I have just done you an immense favor in killing you."

He swished the blade through the air and the head came sliding off. Though the vampire's eyes still worked, they didn't for long. The last thing they saw was Willoughby's boot coming down and smashing the skull of the monster to pieces.

When he turned around, he saw Darius and Marcus sitting there, watching him.

"I didn't need your help, grandpa," said Willoughby.

"See how ungrateful he can be," said Marcus to Darius.

"Yes, it is quite sad when they talk like that to their elders."

Marcus took a deep breath, ready to let the youngest hunter in the group know exactly what he thought of his comment.

"Haven't you three forgotten something?" asked the sheriff.

They looked at him, thinking he was referring to Seth and his injuries.

"Joshua got away," wheezed Seth.

Marcus and Darius jumped up and looked around. They were sure he was still in the cavern, in some smaller form.

"He's not here," gasped Seth. "I guess a raven is his favorite animal form, because he changed into one and flew out of the cave. I tried to shoot him, but I'm out of bullets."

"Jesus, Hell's Gate," mumbled Willoughby.

"Alright," said Marcus, "We have to get back there, but we also have to get Seth out of here and then burn all these bodies."

Immediately, the four uninjured men began dragging the bodies of the dead vampires, birds and rats to the center of the cave and piled them up. Willoughby pulled a white cloth sack off the back of his belt and began sprinkling gun powder over the pile of bodies.

"Get him out of here," said Willoughby, pointing to Seth. "I'll give you five minutes to get out of here before I set this bunch alight. It's going to smell something awful."

The other three gathered their weapons and supplies and then lifted Seth to his feet. They began moving back up the ledge toward the opening and once they got there, Seth grabbed Darius by the front of his shirt.

"Get out of here now," he groaned. "Get back to town!"

Darius looked at the sheriff and then at Marcus. The old hunter just nodded to him and Darius took off up the tunnel as fast as he could go.

Before he got to the bottom of the well, he

could smell the smoke wafting out of the cave. It was a smell he was very familiar with.

Roasting vampires.

He didn't envy the four behind him having to endure the smell until they all got out of the hole.

Looking straight up, he could see a storm of black clouds had rolled in. It was just right for a vampire to raise havoc. He found the ropes still hanging from the top of the well and called up to Midnight to get a little help getting out of the hole.

And where is everyone else?

"They're coming. We're heading for Hell's Gate as soon as I get up there."

Grab a rope and I'll have you pulled up.

Darius grabbed a rope and wrapped it around his wrist and yanked on it. Instantly, he was lifted off the ground and it only took a few seconds to reach the top of the well. What he found was a bit confusing.

It had been Seth's horse that pulled him up.

They forgot to lower a rope for you before they went down.

"Okay."

Lily wants to know where Seth is?

"He's coming, but he's hurt," said Darius as he looked into Lily's eyes. "He's going to be okay, but you need to get him back to Anna Marie as quickly as you can."

Lily just nodded her head up and down as Darius took the rope and dropped it back down the well.

"Did that black bird fly past you?"

Yes, it did. Wasn't much we could do about it, either. It headed straight for the town.

Darius got all of his weapons and supplies situated on Midnight and climbed into the saddle. He looked at the other four horses and hoped they could take care of getting the others out of the hole, but Midnight assured him they were up to the task.

With a quick turn, they set off across the desert, heading back to town. He could see the soft glow of lights as the town was getting itself set for another night.

They just did not know what was coming their way.

29 – Took Your Eyes Off The Ball

It took less than fifteen minutes for Midnight to cover the distance, even though it had grown dark and footing was treacherous. It was as if the horse had an innate ability to avoid setting a hoof wrong.

As they got closer to town, they could tell the horror had already begun. There were gunshots splitting the night, women screaming and the roar of a monster set on destroying the town.

The two of them charged between a couple of buildings and onto the main street. There was plenty of light to see by because the jail was on fire, along with a couple of other buildings.

What broke Darius' heart was the bodies laying in the street. There were half a dozen men and women laying face down in the dirt, blood pooling around their bodies.

Jumping down from Midnight's back, he ran across the street and slammed through the doors of the boardinghouse, causing Abbie and Anna Marie to scream. When they saw it was him, they ran to him and into his arms.

"Give me a quick idea of what's going on out there," he said.

Both the women began talking at the same time, but Abbie stopped so her daughter could fill him in.

Joshua had arrived just about twenty

minutes ago, appeared right in the middle of the street and when the men tried to kill him, he just attacked and killed them. When the women ran to the aid of their husbands, he killed them, too.

"Do you know exactly where he is?"

"Why, Darius James, I'm right here."

Looking up, they saw the vampire standing at the top of the stairs leading to the rooms. The ladies screamed and Darius stepped in front of them, putting himself between them and the monster.

It wasn't the sight of the vampire that caused the ladies to scream, though. It was the fact that Joshua had a hand firmly clamped around the back of Jason's neck. The boy was standing there, shaking with terror.

"Kill him, Mr. James," whispered Jason.

Darius just nodded slightly.

"Now, is that any way to talk about your own father?" intoned Joshua.

"You ain't no pa of mine!"

Joshua turned Jason's neck to face him and looked into his eyes. The vampire's eyes glowed red as he stared into the frightened eyes of the boy.

"If that is how you feel, then I have no use for you, do I?"

Darius cocked one of his pistols and took careful aim at the head of the monster, just trying to calm his fingers long enough to shoot.

Without even looking down at him, Joshua said, "Careful, vampire hunter. You fire and you will hit this poor, innocent boy."

That was the only thing that stayed Darius' hand. He knew if he fired, Joshua could whip the boy in front of himself and the bullet would hit him.

"Don't worry about me, Mr. James," yelled Jason. "Kill this demon that killed my family!"

Darius could still feel the women behind him. Abbie was shaking with fear, seeing this evil with her own eyes. But Anna Marie ran a hand up his back, to his shoulder. He felt a surge of warmth and energy wash over him from her touch.

"Shoot," she whispered. "Jason will be okay."

Darius took another breath and watched as Joshua's lips curled up in one of the most evil grins he'd ever seen. He could see his fangs were extended and thirsting for blood.

Darius adjusted his aim by a fraction of an inch and fired. Joshua whipped Jason off the floor, but Darius had aimed a little further back than the vampire was expecting.

The bullet clipped Jason's left ear and then took off a good piece of the back of Joshua's head. The vampire howled in pain and dropped the boy, who tumbled down the stairs.

Anna Marie ran around Darius and ran toward the stairs, even though he tried to grab her and hold her back. She reached the bottom of the stairs at the same moment Jason bounced off the bottom step. She gathered him up in her arms and looked up the stairs.

Joshua was staring right at her and she

could feel his hypnotic gaze cut right through her.

The sound of Darius' gun blasted again and Joshua moved slightly and the bullet missed, hitting the wall behind him.

It was enough to break the spell Joshua was trying to cast over Anna Marie and she lifted Jason and hustled him away from the stairs.

Darius fired again, but Joshua disappeared in a cloud of black smoke. The hunter started turning in a circle, keeping both of his pistols out and searching for a target.

"Miss Abbie, you know how to fire one of these guns?"

"Ever since I was a little girl."

He handed one pistol to her and she cocked it and held it with both hands, continuing to search the room for the vampire.

"Maybe he's gone," whispered Anna Marie.

"Oh no, he's not gone," said Darius, raising his voice. "He is too far into this game to leave now. But, he likes to hide behind women and children. He's a coward like that."

Everyone jumped when the pistol in Abbie's hand thundered and he looked to see the black cloud she had been shooting at.

"How in tarnation are we supposed to kill him if he keeps disappearing?" she growled.

"He's going to make a mistake," said Darius. "Hell, he's already made the biggest mistake of all in trying to fight me."

Just then, there was a scream from outside

and another round of shots from other men. Darius moved to the door of the building and looked outside to see Joshua had another woman by the neck and was set to sink his teeth into her throat.

"By the power of God in Heaven, I command you to stop this!"

Darius looked to his right and could see the preacher standing in the middle of the street, holding a crucifix in his hand.

"Preacher! Get the hell out of there!" Darius yelled.

Smythe looked at him and Darius could see the conviction in his eyes. But, he also knew that crucifix wouldn't do anything to protect him from this monster.

Joshua straightened up and laughed at the preacher. The sight of the old man holding the cross in his shaking hand was funny to him.

The vampire started walking along the street, toward the preacher. He still had hold of the woman by the throat and was holding her up as a shield between him and Darius. The hunter didn't have a clean shot.

As the vampire got closer, the preacher was reciting the Lord's Prayer, clenching the crucifix even tighter. Darius stepped out of the boardinghouse, still trying to get a shot at the vampire. Joshua wasn't even looking at him as he held the struggling woman at arm's length and perfectly positioned to stop Darius from shooting.

Darius stepped down off the porch and into the street, still looking for a shot.

The last thing he expected was for the preacher to pull a gun from behind his back with his other hand and point it and shoot.

Before Darius could shout, "Stop!" Joshua moved the woman as if she was nothing more than a rag doll. The bullet tore into her chest, killing her instantly.

Dropping her dead body in the dirt, Joshua swarmed over the preacher and then disappeared into the night in a cloud of smoke. Darius could see the raven fly away into the darkness and he tried to get a couple of shots off at it, but missed.

When he looked back down from the sky, he saw Preacher Smythe standing completely still in the middle of the street, staring at the body of the woman he had just shot. His face was as white as flour and mouth was open and moving slightly, but no sounds were coming out.

Darius knew what had happened, but didn't want to see it finish. He closed his eyes and hung his head.

Blood began pouring from the preacher's neck and he fell backwards. When he hit the ground, his head rolled free, coming to rest near the body of the woman.

Darius fell to his knees and raged against the darkness.

"You goddamn coward! Come back here and face me!"

Someone was running up behind him and he jerked around, ready to fire, but found his pistol aimed squarely at Anna Marie. She skidded to a stop as he lowered his weapon.

When she saw the preacher and the woman, she let out an anguished cry. Dropping to her knees near the woman, she stroked her cheek.

"Oh, Suzy," she cried. "I'm so sorry. Fly away home to our Heavenly Father. You, too, Preacher Smythe."

Before she could say anything else, four horses came galloping into town and straight to the scene in the street.

Marcus and Willoughby climbed down and went to Darius, as the sheriff began helping Seth down from his horse. Anna Marie ran to him and could see he was hurt.

"What happened, Seth?"

"Vampires, sweetheart. It's always the vampires."

She put his arm over her shoulders and helped him out of the street and into the boardinghouse. After she got him settled into a chair, she charged back outside.

The three hunters were gathered in a small group in the middle of the street and it looked like none of the townsfolk wanted to go anywhere near them.

No one except Anna Marie and Jason.

The boy walked up to the men and looked at the three of them.

"Thank you, Mr. James for coming to get me."

Darius forced a smile and said, "Hey, Jason. It's what we do."

"I'm sorry my pa is causing all this

trouble."

Willoughby reached out and put a hand on the boy's shoulder and squeezed it.

"You have nothing to be sorry for, young man. This is not your fault."

Anna Marie walked up behind Jason and wrapped her arms around his shoulders and hugged him close.

"Gentlemen," she said as she looked at the three of them, "talk is going around to have you three leave town and I don't think we'll be able to stop it this time."

The three of them looked at the gathering crowd about a hundred feet away and knew she was right.

As they stood there, the undertaker came rolling up in his wagon. He had eight pine boxes stacked in the back. After he jumped down, the hunters helped him pull down two of them and then helped him lay Suzy and Smythe in them.

Then they followed him up the street, stopping at each body and picking them up. For some reason, the crowd kept backing away as they moved to each new body. It was as if they didn't want to have anything to do with the bodies or the hunters.

As they were gathering up the last body, the sun set over the mountains to the west and Darius could feel a sense of terror wash over the town. The darkness had its own feeling of doom. The light of morning seemed to chase that atmosphere of terror away, but they now had to make it through the next ten hours.

After a quick word with the undertaker, they followed him to the cemetery and began digging the graves. Torches were placed all around the graveyard to keep the place lit. It took all evening and until close to midnight for them to finish. With only the six of them working, it took a lot longer than it should have.

After they had laid all eight bodies to rest, Marcus pulled a small Bible from his pack and began reading over the new graves. The light cast by the torches lent a surreal atmosphere to the cemetery. The three hunters kept their weapons in their hands, constantly searching the night sky for Joshua.

Jason was standing with Anna Marie and even though both of them were covered in sweat and grime, she hugged him close and wouldn't let him go. He had tears streaming down his face and everyone knew he was feeling the guilt of being associated with the monster that was causing so much pain in this little town.

"The LORD is my shepherd; I shall not want. He maketh me to lie down in green pastures: he leadeth me beside the still waters. He restoreth my soul: he leadeth me in the paths of righteousness for his name's sake."

"Yea, though I walk through the valley of the shadow of death, I will fear no evil: for thou art with me; thy rod and thy staff they comfort me. Thou preparest a table before me in the presence of mine enemies: thou anointest my head with oil; my cup runneth over. Surely goodness and mercy shall follow me all the days of my life: and I will dwell in the house of the LORD for ever."

As the men began filling in the graves, some of the folks from town joined them and got the job done faster. Darius thought it was because they wanted the hunters done with this job and back in the safety of the town. Nothing could have been further from the truth.

30 – Not Wanted Anymore

After they were finished, the group walked back to town, carrying the torches. Marcus couldn't help but remember all the times he had been in the Old World and seen crowds like this. They would be carrying torches just like these and seeking those they suspected of being witches. Most of the time those crowds had been wrong in their accusations of innocent, young women.

They went straight to the boardinghouse, where Abbie had set a table for them with sandwiches and water. Their table was the only one occupied in the dining room.

Seth was sitting in one chair, having been bandaged up. Even though he could still be heard having breathing problems, he would not leave the room and get some rest.

When each of them said they didn't feel right eating without cleaning up, Abbie demanded they all sit down and eat. She even forced Anna Marie to sit and not do any work. She could see the pall of sadness hanging over all of them and wanted to do whatever she could to drive it away.

When they finished eating, Darius stood up and said he was going upstairs to get cleaned up. It was about this time the sheriff came in and joined them. He motioned for Darius to sit back down and everyone could tell he had something he needed to get off his chest.

"I guess I don't need to tell you the town is ready to explode," he said.

"No, sheriff, I don't think you do," said Marcus. "Can we assume it's as bad as the look on your face?"

The sheriff nodded and looked around the table.

"The others are demanding you leave and let us deal with this vampire in our own way."

Darius was sitting, with his head hung low, just staring at the table in front of him. Marcus reached over and gripped his shoulder. He knew very well the pain the younger hunter was feeling, having experienced it with him before. Leaving a town that was under attack was never a good thing, but there came a time when they couldn't argue against it.

"Please don't leave us," squeaked Jason.

Darius raised his head and looked into the boy's eyes. He could only shake his head slightly and the rest knew the hunters would do whatever the town citizens would ask of them.

"Take my Anna Marie with you."

They looked up to see Abbie standing there.

"Do not leave this town without her."

"I'm not leaving this town, mama."

"Yes, you are," said Seth. "When they ride out, you will be with them. You, too, Jason."

"I'm stayin' and fightin' this demon," said the boy.

"No!" thundered Seth, even though raising

his voice caused him severe pain. "You will be on a horse, along with Anna Marie and you will get out of this cursed town!"

He fell into a fit of coughing and Anna Marie jumped up and grabbed a towel and held it to his mouth. When he finished coughing, she pulled the towel away and it had a puddle of blood in the middle.

She stroked his cheek and said, "If anyone needs to leave it's you. And you, mama."

"I am part of the law in this town, sweetheart," said Seth. "I can't go running just because things look bad."

The sheriff just shook his head.

"Seth," Anna Marie said with her hands on her hips, "right now a seven-year-old girl could kick your behind. Just how much help do you think you'll be in your condition?"

He looked around the table and then at her and said, "I'll go if you don't argue anymore. You leave this town with me and I won't put up a fuss."

"Mama?"

"I'm staying," said Abbie. "Someone needs to look after this fool town and try to pick up the pieces later."

"There may not be a town to look after by tomorrow," said Anna Marie.

"Be that as it may, I've had a good run. If it ends here, then that's God's will."

She looked at Seth and said, "You take good care of my baby."

He just looked at her and nodded.

"Midnight," said Darius, "you still out

there?"

Yes, Darius. I've been standing in the street all night.

"I'm sorry about that. See if you can gather all the other horses near the front of the boardinghouse and get ready to move out."

Already on it.

The three hunters stood up and headed for the stairs, with Anna Marie following them up to her room. When she was finished, she ran to Seth's room and grabbed his things. Within five minutes, they were all gathered back in the dining room with packs and travel bags ready to go.

When they walked out to the porch, they could see the crowd had gotten bigger, but were still reluctant to get any closer.

Darius looked at the horses and asked, "Where's Lily?"

She went down to the stables to find a horse for Anna Marie and Jason.

The group began walking toward the stables and the crowd just parted in front of them. There was so much hate coming off the group, the hunters felt like they were the monsters and not the vampire.

When the sheriff saw the weapons some of the townsfolk were carrying, he pulled his own pistol and walked in the middle of the group.

"Ya'll just go on about your business," he told the crowd. "You're getting what you wanted. They are leaving and we will be unprotected."

"A lot of good their protection has done

us," yelled one woman.

A murmur of discontent rolled through the crowd and they pressed in a little closer. The sheriff cocked his gun and leveled it at the closest person to them and the crowd stopped.

Marcus reached out and put a hand on the sheriff's forearm.

"That won't be necessary, Caleb."

"I ain't never seen this town act like this," said the sheriff as he relaxed his aim.

"I have," said Marcus. "We all have. When people are trapped on a slowly sinking ship, they will lash out at anyone they feel is to blame."

"It just don't seem right."

"There is nothing about this God-forsaken mess that feels right," said Seth with a cough.

When they reached the stables, Lily came out with Clem's horse, saddled and ready to go. The stableman came out with the poles for the travois and he and Darius went about setting it up and then getting Seth laid down on it.

Then the stableman disappeared and then came back out with another saddled horse.

"That's my horse," yelled one man in the crowd.

"Carl, you ain't paid your bill in over six months. I'm taking Sissy as payment for your account."

"Sheriff!" yelled the man.

"He has every right to claim this horse as his property if you haven't paid your bill," said the sheriff. "Are you ready to settle your bill in full this minute."

The man remained silent.

"I didn't think so," said the sheriff.

They got Anna Marie up into the saddle on Clem's horse and then helped Jason up behind her.

The hunters climbed into their saddles and Marcus looked down at the sheriff.

"May God watch over you and your town, Caleb."

"I think God left this town long before any of you got here."

Abbie was standing near Anna Marie's horse, holding her hand. Neither one was saying anything. Darius reached down and tapped her on the shoulder. When Abbie turned to face him, he put his hand on the top of her head and she gasped.

She could feel him inside her head, planting a piece of his mind there. As he did it, she could feel a calm settle over her and she knew that what she saw and thought, he would see and think. After a few seconds, he lifted his hand and she had tears in her eyes.

She looked into his eyes and nodded at some silent words that passed between them.

Marcus just bit his lip and turned his horse and led the small group out of town. Darius looked ahead and could see the sun was beginning to brighten the eastern sky.

Deep inside his chest he knew Hell's Gate would be wiped from the face of the Earth before the sun came up two mornings hence.

31 – A Plan Is Hatched

The group only traveled about five miles before stopping and setting up camp near a small creek. There was a small copse of trees that rustled in the breeze.

The men gathered four rocks and set them in a long square and then laid Seth's travois on them, providing him a bed off the ground.

Darius picked up his pack and walked a hundred yards away from the camp, to a place behind some bushes at the edge of the creek. Stripping off the grimy clothes he'd been wearing since the day before, he waded into the cool water and sat down.

He grabbed a handful of mud from the bottom of the creek and began using it to scrub his body. He rubbed harder and harder, trying to wash the shame of failure from his skin, but the only thing he accomplished was rubbing his skin raw.

He stopped and dropped his head and could feel tears falling from his eyes into the water. He rubbed even harder, feeling his skin beginning to bleed.

"That will not help, no matter how much you rub."

He opened his eyes and stared into Anna Marie's blue eyes. She had sat down on a rock near the edge of the water and was just watching him.

"Anna Marie, it's not a good idea for you to be here right now."

"Why? Because you think I've never seen a man without his clothes before?"

"No," he said as he looked at her. "It's because I'm not in a very good place right now."

"What? Do you think you're some sort of man that is above feeling sadness and despair? Get over it, Darius. You're human, just like the rest of us. Maybe you'll live longer than any of us, but you're still a man."

"There are days I wish that wasn't so," he said as he washed water over his face to clear away the tracks of the tears.

"Do you really think Hell's Gate will suffer the same fate as the little town in France? What was the name of it again?"

"Courville and yes, I think Hell's Gate will just be another version of that town. Just because the hunters have left doesn't mean the vampire will walk away. He won't leave until there is not one living person in the town."

This time, it was her turn to hang her head. The thought of her mama still in town brought a wave of grief over her, stronger than any she had ever felt.

Darius rinsed off the last of the mud and stood up, not caring one bit that he was completely naked to her. As he waded to the shore, she picked up the towel from his pack and handed it to him. As he dried off, she stood up and picked up his clean pants and shirt. She shook them to get any dust and dirt out of them. She waited while he pulled on his longjohns and then handed him his clothes.

While he got dressed, she asked, "Is there nothing we can do to save the town?"

He stopped what he was doing and looked at her. He hadn't seen such sadness in a pair of bright blue eyes in many years.

"Contrary to what you and the town may think, we're not quite ready to give up. I'm sure Marcus and Willoughby are sitting down right now and plotting some sort of crazy scheme to take the town ..."

He stopped and cocked his head as if listening for something.

"What is it?"

"Something has changed," he whispered.

He pulled on his boots and picked up his dirty clothes and the two of them headed back toward the camp. When they got to within a few yards of the spot hidden by a small hill, they saw what had changed. There weren't five people in the camp anymore.

There were seven. The old medicine man had arrived, along with one brave.

The old man smiled when he saw Darius, knowing he was looking at a kindred spirit. He greeted the hunter in his native tongue and Darius nodded.

"What did he say, Mr. James?" asked Jason.

"He said he heard the voice of the Great Spirit telling him to join us."

He turned back to the old man and said, "We face a threat far greater than the one you and your men faced before."

"Greater or not, my son and I are here to help bring about the end of this evil that hangs over these people."

Marcus said something and the old man nodded. The brave went to his pony and came back with a lance and a set of knives. Marcus pointed to Willoughby and the brave handed the weapons to him.

Willoughby walked over to the fire pit and began melting down a couple of small ingots of silver in a small pot. Jason stood over his shoulder and watched.

"Wanting to learn something, young man?" asked Willoughby.

"If I am to be a good squire, I should know these things."

Looking up at the boy, Willoughby motioned for him to sit down.

"Does the silver kill the vampires?"

"No, it doesn't, but it does cause them considerable discomfort. As long as any silver remains in their bodies, it will hinder their abilities to move and fight us. That's why we put a small amount on the blades we use. It flakes off in the vampire's body and they can't get it out easily."

"So, how do we kill a vampire?"

"Well, beheading always does the trick, but you need to be careful with that. If a severed head is brought close to its body, they can rejoin and come back to life."

"Is that why you always burn the bodies?"

"Correct. Once a vampire's body is burned, there is nothing to come back to life."

"So, beheading and burning are the only ways to kill a vampire?"

"Well, there is actually one other way, but we try to avoid it."

"Why avoid it if it works?"

"Because it can be rather ... messy. A wooden stake through the heart will kill a vampire. However, you usually need to be right in front of them to do that and we tend to avoid getting that close."

By then, the silver had melted and Willoughby had Jason hold the knives and the lance while he carefully poured the silver along their edges. Once the molten metal had cooled, it had become part of the blades.

Willoughby took one knife and flicked a thumbnail over a piece of silver and it flaked off on his finger. He held it so Jason could see it.

"See that? That tiny piece of silver is enough to cause a vampire to have a terrible day."

Jason looked at the tiny piece of silver, no bigger than a couple of grains of sand, and marveled at how such a small thing could cause a vampire any pain.

Willoughby stood up and looked at Jason.

"Now, I want you to promise me one thing, Jason. You are going to stay here with Miss Anna Marie and Seth."

"But I can help," said the boy. "I am Mr. James' squire."

"You are also the one the vampire wants more than any other. He may not remember you were his son, but something in his cold, dead heart is reaching out to you. We need to keep you away from him at all costs."

Jason dropped his head and looked at the ground, while Willoughby turned and walked back to the others. He handed the weapons to the brave, who looked at the edges of the blades and nodded.

"So, any plans?" asked Willoughby.

"I am heading back to town in a few hours," said Darius. "I want to be back there as the sun goes down."

"The townsfolk may not take too kindly to you waltzing into town."

"I'll be waiting just outside of town until dark. I should be able to come in from the north and not be seen."

Willoughby looked at Marcus.

"What about us?"

"We will come in from the south."

Then Marcus said something in Pueblo and the brave just nodded. He was going with Darius.

"Well," said Anna Marie, "we can't be having you men going off to fight this monster on empty stomachs."

She stood up and walked over to the packs, pulled out some wrapped sandwiches, preparing for lunch. Seth groaned as he sat up on his bed and watched her.

"Just what do you think you're doing, Seth?"

"Trying to figure out how I can help you, sweetheart," he said with a grin.

"You can help me by laying back down and resting. I can hear your breathing from here. It doesn't sound good."

The medicine man stood up and walked over to Seth and was getting ready to see if he could heal his wounds. Darius called over to him and told him not to.

"Should he not be made whole?" asked the old man.

"After we leave, you can mend him."

Marcus looked at the medicine man and nodded his agreement with Darius. The old man understood what they were asking. Healing Seth would give him a sense of being able to help in the coming battle, but he would still be weak and unable to fight. Better to keep him wounded and out of the fight.

As the men continued to go over their plan, Anna Marie finished setting out the meal and called them over to get something to eat.

During the entire time, Jason was unusually quiet and Darius could almost read his mind.

He whispered to Anna Marie, "Look after the boy. I think he is trying to figure a way to go to town."

"Why don't you just bind him with the power of Heaven?" she asked dryly.

He just smiled at her.

After lunch, Darius and the other hunters laid down to get some rest. They knew it was going to be a long night.

The brave left the camp and headed north, across the creek and into the low hills that ran behind the town. He and Darius had plans to meet at a certain point just above the town.

There was only one thought running through Darius' mind as he sat back against a tree, pulled his hat down low and closed his eyes.

This ends tonight.

32 – Please, Don't Make Me Do This

As the sun was setting, Darius found the brave in a good spot overlooking the town. Hidden among the trees on the hill, they could see the people of the town setting guards and Darius knew it wouldn't do them any good.

When Joshua attacked, it was going to be swift and without mercy. Darius prayed that he and the others could keep the casualties to a minimum. He knew they would lose some of the townsfolk, but with any luck, it would only be a couple.

Almost as if a signal had been given, as soon as the sun disappeared behind the horizon to the west, the first shots rang out. Without fail, the men that had been guarding the northern perimeter of the town abandoned their posts and ran for the middle of town.

Darius pointed to the right, telling the brave to enter the town between a couple of buildings. He was going to come in from further to the east.

As the indian moved away, Darius looked at Midnight.

You be careful, Darius.

"And you stay hidden here with his pony. I don't want either of you to get hurt."

Midnight just bobbed his head up and down as Darius began moving toward the buildings of the town.

As he approached a couple of the

buildings and walked between them, it reminded him of his earlier failures. High on the wall of the saloon, he saw the smear of blood left by old Ben. Even though the saloon owner had tried to clean it off, there was always going to be a reminder of that night of horror until he decided to paint the wall.

He stopped for a moment and let his rage subside. Getting angry would not help him in the coming fight. Anger and rage did nothing but cause you to make mistakes. Mistakes he couldn't afford to make.

Another round of shots snapped him out of his thoughts and he headed toward the main street and more horror.

It wasn't too long before he came to the first body. One of the young ladies from the saloon was lying on her back, her lifeless eyes staring up at the starry sky. The monster had ripped her throat out, looking like the vampire had used his teeth to do it.

Moving onto the main street, he saw more bodies scattered up and down the dirt road. He realized Joshua intended to finish this town in one night.

Then he saw a couple of men come backing out of an alley, firing their guns at something he couldn't see yet. They fired and kept retreating, never taking their eyes off their target.

With a motion faster than the eye could see, Joshua swept out of the alley and overwhelmed one man, tearing his head from his shoulders with no trouble at all.

As the other man turned to run, Darius fired one shot. The bullet whistled past the man's ear and hit Joshua in the chest, knocking him back a couple of steps. This allowed the man to escape and he ran past Darius, looking like he would not stop running until he got to California.

"I told you to leave," growled Joshua as he swayed back and forth on his feet.

"Well, my mama would be the first to tell you I'm a stubborn cuss. I never listen when it comes to monsters telling me what to do."

"She should have raised you better."

"You mean like the way you raised Jason?"

"Where is my boy?"

"I don't really think he would call himself *your boy* anymore. I believe he's come to realize you are not his father anymore."

Joshua was moving from left to right, allowing his body to repair the damage Darius' bullet had done. Why the hunter was allowing him the time to heal was a mystery to him.

Just then, Marcus and Willoughby came out from between a couple of buildings behind the vampire and the old hunter wasted no time. He fired one shot that hit Joshua in the back, almost driving him to his knees.

Darius was just about to wonder where the brave had gotten off to, when he saw him come creeping out of the shadows beside the boardinghouse. He had his knife in one hand and his lance in the other.

Darius wanted so much to warn him to stay back, but giving any kind of warning would have alerted Joshua to his presence. If he didn't already know.

The indian ran silently toward the hobbled vampire and just before he was ready to sink the lance into his back, Joshua snapped his left hand out and grabbed the lance. In the blink of an eye, he wrenched the spear from the brave's hand, turned it and rammed it through his chest.

The hunters could hear the breath get knocked out of the brave as the silver-coated spear head tore through his heart.

All three hunters yelled in rage at the same time and unloaded every bullet they had.

They might as well have been firing at a tornado because their bullets were not affecting the monster. The couple of bullets that did hit him only slowed him down and become more enraged.

But they didn't slow him down much. He vanished into a cloud of black smoke as the hunters fired more shots at him. Then the cloud of smoke flew with the speed of lightning and crashed through the doors of the boardinghouse.

As the doors slammed shut, Darius ran to the brave and fell to his knees. He could see there was no saving the indian from his coming death.

The young man reached up and gripped Darius' arm as pain burned through his body.

"Bring an end to this evil," he gasped.

"I promise, I will."

The indian's eyes glazed over as Marcus

and Willoughby walked up to them.

"Tell my father I go to the great buffalo hunting lands."

Darius clasped his hand and said, "Save some buffalo for your father."

The young warrior smiled and nodded slightly and then his head fell to the side.

Darius stood up and looked at the other two. There was a silent agreement between them this night would end with the death of Joshua and the end to his reign of terror.

The only thing that snatched their attention away was the sound of some crashing glass in the boardinghouse. It was at that moment Darius realized Abbie was probably still in there.

Then he felt the bond he had with her mind light up like a blazing fire. He could see through her eyes. Joshua had her cornered while she tried to hold him back with a knife. Then the image went black, as if a curtain had fallen over the scene.

Turning and sprinting toward the door, he cleared the three steps in one leap and slammed through the door and into the dining area.

Joshua was standing in the middle of the room and he waved his hand at the door. It slammed shut in the faces of Marcus and Willoughby as they were about to come in.

Darius could hear them pounding on the door, trying to break it down. Even the glass held when they tried to break it.

"You and your hunter friends have come to

the end of your road," said Joshua.

"Getting a little ahead of yourself, aren't you?"

"Oh, I don't think so. We have been walking the face of this planet long before you hunters came around."

"And yet, we seem to be killing you at a good pace."

"Oh really? Is that what you intend to say to Sophie and Richard when you see them."

Darius felt like he'd been gut-kicked by a mule at the mention of his friends. Without a second's hesitation, he fired one of his pistols from his hip. The bullet was streaking straight at the vampire's head, but never got there.

Joshua snatched it right out of the air with his hand and held it between a couple of fingers. They could hear sizzling skin as the silver in the bullet burned his fingertips. Then he dropped the bullet to the ground.

"Your bullets are nothing to me anymore," sneered Joshua.

"Let's find out!"

Darius let loose with a barrage of bullets and none of them found their mark. As the sound of his guns died, the only thing he could hear was Marcus and Willoughby still trying to break through the door.

"I tire of your weak efforts," growled the vampire. "I am going to kill you now, but there is one thing I want to show you before you die. Something that will cause you great pain and suffering as your life leaves your body."

Joshua held out his hand and motioned

with his fingers. Stepping out of the kitchen, Darius saw Abbie walk to Joshua's side. Her face was a ghostly white, her lips redder than an apple and her eyes glowing with fire.

"No," gasped Darius.

"Miss Abbie has consented to be my bride and help me raise up a new family in place of the one you slaughtered yesterday."

Darius was fighting to control his breathing as he looked into the woman's eyes.

"Did you really give her much choice?"

"They always have a choice, Darius. The choice to join me or die. I think she chose wisely."

Marcus and Willoughby had stopped pounding on the door. They could see Abbie through the glass and could hear everything that was being said.

"I am going to let you be her very first kill," said Joshua. "It should be very poetic when you realize she really liked you."

Joshua gave her a small push and she started walking toward the hunter.

"When we are finished with you and this town, I intend to find Miss Anna Marie and turn her, too."

At the sound of the young woman's name, Darius could see a slight change in Abbie's eyes. It was a look of sadness and despair.

"Kill me," she mouthed silently. "Save Anna Marie."

Darius brought his pistol up and pointed it at her forehead, but he couldn't pull the trigger.

"Please, Abbie, stop right now," he said,

almost wanting to cry.

"She will do whatever I ask of her," laughed Joshua. "And just think of all the young she and Anna Marie will bring into this world for me."

Darius pulled the hammer back on his pistol and aimed right between her eyes as she continued walking across the floor toward him.

"Please stop," he whispered as a tear rolled down his cheek.

He could see the pleading in her eyes for him to do what he needed to do.

"Do what is right, boy!" yelled Marcus.

Joshua waved his hand again and the windows of the boardinghouse went black and they could hear no sound from outside.

"You can't do it, can you?" said Joshua with a sneering laugh.

Abbie stepped up in front of him and raised one of her hands. The claws of her fingers grew and her new fangs were growing out from behind her lips. But there was something else. Something Darius had never seen with a vampire before.

A single tear crawled slowly down her cheek.

Then she stepped forward and leaned her forehead against the barrel of Darius' gun.

"Kill him!" raged Joshua.

"Kill me," implored Abbie softly. "Tell Anna Marie I love her."

Darius couldn't see through the tears welling up in his eyes, but he could feel her head press harder against the barrel.

"Kill him!" screamed Joshua as he stretched out his right hand, trying to conjure obedience from his newest bride.

It was over in a split second. Darius' finger tightened on the trigger and the bullet slammed through her head, blowing the back of her skull off.

"No!" screamed Joshua. "What have you done?"

Darius fired three more shots and was out of bullets. Those shots didn't matter, though. Joshua vanished, causing Darius to scream at him to come back and face him.

Just then the doors of the boardinghouse flew open and Marcus and Willoughby rushed in. They found their fellow hunter standing over the body of Abbie, his two guns hanging at his sides.

Both of them had their guns sweeping the dining room, but it was clear Joshua had fled. Willoughby grabbed a tablecloth from the nearest table and swept it over Abbie's body.

Marcus stepped up and gripped Darius' arm.

"You had to do it, Darius. You know that better than anyone."

"It doesn't make it right," he mumbled softly.

"No, it doesn't. But what you did was save her from an eternity of torment at the hands of that monster."

Willoughby stepped up and said, "We need to find him. I doubt he is going to flee this town tonight."

"Why not?" yelled Darius. "Why not, Willoughby? He can just wait us out!"

"Calm down, Darius," said Marcus as he stepped in front of the younger hunter.

"Calm down? You didn't have to look into her eyes as the trigger was pulled!"

Marcus let go of his arm and walked a few steps away, and swept the room with his gaze. They were the only three living souls in the building.

Swinging back around, he stared at Darius.

"Do you really think you're the first and only hunter to kill a loved one?"

Darius tore his gaze away from the covered body on the floor and looked up at him.

"Maybe it's time for you to realize you might be the great Darius James that strikes fear into the hearts of monsters all over the world. But, you are not the only hunter in Heaven Sent and you certainly aren't the only one to kill someone you didn't want to."

Darius settled his eyes on the old man as he saw grief wash over him.

"I had to kill my second wife, because like Miss Abbie, she was turned and there was nothing I could do about it. So get over feeling sorry for yourself. We still have work to do and Willoughby is right. Joshua isn't leaving until he's finished with this town."

Willoughby stepped up next to Darius and bumped shoulders with him.

"Let's kill this monster for Miss Abbie," he said.

Darius bumped his shoulder back. Even

though Willoughby could be an arrogant ass sometimes, he was okay.

33 – Final Battle

Just as they were about to head out the door, Marcus went flying through the door and into the street. The other two could hear him groan in pain as he hit the dirt outside.

Joshua appeared and swiped at Willoughby, knocking him back across the dining room and crashing into the far wall. Darius could tell immediately he was unconscious before he hit the floor.

He went to pull one of his pistols, hoping to blow this monster's head off, but Joshua just knocked the gun from his hand and then slammed a fist into his chest, knocking him through the door and into the street. He landed near Marcus, who Darius could see was also unconscious.

Struggling to his feet, he went for his other pistol, but remembered he hadn't had time to reload. He just left it in the holster.

Fighting the feeling of cracked or broken ribs, he turned and looked at Joshua, who was slowly stepping down from the porch and toward him.

"I am quite displeased with you, but also amazed. That you could actually shoot my wife like that, I didn't think you had it in you."

"You left me no choice," growled Darius.

"We always have a choice, hunter. Just like right now. I'll give you the choice to join me and live forever. Or ... you can just die right here, face down in the dirt."

"I'd rather die a hundred times than join you for five minutes."

"I was hoping you would choose death. And just remember this, I will make sure to remind Anna Marie every single day it was you that killed her mother. Every single day she is bearing my children, she will hate you for what you've done."

"I think you underestimate her. If you are successful in turning her, you better be sleeping with one eye open for the rest of your miserable life. She will kill you the first chance she gets."

"And you underestimate my power over those I turn. She will feel nothing but love for me. It will be beyond her power to do otherwise."

Joshua had come to a stop about ten feet from Darius and stood still, just looking at the hunter with as much disdain as he could muster.

Darius looked around, seeing dead bodies scattered all around him. He could see Marcus was breathing, but was still unconscious. He even found time to hope Willoughby was okay inside the boardinghouse.

He looked at the brave warrior laying a few feet away. There was something wrong with his body. Something different, but Darius couldn't put his finger on it. Something was missing.

Joshua looked at Darius' belt and the hunter undid the buckle and dropped the belt with holsters on the ground in front of Marcus.

"Not going to use your beloved guns?"

"Out of bullets," said Darius, as he felt the spikes press against his chest under his vest.

"Not very good planning on your part," said Joshua.

"Yeah, well, you know. It happens."

In a flash, Joshua moved forward and grabbed Darius by the throat, lifting him off the ground.

"Where is my boy?" demanded the vampire.

"What do you care?" gasped Darius through his closed throat.

"He is my son and should take his rightful place at my side."

"He will never make that choice."

"We shall see."

Joshua doubled up his fist and slammed it into the hunter's chest, breaking more ribs and sending him flying twenty feet through the air. When he hit the ground, he could feel the ribs grating inside his chest and driving the breath from his lungs.

The vampire casually walked the few steps to Darius and reached down and grabbed him again by the neck. Lifting him up again, Darius could feel his neck being stretched nearly to the point of breaking.

In a desperate bid to win this fight, he snatched a spike from inside his vest and jammed it into the chest of the vampire. Joshua screeched in pain as the silver spike burned his undead, gray flesh.

He dropped Darius, who crumpled into a

heap on the ground and tried to grab the spike and pull it out. Each time his claws came in contact with the spike, it burned. After a couple of attempts, he was able to pull it out and drop it into the dirt.

Darius was fighting consciousness as the spike fell into the dirt in front of his face, covered in vampire blood. He could see it sizzling on the metal, but knew Joshua could heal himself in a couple of minutes.

The monster reached down and grabbed Darius' vest by the back and ripped it off his body and flung it away.

"That wasn't very nice of you," growled Joshua.

Darius still had his face in the dirt as he mumbled, "I don't believe anyone has ever accused me of being nice."

Each time he tried to draw a breath, the pain pushed it back out of his mouth and he could see the small cloud of dust rise each time it happened.

The only thought running through his mind was this is where it was going to end. He was going to die face-down in the dirt, in the street, in Hell's Gate, New Mexico.

Damn, they should change that name.

Joshua kicked him in the gut and rolled him onto his back.

"Where is my boy?"

"Your boy hates you for what you did to his mama," gasped Darius.

Joshua picked up a foot and placed his boot on Darius' throat and pressed down.

"I won't ask again. Where is my boy?"

"Good. That means I won't have to listen to your voice ever again," croaked Darius.

"WHERE IS MY ..."

Joshua's demand was cut off and as Darius looked up at him, he realized what was missing when he looked at the indian warrior.

Joshua looked down and saw a silver-coated spear tip poking out of his chest, attached to a wooden lance. His body froze as he realized his heart had just been pierced with a wooden stake.

"I'm right behind you, pa."

Joshua took a step forward and then slowly turned around, clutching at the spear protruding from his chest. He looked into the twelve-year-old eyes of his son.

"But, you ain't my pa anymore," said Jason. "You kilt him and he's gone."

Joshua fell to his knees, knowing a final blow had been struck against him.

Darius rolled onto his side and picked up the gore covered spike from the dirt and held it out to Jason. The boy took it from his hand and looked at it.

"Right between his eyes, Jason," gasped Darius in pain.

Jason looked at the spike and then at the vampire kneeling in front of him. Joshua was still trying to grasp the spear, but being a wooden stake, its damage was done.

He looked up into the eyes of his son and could see nothing but hate in them.

Jason re-gripped the spike and said, "This

is for my ma and pa."

Then, taking one step forward, he slammed the spike through the right eye of the vampire, driving it completely into its head. Joshua's body seized up as the spike drove into his brain, punching a small hole in the back of his skull.

With a small gasp, his final breath escaped his mouth and falling forward, the ground pushed the spike out of the back of his skull. The lance tip broke off, leaving the wooden lance sticking straight up in the air from his back.

Just then, Marcus and Willoughby staggered over and looked at the scene. Willoughby pulled his sword and made quick work of beheading the vampire and kicking the head away from the body.

"How you doing, boy?" said Marcus.

When Darius realized he was talking to him, he croaked into the dirt, "Would you stop calling me boy, grandpa?"

The survivors of the town began filtering into the street, checking on the dead. Willoughby asked them to gather some firewood so they could burn the vampire's body and they went right to work doing it.

Jason stood and looked around. All he could see was the death and destruction his pa had visited in this town. He felt ashamed for a moment, but when Marcus laid a hand on his shoulder, he felt the shame pass from his soul.

"You did good, young man. I'm not too happy that you snuck away from the others, but I can't argue with the results."

Jason had no words for what he was feeling at that moment, so he just nodded.

"Jason Dalton! You and me are going to have words!"

The boy tensed up as he saw Anna Marie stalking toward him, looking like she was ready to breathe fire. Marcus took him and moved him behind, placing himself in front of the raging woman.

Willoughby reached and grabbed her by the arm and stopped her.

"Miss Anna Marie, he did good."

Then he stopped and took a breath, before turning her around and started walking away with her.

"We need to talk," he said as they headed toward the boardinghouse.

A group of men came over and placed Darius on a blanket, picked it up and carried him toward the boardinghouse. He was slipping in and out of consciousness, but not so much he didn't hear the cries of anguish from Anna Marie.

By the time they reached the boardinghouse, he was out and didn't feel the trek up the stairs to his room.

The dream that overtook him had nothing to do with vampires, wendigos or demons. He found himself standing on the banks of a river, throwing rocks into the water.

"Darius, come eat your meal."

Turning, he ran back up the hill, saying, "Coming, mama."

34 – Returning To Normal

Laying alone in the dark room, he stared up at the wooden beams over his head. It was late at night, or early in the morning. He couldn't really tell because it was deathly quiet downstairs. But it had been that way for three days now, as Anna Marie was in no condition to open the dining room.

He prayed she could move past what had happened. Though she put on a brave face when she was in the room, he could tell she was having a hard time being around him. She knew he did what he had to do, but he was the one that shot her mother and it was going to take time to get over that.

Willoughby and Marcus had left town the day before. Marcus was heading to Canada after receiving a telegram saying there was a werewolf causing trouble in Edmonton.

Willoughby was being sent to London. The slasher he had failed to stop in Boston appeared to have started up again and the Britishers were begging for help from Heaven Sent. He was tiring of this ghoul ripping up the lovely ladies of the night and he was going to put an end to it.

The old medicine man had done what he could to repair the injuries Darius had suffered, but he told him he still needed to stay in bed for a few days and rest.

Darius leaned over and looked to the floor and saw a sleeping figure, wrapped up in a couple of blankets.

Jason hadn't left his side for these three days, choosing to sleep on the floor of his room rather than in the jail cell. Of course, there was no jail as it had burned down a couple of days ago. Work had already started on rebuilding it, but it wouldn't be complete for some time.

When the sun rose the next morning, he felt a lot better and knew it was time to get out of bed. The blankets on the floor had been folded neatly and were stacked in the corner.

After getting dressed, he looked at his weapons and decided he could leave them there for the time being. The vampire threat was over and he felt safe for the first time in weeks.

As he stepped down the stairs, he realized how eerily quiet it was. There was no one in the dining room and from what he could gather, he was the only one in the building.

Looking through the window, he could see some people walking to the west, all dressed in black and he knew what was going on. Walking out the door and into the street, he joined the procession as it made its way to the cemetery.

They had completely dismantled the tent village, leaving an unobstructed view of the hill outside of town where a large crowd was gathering.

The preacher from Sage Springs had come

over to officiate over the funerals of all those lost. Though he didn't understand how so many could have died, he spoke with the softness and reverence the situation deserved.

Darius walked through the gates of the cemetery and saw Anna Marie and Seth standing near one coffin. When he went to stand somewhere else, Anna Marie walked over and took his hand and led him back to Seth's side. Her touch was gentle and reassuring.

As they stood there, Darius looked at the coffin in front of him, but had to wonder about it. Seth leaned over and whispered and removed his doubts.

"Obviously Miss Abbie isn't in there. We needed to burn the body, just like any other vampire. We just felt we needed to do something."

Darius just nodded to him as he reached over and put an arm around Anna Marie's shoulder.

As the preacher moved from grave to grave, he reached Abbie's spot and Anna Marie turned and buried her face in Seth's chest and he held her close. The preacher talked about how Abbie had brought comfort and joy to those who frequented her house and she would be missed.

It took the better part of three hours to lay the twenty-three departed souls to rest and no one left the cemetery early. When the last words had been spoken, all the men jumped in and began lowering the coffins and filling the graves. Not much was said during this time.

After it was done, everyone began filtering out of the graveyard and back home. Jason walked next to Darius, while Seth and Anna Marie walked together, holding hands.

When they got to the boardinghouse, Anna Marie told them to take a seat and she would get some food for them. When they tried to tell her not to bother, she gave them a look that told them they best be quiet.

While they sat at their usual table, the sheriff came in and sat with them. He just looked out the window at the passing people and shook his head.

Quietly, he said, "Thank you, Darius, for not abandoning this town."

He was still looking out the window as the hunter looked at him.

"It wasn't just me," said Darius.

Caleb looked at him and said, "Oh, I know. I already thanked Marcus and Willoughby before they left. And I will send a telegram to Father Benedict, thanking him for sending the three of you."

"I only wish we had put a stop to the killing sooner."

The sheriff bit his lip and just nodded. Then he looked at Jason.

"The men tell me they should have the jail done soon, so you can go back to sleeping there sometime next week. For a few years anyway. Your family's farm is yours now, but you might be a bit young to take it on right now."

"Thank you, sheriff, but someone else is

giving me a place to live."

"Really?"

Seth nodded and smiled.

"Anna Marie and I have told him he is welcome to live here in the boardinghouse with us. He will have a job working with her when she is ready to reopen for business."

Anna Marie walked up with a platter full of sandwiches and set them down.

"I may not be your mama, Jason, but I will still set some rules around here."

Jason looked at her and grinned.

"Yes, ma'am."

Darius leaned over and bumped shoulders with him.

"Best listen to her, Jason. She's a tough lady."

Jason just nodded.

Darius looked at Seth and asked, "When will your blessed day be?"

"Tomorrow," said the deputy.

Anna Marie said, "We weren't sure how long you'd be here, so we wanted to do it before you left. The preacher from Sage Springs will do it before he heads back."

Then she looked at Darius and asked, "Can I speak with you, Darius?"

Without waiting for a reply, she turned and headed for the front door and the hunter got up and followed her. He found her waiting in the street and when he stepped down off the porch, she turned and started trudging toward the stables.

Neither one said anything for a moment.

Then she broke the silence.

"Before they left, Marcus and Willoughby told me what you faced the other day. About how you pleaded with my mama to step back so you wouldn't have to shoot her."

"It was one of the hardest things I've ever had to do in my life," said Darius softly.

"Before they talked to me, I wanted to hate you so much. I just knew there had to have been a way to save her, but they assured me that's exactly what you did. You saved her from an eternity of being a monster. She knew that and that's why she wanted you to kill her."

As they walked, he reached up and put a hand on the back of her neck and gave it a gentle squeeze.

"The very last thing she said was to tell you she loved you very much."

Anna Marie came to a stop and they looked at each other. Then she threw her arms around him and buried her face in his chest.

"I'm so sorry I thought ill of you," she cried.

"Hey, hey, hey. Don't you be sorry. You have nothing to be sorry for."

He held her for a moment before she pulled back and wiped her face.

"Come on," she said. "I have something I need to take care of."

They walked into the stables and Midnight was standing in his stall, looking like he was expecting them. Anna Marie fished an apple out of her pocket and held it up for him, which he gratefully began munching on.

Maybe I'll stay here and be a plow horse for Anna Marie.

"She don't have any fields to plow and I'm sure she could do better than an old nag like you."

Anna Marie giggled and kissed Midnight on the nose.

"Don't you listen to him, Midnight. Between the two of you, I'd keep you here."

I wish I could stay Anna Marie, but he needs someone to look after him.

"And you are the best one for the job."

"Hey," said Darius, "I'm standing right here."

The next day was a joyous one, especially considering the days before. Everyone for miles around gathered in the small church, with a crowd so large it spilled out onto the sparse grass lawn in front.

The sun came out and shined down through the stained-glass window, right on the beautiful bride as she walked down the aisle. She was wearing her mama's wedding dress and being escorted by the rugged, but handsome monster hunter.

Seth watched her walking toward him and he had the look of a scared rabbit about ready to bolt. His best man reached out and put a hand on his arm and squeezed it, saying she sure looked pretty.

Seth looked down at Jason and all of his

fright evaporated.

"Yes, son, she surely does."

After walking her to the altar, Darius took a seat next to the sheriff and both of them looked like they were having a contest to see who could smile the biggest.

After the ceremony, everyone gathered outside, wishing the new couple well. While they were talking and laughing, the man from the telegraph office walked up and handed Darius a telegram. Those right around him went silent as he read what it said.

"Well," he said as he folded the piece of paper and stuck it in his pocket, "looks like I'm needed over in Oklahoma. There's a town that appears to be having some demon trouble."

"Are demons worse than vampires?" asked Anna Marie with a look of fear on her face.

"Oh no, Anna Marie. They are more like rowdy kids that need a good whippin'."

"Oh, that's good," she said with a sigh of relief.

"Of course, their daddy is Satan, himself. That always makes it interesting."

Her mouth dropped open as he stepped forward and kissed her on the cheek.

"Don't you worry about me. Besides, you have a new man that needs your guidance and strength."

She smiled and pulled Jason in front of her and wrapped her arms around him from behind.

"Two men, actually," she said.

He smiled and looked toward the main street in town. The stableman was leading Midnight to the church, all saddled and ready to go.

He held out his hand to Seth and shook it.

"Remember what I told you," he leaned in and whispered. "The woman is almost always right."

Seth looked him in the eye and said, "I've never known Anna Marie to be wrong yet."

Darius nodded, turned and walked through the gate to his horse. Everyone was watching him go.

The sheriff stepped up and said, "Thank you for being here, Mr. James. Oh, and when you reach the other side of town, take a look. The town voted and ... well, you'll see."

Darius shook his hand and climbed into the saddle. He gave one last look and wave to the people gathered around and then turned Midnight to the east and began trotting through town.

When they reached a spot about half a mile out of town, he found a couple of men putting the finishing touches on a new sign. When he walked past it, he turned and looked to see what it said. Then smiled.

WELCOME TO
ABBIETOWN, N.M.

The End

I hope you've enjoyed this story about Darius, Anna Marie and the rest. These *Campfire Stories* are meant to be stand-alone novels and they are meant to be a little darker than my other series, ***A Cold Shivers Nightmare***. Though they are to be stand-alones, that doesn't mean that there won't be more stories with Darius, Marcus and Willoughby.

I would appreciate it if you could visit the website of your favorite bookseller and leave a review. Obviously I would love to get 4 and 5 star ratings, but more than that, I'd like to get honest ratings so I can see how these stories are being received. Thank you for taking the time to read my stories.

362

Coming in late 2022
The City of Time

"Liessel, can't we talk about this?"

Dylan stalked after the young woman, who had turned and walked away from him when he asked her a question. The question every young woman would love to hear from the man she's in love with.

Dylan reached for her shoulder and turned her around to face him. She had a defiant look on her face and he knew that her mind was made up. It didn't matter that she had made up her mind without talking to him. She wasn't going to give in to him.

"No Dylan! We are not going to talk about this. I believe I've made myself perfectly clear and my decision is final."

Dylan racked his brain, trying to find the words that would swing the argument in his favor, but those words were nowhere to be found. He ran his hands through his bright, red hair and clutched at it, as if he were going to pull every strand right out of his head.

"Stop that," she said. "I won't love you nearly as much if you pull your hair out."

He opened one eye and looked at her.

"Woman, if I were to pull my hair out, it will be because you are one of the most exasperating creatures I have ever encountered."

"Surely not as frustrating as my mother," she said, with an impish grin.

He dropped his hands to his side and shook his head.

"I'll give you that, but I can see where you learned the art of confounding a man and you've learned it well."

"My mother is a wise woman."

"Your mother hates me!"

Liessel laughed and said, "She doesn't hate you. She just thinks I can do better."

"Well, that's true. You could do a lot better than me."

Liessel stepped forward and placed a hand on his chest and looked up at him. Her sparkling green eyes danced in the moonlight and the glow from the city.

"No Dylan, I can't do any better than you. I love you dearly and nothing is going to change that."

Dylan looked down at her and said, "But, you won't marry me."

"I didn't say that."

"I just asked you if you would marry me."

"Right, and I said, not right now."

Dylan took a deep breath, still reveling in the touch of her hand on his chest.

"But, what does that mean?"

"You know exactly what that means," she said, as she stepped back and put her hands on her hips. "I do not need to explain it to you. Until you complete your final trials and become part of the council, we will remain apart. I am not going to do anything to stand in the way of you attaining what you've worked your whole life toward."

Dylan dropped his head and took a few deep breaths. Then he turned and faced the city and raised his fist and yelled, "Curse you and all you stand for!"

Liessel giggled and stepped up beside him and wrapped her arms around him.

"Stop that. The city might hear you."

"I doubt that," said Dylan as he looked down at her. "The city never listens to me."

"Well, sometime in the not too distant future, you will be the one that speaks and then, the city will listen."

They both stood there on the mountaintop, looking out across the void, to the floating city that hovered above the clouds below. The lights of the city were shining brightly in the dark, night sky. The city cast its warm glow on the clouds and they looked like a soft bed of yellow cotton.

The glow of the disc around the black hole was visible in the night sky, powering the city and the galaxy, itself. To Dylan's ear, the furnace of the black hole was a deep rumbling; churning out massive amounts of energy used to keep the galaxy spinning like it had since the beginning of time.

As they stood there, Dylan could feel the heartbeat of the city and could almost see it with his eyes. The lights pulsated almost imperceptibly to most eyes, but he was one of the rare few that could see it with ease.

"It won't be much longer," said Liessel, "before you become a fully sanctioned Time Keeper, with your trials behind you and then you can ask me that question again."

Dylan sighed and then said, "You best hope that I don't find someone better in that time."

She looked up at him with fake shock, "You couldn't possibly find someone better than me."

He looked down at her and smiled, "I know ... and believe me I've tried."

"We've known each other for well over ten years now. I think if there was another out there better suited to you than me, you would have found her by now."

Dylan turned toward her and put his arms around her.

"Sweetheart, I stopped looking about seven years ago. I knew then exactly what I know now. You are my one and only."

She looked up at him with a wry grin and asked, "You knew at thirteen years old that I was the one for you?"

"Absolutely."

She put her arms around his neck and drew him down for a long kiss. She sank into the feeling of his strong arms around her and she knew that it was only a matter of time before they would become one.

They parted and looked into each other's eyes and then he took her by the hand and led her back to the blanket they had spread under the tree. He sat down and leaned back against the tree trunk and she sat down and leaned up against him. He put his arms around her and they both sat there and stared at the city.

"You know," she said, "once you become a Time Keeper, you won't be able to take off and see the other parts of the galaxy, like you do right now."

"Sweets, when I become a Time Keeper, I will be the lowliest member of the council and my duties will be sparse."

"But, you will still need to learn your duties, won't you?"

"I've been preparing for those duties for over twelve years now. There isn't much more to learn. D'more has made sure of that."

"How is D'more feeling these days?"

"Like the crotchety old man that he is,

always looking for ways to make me sweat and doubt my abilities."

"He is rough on you because he believes in you and sees greatness in your heart. He knows you are the future of the council."

Dylan nodded and sighed to himself.

D'more was the oldest Time Keeper and the leader of the council. He was ancient when Dylan was presented to him as a prospect and he had gotten even more ancient since then. He still remembered that day as a lad of eight years, looking at the old man across the large desk and wondering how in the world someone could live as long as he obviously had.

The Time Keepers could live for hundreds of years, some even got past the thousand year mark. D'more was closing in on eleven hundred years old and almost nine hundred years of that spent as a Time Keeper.

"Well, once I become a Time Keeper, I intend to volunteer for every single mission that will take me to some place else in the galaxy. I've seen a lot on my previous trips, but I don't think I've come close to satisfying my urges to see more."

Liessel snuggled up against him and said, "But, that will take you away from me for years at a time."

"No, it won't. Once I become a Time

Keeper and we are joined, I will be allowed to take you with me on those trips."

She pulled away and sat up and looked at him.

"You think I want to spend months or years cooped up in a tin can, flying through space with you?"

Dylan looked at her, with a bit of apprehension spreading across his face. He had never considered she might not want to go off-world with him.

Then she laughed and threw a leg over his and sat on his lap. She leaned down and kissed him.

"I can't think of anything I'd rather do than to see the galaxy with you," she said. "Just the two of us, flying around and seeing the wonders of all there is to see."

"Well, the two of us and the fifty or sixty members of the crew. Those ships don't fly themselves."

"Pity," she said, as she leaned in for another kiss.

His hands ran up and down her back as she pressed her lips even harder against his. He could stay right there, on that mountaintop, for the rest of all eternity and never want to leave. He could smell the sweet scent in her midnight black hair and he could taste the intoxicating moistness of her mouth with his.

As they were getting lost in each others passion, he stopped suddenly. She pulled away and sat up and looked at him. She could tell his thoughts were not with her anymore. Something had pulled him away.

"What's the matter, Dylan?"

He shook his head slightly and held a couple of fingers up to her lips, letting her know to be quiet.

Then he rolled her off his lap and jumped to his feet. He reached down and pulled her up and then he turned and looked toward the city.

Stepping up beside him, she wrapped an arm around his waist. The city didn't appear to look any different than before, but she couldn't hear, see or feel the things he could, but she could tell that he knew there was something wrong.

"Dylan?"

She looked up at him and he closed his eyes and turned his head slightly, turning his left ear toward the city. She could tell he was listening to something that she couldn't hear.

Then he opened his eyes and took her hand and started toward the aircycle they had used to get to the mountain.

"We have to go now," he said, pulling her along.

He swung his leg over the cycle and got himself situated and then she climbed on behind him.

As she wrapped her arms around his waist, she asked, "What's the matter? What's happened?"

"I don't know Liessel, but it isn't good," he said as he started the engine and flew off the mountaintop and headed for the glowing lights of the city.

He couldn't put his finger on it because he had never heard anything like it before, but the city had shuddered right down to its core. It sounded almost like a large animal gasping and fighting for its life.

And the City of Time was losing.

Other books by D Glenn Casey

Beware The Boogerman
A COLD SHIVERS NIGHTMARE
by D Glenn Casey

**How do you fight the thing
even monsters are afraid of?**

After Debbie Dinkendorfer did her tour in the Army as an MP, she returned to her home town, marched into the sheriff's office and demanded a job. Her daddy is the sheriff. Now, you can call her Deputy Debbie -- or if you're really brave, Dinkie.

Her hometown of Prattville isn't like other towns. It's where the monsters go when they retire. The sheriff's job is to keep the peace between the human folk and the vampires, goblins, werewolves and such that call the town home.

It's a good place, and with a slightly alien past, it's a place Debbie can call home.

But, when a tragic past reemerges and Debbie's bestie disappears – again – in the midst of a spate of attacks on monsters, Debbie fears the worst.

What's killing monsters? Where is it hiding Debbie's friend? And how is one little, human woman supposed to fight something that can shred a goblin, decimate a vampire and put two large trolls in the hospital?

All she knows is that she's got to try. Her friend's life depends on it.

Shattered Prisons
A Cold Shivers Nightmare #2

When things go bump in the night, maybe you should just sell the house and move.

For the last few months before her death, artist Julie's beloved Nana started to talk about strange things - evil demons, dark angels and bad humans. Julie let her prattle – it was just harmless talk, wasn't it? Wasn't it?

Now on her own with her grief in a big empty house, Julie's beginning to think that maybe there was something to Nana's wild talk. Most normal families have skeletons in the closet. Julie's family is a little more unusual ... her closet has demons.

Demons are on the loose, a friend is in peril, and a family legacy has been thrust upon her surprised shoulders. Can Julie transform into a badass demon fighting machine or will she cower behind her easel?

With the forces of evil on the prowl – released from their prisons by a clumsy friend – Julie must scramble to train and take her place beside Templar Knights, demon-fighting monks and a feisty Dominican nun who has an obsession with cherry pie.

Paranormal horror with a touch of humor and dose of hair-raising shivers, this is the perfect novel for the Goosebumps kid who has outgrown Goosebumps.

Into The Wishing Well
by D Glenn Casey

Welcome to the afterlife. Please take a number.

Melanie lived a good life. She played by the rules, loved her friends and neighbors, and was always kind to strangers. But when an "accident" sends Melanie to the Pearly Gates, she's shocked to find Heaven is closed for new arrivals! How was she supposed to know she needed a number to get in to the afterlife?

While she waits for a spot to open up, Melanie discovers she isn't the only spirit walking around her old town. A diabolical demon also walks the earth. And this sinister entity has made it his mission to capture Melanie's soul for his master. A war is brewing between Heaven and Hell, and poor Melanie is caught squarely in the middle.

With Angels and archangels sworn to protect her, and Lucifer's own minions eager to take her captive, it seems like death is only the beginning of Melanie's problems. And the fate of both Heaven and Hell may rest in her ghostly hands.

Buy *INTO THE WISHING WELL* today and find out if a small town girl can keep the darkness at bay and give the rest of us a little more time to work things out.

Wicked Rising
The Chronicles of Wyndweir
Book One

by D Glenn Casey

Garlan has finished his trials in the Land of the Dragons and he is heading home. The only thing he can think of is being reunited with the woman that has stolen his heart.

But, there is evil rising in the Eastern Desert and war is on the horizon. Everyone he knows is expecting him to rise up and be a leader and vanquish this evil. He'd rather they find someone else.

The Tales of Garlan
Prequel to the Chronicles of Wyndweir
by D Glenn Casey

Garlan went to live with the old wizard, Sigarick when he was eight years old. Now, in his twenty-third year it's time to prove he's actually learned something.

These four short stories tell of wizard duel, clearing thugs from villages and facing a final set of trials that could very well kill him. All in a days work for Garlan.

Printed in Great Britain
by Amazon